BLIND
BETRAYAL

Books by Nancy Mehl

Finding Sanctuary

Gathering Shadows
Deadly Echoes
Rising Darkness

Road to Kingdom

Inescapable
Unbreakable
Unforeseeable

Defenders of Justice

Fatal Frost
Dark Deception
Blind Betrayal

BLIND BETRAYAL

NANCY MEHL

BETHANYHOUSE

a division of Baker Publishing Group
Minneapolis, Minnesota

© 2018 by Nancy Mehl

Published by Bethany House Publishers
11400 Hampshire Avenue South
Bloomington, Minnesota 55438
www.bethanyhouse.com

Bethany House Publishers is a division of
Baker Publishing Group, Grand Rapids, Michigan

Printed in the United States of America

ISBN 978-0-7642-1779-1 (trade paper)
ISBN 978-0-7642-3142-1 (cloth)

Library of Congress Cataloging-in-Publication Control Number: 2017961600

Scripture quotations are from the King James Version of the Bible.

This is a work of fiction. Names, characters, incidents, and dialogues are products of the author's imagination and are not to be construed as real. Any resemblance to actual events or persons, living or dead, is entirely coincidental.

Cover design by Dan Pitts
Cover photography by Mike Habermann Photography, LLC

Nancy Mehl is represented by The Steve Laube Agency.

18 19 20 21 22 23 24   7 6 5 4 3 2 1

To my mother and father,
Barbara and Jack Harper,
for introducing me to God
and encouraging my love of books.

CHAPTER
ONE

As Martin Avery waited to be murdered, he was surprised to find that, more than anything else, he felt offended. He wanted to explain to his killer that he was a good son. That he'd been a loving brother to his special-needs sister. He'd always tried to be a decent man. He cared about people and had dedicated his life to protecting the environment. Somehow he felt it should matter that on Christmas he worked at the downtown shelter and served dinner to the poor and homeless. Then there was the time he stopped to help a woman who'd run her car off the road and into a tree. Martin had smelled gas and pulled her out before the car caught fire. Shouldn't that mean something now?

He scooted a little closer to the dumpster. He retained a small spark of hope that the man who wanted him dead wouldn't see him hiding beneath all this trash. He was struck by the absurdity of his situation. There were plastic bottles, aluminum cans, and newspapers strewn all around him. Normally he'd be angry at a business that clearly wasn't recycling. In fact, he would probably stop by and speak to the owner, reading him the riot act about how he was damaging the environment for upcoming generations. But now, the very items he'd spent the last few years fighting against could actually end up saving his life. Of course, his chances weren't great. How many times had Martin yelled at the TV when a character running from someone who wanted to kill him headed into an alley with no exit? Yet he'd just done the same thing. Problem was, he didn't know much about the streets of Pennsylvania. The man who'd chased him from the warehouse had to know he was here. It would likely just be a matter of time.

He could hear footsteps getting closer. Then he remembered his phone. All his texts to Valerie. He had to protect her. He slowly pulled the phone out of his pocket, trying not to shake the newspapers that covered him. Martin quickly slid it under the dumpster. Hopefully his killer wouldn't take the time to look there after Martin was dead.

At that moment, the sadness finally came. Martin didn't want to die. There was so much he wanted to do. How could this be happening? He was an environmentalist, not a criminal. Not a law enforcement officer. How could protecting the earth cost him his life? It was ridiculous.

Something his mother once told him whispered in his mind. When he was twenty, he'd told her he didn't believe in God anymore. He could still see the pain in her eyes. But instead of chastising him, she'd said, *"You may not believe in Him, Marty, but He believes in you. Just remember that*

He's always close. All you need to do is call on Him. He'll answer."

Martin closed his eyes and silently called on God. He was still praying when someone grabbed the newspapers and pulled them away.

"We need to get her ready to move."

Doug nodded. "I'll call the office. You tell her."

"Sure." Casey Sloane knocked on the door to the adjoining room while Doug took out his phone. She and Doug Howard, both Deputy U.S. Marshals from St. Louis, had been assigned to transport a witness to Washington, D.C. Valerie Bennett, a local newspaper reporter, had been called to testify before a grand jury. According to the chief, Valerie had been interviewing a well-known environmentalist when she'd supposedly stumbled across the possibility that a sitting U.S. senator dedicated to environmental issues might have ties to terrorism. Casey wasn't sure how the jump was made from tree hugger to ISIS, but somehow things had taken a really perilous turn and there was real concern that Valerie Bennett's life was now at risk. Casey had no idea if those fears were valid. It was the Marshals' job to deliver their witness safely to D.C. Period. Once their assignment was done, it was up to the Feds to figure out what was true and what wasn't.

Not getting a response, Casey rapped a little louder. "Ms. Bennett, it's Casey Sloane. We'll be leaving in about fifteen minutes. Any problem with that?"

The door swung open to reveal Valerie Bennett, dressed

and seemingly ready to leave for their meeting at the U.S. Marshals Office.

"I'm all packed. Ready whenever you are."

"Good. Why don't you give me your suitcases? We'll put them in the car for you."

"Sounds good. Come on in." Valerie retrieved her two suitcases and had started to hand them to Casey when she paused. "Wait a minute. I don't think I checked the bathroom. Sorry to make you wait."

"Not a problem. We still have a little time. Our office is just down the street."

"I'll be right back." Valerie put the bags down, turned, and went into the bathroom.

As she waited, Casey's gaze swung slowly around. The rooms here were nice. Dark wood furniture, colorful bedspreads, and the obligatory pictures that were screwed into the walls just in case you wanted to take them home. Casey found those concerns a little strange since she'd never seen a painting in any hotel she'd actually want in her house. There was also a desk in each room, which was handy. Of course, the most important amenity to Casey was the coffeemaker, something she looked for first whenever she was assigned to stay with a witness.

The general public didn't know that most safe houses used by the Marshals were actually located in hotels. That was fine with Casey. The last thing she wanted was to get stuck someplace where she couldn't get her daily caffeine fix. She could easily down six cups of coffee before noon. It had become a necessity, not a luxury. The minutes ticked by, and Casey checked her watch. She was just about ready to say something when Valerie came out of the bathroom carrying some clothes and a makeup box. She really had forgotten to pack everything. Casey couldn't blame her for being a little scatterbrained. The reporter was under a lot of pressure.

"Do I have time for one more cup of coffee?" she asked as she added the additional belongings to one of the suitcases.

"I'm not sure there's time to drink it here, but you can certainly take it with you. Do you have everything now?"

Valerie nodded. "I hope so." She moved toward the coffee-maker. "The hotel staff put at least a dozen packets of coffee in my room. If I drank all of it, I'd be up for a week."

Casey smiled. "The people here are great. Very supportive."

"I'll make a quick cup and be right out."

Casey picked up the suitcases and put them next to the door leading to the hallway. "Do you want to take these to the car?" she asked Doug, who sat at the desk, frowning at the cellphone in his hand.

"Not yet."

"What's going on?"

"Just finished talking to the chief. There's a problem."

Casey and Doug worked under Richard Batterson, Chief Deputy U.S. Marshal for the District of Missouri's U.S. Marshals Office. Batterson was tough but fair. The deputies who worked under him respected him immensely.

"What kind of problem?"

Doug stood. When he was upset, he'd purse his lips, and right now they were almost tied up in a bow. "Chief says the office isn't secure. There was a call. A bomb threat. They were checking it out when someone noticed a new deputy had signed in a couple of hours earlier."

"So?"

"The real guy's actually in Kansas City for special training. Until they figure out what's going on—and who's using his identification—we're to stay here. Valerie is our only high-profile witness right now. The chief's afraid whatever's going on is connected to her."

Casey's stomach tightened, and she took a deep breath. The news was disturbing. "But how . . . ?"

"They don't know how it happened yet. I'm sure they're reviewing all the security cameras and talking to the real deputy. Maybe there's a plausible explanation, but just in case they've notified the Federal Protective Police and they're evacuating the building."

Casey sat down on the bed and shook her head. "Sure sounds like someone infiltrated our office." She frowned. "But why?"

"We can't be sure, but you can see why the chief is concerned."

"What about the guy from D.C. we were supposed to meet up with?"

The D.C. office had sent one of their deputies to travel with them. Although it wasn't without precedent, the move made Casey feel uneasy. Was it because they didn't trust St. Louis to safely transport their witness? She was also worried about who might show up. Casey had worked in D.C. for a couple of years, and there were some people she really didn't want to see again. She'd left abruptly, for her own personal reasons, and she had no desire to deal with anyone who felt the need to poke their nose into her business.

"What do you mean?" Doug asked. "You're wondering

if he might be involved?" He shook his head. "The chief had him checked out. One of D.C.'s best. Besides, he's been staying in a hotel near the airport. Batterson contacted him, and he's on his way here. We're to wait for further instructions, but as of right now, we'll leave from the hotel and go straight to D.C." He patted the breast pocket of his jacket. "I've got our tickets, and we've already been briefed, so we don't really need to meet with the chief again anyway. The D.C. Deputy Marshal will get us from Reagan National to the final drop-off point. It's not complicated."

"Something feels off," Casey said. "I mean, our offices get breached right before we leave town with a witness?"

Doug ran his hand over his short strawberry-blond hair. It was obvious he was bothered too. "I'm not going to disagree with you. Until we know what's going on, maybe we should be extra careful. I think I'll wait in Valerie's room until we get the all clear."

"Good idea."

Doug got up and knocked on the adjoining door. When Valerie opened it, he said, "If you don't mind, Ms. Bennett, I'd like to stay with you until we're ready to leave. Just an extra precaution."

The door closed behind him, and Casey walked over to the sliding glass door that led to a small balcony. She carefully pulled the drapes back and checked the street. Everything looked normal. She couldn't stop wondering once again who D.C. had sent. Was it someone she knew or a deputy who'd never met her? Would they be surprised when they saw her? Casey was tired of the expressions of disbelief on the faces of her colleagues in law enforcement. She had a slight build and had been told more than once that she looked like a teenager, even though she was twenty-seven years old. However, anyone who marginalized her would be seriously mistaken. Batterson had praised her many times for being one of his toughest deputies.

She checked her watch again. A quarter to ten in the morning. If they hadn't gotten the call from Batterson, they would be leaving for the office right now. She was headed toward the coffeepot when a loud explosion rocked the room and she was thrown to the floor.

CHAPTER
TWO

"Casey! Are you all right?"

She'd just gotten back on her feet when Doug and Valerie came through the door. "I'm fine. What the heck was that?"

"I'm not sure," Doug said, "but I have a bad feeling."

Casey had trouble catching her breath as sudden realization hit. "No. It can't be," she choked out. She ran over and grabbed her phone, punching in the number for the U.S. Marshals Office. There wasn't any answer, just a fast busy signal.

Valerie turned on the TV. "Should be some kind of report soon."

They waited a few minutes, everyone deathly quiet. Casey wanted to know what had happened, yet she also dreaded hearing what she feared was true.

Finally, a grim-faced reporter broke into the program, looking as if she'd rather be anywhere else than at the television station downtown. "We're just now getting information that there's been a major explosion downtown. We're not sure yet exactly where the incident took place, but police are asking everyone already in the area to stay inside and off the streets until they can investigate. They are setting up roadblocks, so if you're headed into downtown St. Louis, they're asking you to turn around. Until authorities know what they're dealing with, they don't want anyone in the area around Tenth Street. Please stay tuned. We'll bring you more information as soon as we have it."

"I'm worried," Casey said to Doug. "I can't get through to the office."

"I know. I just tried too."

"What should we do?" Valerie asked, her eyes round with fear.

"We sit tight until we get further instructions," Casey said. "Our people know we're here. You're our first priority. Someone will contact us."

"I agree," Doug said.

A knock came at the door. Doug drew his gun and went to see who it was. He peered through the peephole. "It's the hotel manager." He looked back at Casey. "He appears to be alone, but I can't be certain. Back me up."

Casey pulled her gun, pointing it toward him. Doug stayed to the left of the door in case she would need to take a shot. When she was ready, Doug opened the door.

"What can I do for you?" Doug asked the manager, a short chubby man with a florid face. He noticed Casey's gun was drawn and took a quick breath.

"The word on the street is that your office has been bombed," he said, looking around him as if people were hiding out, listening. Since the entire floor had been cleared,

Casey wasn't certain who he was worried about. However, she noticed Doug checking the hall too. He turned and nodded at her.

"Are you sure?" Casey asked, putting her gun back in its holster.

The manager shook his head. "No, not one hundred percent, but I've heard it from more than one person. I think you need to prepare yourself. It was a really bad explosion."

"Thanks," Doug said. "We're going to stay where we are for now, but we might need to move quickly. Please continue to keep people off this floor—and don't talk to the press. Revealing our location could put our witness at risk."

"As far as we're concerned," the manager said, "you're not here. If you need anything, please let me know."

"I will. And thanks. We really appreciate it."

The manager left, and Doug closed the door.

"The bomb went off at a quarter to ten," Casey said. "Fifteen minutes before we were supposed to meet with the chief."

"I know," Doug said. "It doesn't sound like a coincidence."

"You think the people who threatened me blew up your office?" Valerie asked. She looked sick. "I . . . I don't know what to say."

"This isn't your fault," Casey told her. "Besides, we're still not sure what exactly happened."

"Hey," Doug said, pointing at the television, "there's more."

The same reporter was back. "We can now confirm that the blast downtown occurred at the U.S. Marshals Office. Although it will take some time to get reliable information, we're told there are casualties. Continue to stay tuned to this station for updates." The reporter put her hand up to her ear as if listening to something in her earpiece. "Once again, for your own safety, the police are asking you to stay away from downtown St. Louis around Tenth Street as law enforcement is working to evacuate the area. Again, we'll get back to you with more details as soon as we have them."

Another knock sounded at the door. This time Casey pulled her gun and got to the door first. She looked through the peephole. A badge belonging to a Deputy U.S. Marshal filled the small space. This was probably the Marshal from D.C., but since someone had used another deputy's ID to breach their office, she kept her gun ready.

When she opened the door, she wasn't sure what to expect, but she certainly wasn't prepared to see the man who stood there.

E.J. Queen.

Her heart sank.

E.J. knew Casey had been assigned to this operation. In fact, he'd asked for her since she was so good at her job. Still, seeing her again gave him a jolt. They'd worked a case together in D.C.—one that didn't end well. He'd always found her fascinating. Strength, commitment, and talent poured into a rather small container. Long blond hair usually pulled back in a ponytail. A young face with large dark-brown eyes that seemed to size up situations and people within seconds. Frankly, she used to make him a little nervous.

If he was truthful with himself, he'd had feelings for her. Feelings he had no right to entertain. He'd worked hard

over the last year to rid himself of Casey Sloane and was
convinced he'd succeeded until this moment.

"Your office was bombed," he said, waiting for her to let
him in. She finally moved out of the way, and he entered the
room. He found their witness and another deputy standing
in front of a television mounted in a dark wood armoire.

"We're seeing it now," Doug said. "Can't get through on
our phones, and no one has called."

"What's your next move?" E.J. asked.

"Since we don't know what's happening, we stay put until
we get orders."

"I agree."

Casey glanced at her watch. "If we're not ready to leave
soon, we'll have to cancel our tickets and get a later flight."

Doug walked over to E.J. and put his hand out. "Doug
Howard. Good to meet you."

"E.J. Queen. Happy to meet you too, but I wish the circumstances were different."

"Amen." Doug stared at Casey, a look of confusion on
his face. He waited a few seconds before saying, "And this
is Casey Sloane."

"Actually, we know each other," E.J. said. "We worked
together in D.C."

"Of course. I forgot you came from Washington, Casey."

"Yeah." Casey walked over to the bed and plopped down,
focusing on the television as if no one else was in the room.
E.J.'s nervousness turned to irritation. If anyone had the
right to be upset, it was him. Casey had left D.C. suddenly,
walking out on his best friend, Jared, without any explanation. She didn't say good-bye to E.J. either, and they'd been

partners. The snub still bothered him. Not long after she took off, Jared transferred to Los Angeles. Although he and E.J. stayed in touch online, he'd only seen his friend in person once in the last twelve months. During his visit, Jared had seemed distant and uncomfortable. E.J. couldn't help but blame Casey. Obviously, E.J. reminded Jared of the love he lost, and he couldn't handle it.

It was clear Doug had also noticed Casey's reaction, but he didn't say anything. Instead he introduced E.J. to their witness.

"Nice to meet you, Ms. Bennett," E.J. said, extending his hand.

"Please, just call me Valerie," she replied, putting her hand in his. "I'm really grateful for your help."

"Just doing my job."

E.J. took quick stock of Valerie Bennett. She looked to be in her early forties. Well groomed, an air of professionalism about her. High-end pantsuit, reddish-brown hair that was expertly colored, and a firm handshake. It was clear she was used to meeting the public. Although her fingernails were trimmed and polished, the edges of several nails were ragged. She'd obviously been biting them, probably something she normally didn't do. And there was something going on behind those hazel eyes. Most likely it was fear, though it could be anything. He'd learned not to read too much into first impressions. Most people had secrets.

"Any coffee?" E.J. asked, directing his question to Doug.

He pointed to the small pot on the dresser. "Cups next to the coffeemaker, along with sugar and creamer."

"Thanks." While E.J. put water in the one-serving coffeepot, he heard a phone ring. Doug quickly picked up. A look of relief washed across his features almost immediately. "Chief," he said, "we were afraid—"

Obviously the person on the other end interrupted him, but Doug didn't seem to mind. He hurried over to the desk and pulled out a pad of paper and a pen, then began to write. E.J. assumed these were their instructions and that they'd soon be on their way. No matter what happened at the Marshals Office, they still had to get their witness to D.C.

Finally, Doug said, "Got it, Chief, but are you really okay? Did we lose anyone?"

After a few seconds, Doug said, "Okay. We'll take care of it right away. Please keep in touch." Another long pause. "I . . . I think so." He turned to look at Casey, who was still staring at the TV. "Casey, we need a burner phone. I didn't bring one."

She nodded at him. "I've got an old one, the kind before they started adding GPS chips."

"What's the number?" he asked.

She rattled it off, and Doug repeated it. Finally he put the phone down. Everyone in the room stared at him as they waited to find out what their next move would be.

"Batterson is concerned that Valerie was the target of the bomber. We need to take off immediately for D.C. We're on our own for now."

CHAPTER
THREE

"What do you mean 'on our own'?" Valerie asked. "Someone set off a bomb hoping to kill me and no one plans to back us up?"

Doug shook his head. "No, that's not what I meant."

Casey went over to Valerie and sat down next to her. "You'll be fine. We're all highly trained professionals, and we'll get you safely to D.C. Besides, we're not sure this had anything to do with you at all. We're just being cautious." She turned to look at Doug. "So what does the chief want us to do next?"

"He feels we may be compromised, but he doesn't know the extent of it. He wants us to take every precaution. We'll need to avoid all public transportation, which makes our airline tickets useless. From here on out, we keep our cell-phones off. All communication between us and the chief will be over the burner and the chief's secure line. Unfortunately, it might take a while for him to get that phone."

"Where is it?" Casey asked.

"Still in his office. But he keeps it in the bottom drawer of his steel desk. He's convinced the phone survived the blast. Of course, authorities won't let anyone into the building unless they're sure it's safe. Thank God they'd already started to evacuate before the explosion or there would have been a lot more casualties."

"Are they concerned about other bombs?" E.J. asked.

"Yeah," Doug said. "Batterson thinks the guy who did it was only in the building for a short time, so hopefully he didn't have time to plant more than one bomb. Of course, they can't be sure. They're proceeding as if there's still a threat." He chewed his lip for a moment. "If this guy was trying to target us . . . or Valerie, why did the bomb go off fifteen minutes before we were supposed to be there?"

"Maybe it went off too soon," Casey suggested.

"Maybe. . . . I still think it's odd, though."

Casey frowned at him. "But if it had something to do with us, someone must have known beforehand about our meeting. How could anyone have found out about that?"

"That's why Batterson's afraid we've been hacked. Somehow the bomber would have had to intercept our communications to find out our schedule."

"What if Batterson can't retrieve his phone?" E.J. asked. "It might be harder to get back into the building than he thinks. I've seen the police, and the Feds shut down bombing scenes for days while they work them, especially if they suspect terrorism. I wonder if your boss is a little too optimistic."

"You don't know our chief," Doug said. "He's not a man who takes no for an answer. If he says he'll get his phone, I'm sure he will."

"What phone was he using when he called you, Doug?"

Casey asked. "I assume he was already concerned about using a secure line."

Doug gave a little shrug. "He didn't have his phone on him. Lost it in the explosion. He borrowed a phone from the paramedic who's treating him."

"Wait a minute. He's being treated by a paramedic? How badly is he hurt?"

"You know better than to ask that. He'd never tell us. Since he's walking and talking, I assume he's doing okay. Thankfully he wasn't in his office when the blast went off. The point of origin was nearby, however."

"Where was he then?"

"Down the hall. Making sure everyone was out of the building."

Casey nodded. "It figures he'd put his people first." Then her eyes widened, and the color drained from her face. "What about Shelly? Where was she?"

"Who's Shelly?" E.J. said.

"Batterson's assistant," Doug answered. "Her desk is right outside his door." He shook his head at Casey. "I just don't know, but I'm sure he would have made her leave right away. He wouldn't tell me anything about who was injured. Maybe for now it's best we don't know any of the details. We have to stay focused on our assignment."

Casey didn't say anything, just nodded.

Doug picked up his briefcase. It held all the paperwork associated with their witness. "Well, we need to get on the road. He doesn't want us to take the SUV." He gave Casey a tight smile. "He wants us to take your car. No government tags, no GPS tracker. Is that all right with you?"

"How old is your car?" E.J. asked. "Most newer cars have trackers."

"You should remember my car. You rode in it several times." Casey spoke calmly enough, but her voice had a definite edge.

There it was again. She was angry with him. But why? She was the one who took off, so it couldn't be that. Was it that last case they'd worked together? It was awful, but that wasn't really their fault. Surely she wasn't still upset about that. Even if she was, why would she direct her anger toward him?

While Casey and Doug talked about the car, E.J.'s mind wandered back to the time he'd spent with Casey. She'd started dating Jared not long after their case concluded. In fact, E.J. had introduced them. The three of them had gotten along well. Almost too well. At one point, he stopped spending so much time with them. It got harder and harder to hide the feelings he'd started to develop for Casey. He still wasn't certain if she knew about it, or if she felt anything for him. It didn't matter. E.J. would never betray a friend. A couple of months after he pulled away, Casey and Jared began having problems. Jared told him they weren't getting along, and he was afraid the relationship wouldn't last much longer. Then suddenly Casey left town. Transferred to St. Louis. Not a word to any of her friends. Certainly not to him. Jared admitted he'd purchased an engagement ring and was hoping they still had a future. E.J.'s friend was left hurting, and E.J. was still angry with Casey for the cowardly way she'd handled the situation.

"So you still have that 2003 purple PT Cruiser?" E.J. asked

after Doug and Casey finished their conversation. "I figured you'd have something newer by now."

"I love that car. Why would I get rid of it? Keeping it in good shape costs less than buying something new."

"And you're sure it's okay if we take it?"

E.J. saw the muscle in Casey's jaw twitch, a sign she wasn't okay with it at all. But always the obedient public servant, she nodded. "It's fine. It's parked downstairs. Shauna was going to take it back to my place later today. I need to call her. . . ." Casey's voice trailed off. "Is Shauna . . . ?"

Doug was quiet as he met her eyes. "I'm sorry. I don't know. We need to have faith."

Casey didn't answer, just looked away.

Doug turned to E.J. "We're going to a spot in Ohio where we're to wait for the FBI. It's not a safe house. Batterson didn't want us to go anywhere that could be traced. Only the FBI and Batterson will know of our location. When we meet the Feds, they'll take charge over our witness. You and I will head back here, Casey. I know it's not what we wanted, but we have to put Valerie's safety first. If we're compromised, we need to hand her over to someone else."

Casey started to say something when Doug waved her comment away. "There's no debate over this. The chief was very clear."

E.J. noticed how quiet Valerie had been. She was clearly concerned, and he didn't blame her. She didn't flinch at the news that she'd get protection from the FBI. Frankly, E.J. felt the same way he guessed Casey did—that the Marshals were better equipped to get her safely to her destination. Yet he understood Batterson's decision, and at this point he was fine with cutting his time with Casey short. She obviously had a problem with him, and that kind of personal stuff didn't belong in a serious situation like this.

"Let's get this show on the road." After getting their own bags, Doug grabbed one of Valerie's suitcases while E.J. got the other.

As they filed out of the room, E.J. noticed that Casey refused to look at him. He couldn't help but worry a little. This could end up being a very dangerous assignment, and everyone needed to be on the same page. If circumstances were normal, he'd wonder if Casey should be pulled off the team. But this wasn't a normal situation. They had no idea which deputies were alive and who had died. Casey was one of the best deputies he'd ever worked with, and he had to believe she would pull herself together. He was determined to make this work and knew Casey was just as committed. Regardless of their personal feelings, they'd never put the life of their witness at risk.

CHAPTER
FOUR

Richard Batterson held a towel to his face, attempting to staunch the flow of blood running down his cheek. He wasn't sure how badly injured he was. Flying glass from the explosion had caused several deep cuts, and his back and shoulders hurt from being hurled across the room and slammed against the pop machine. He assumed that was when he'd lost his cellphone. It didn't matter, though, because he was aware they were vulnerable. Someone had breached their security. The only phone he could trust was the one upstairs in his desk. It was completely secure; the password automatically changed hourly, and he was the only one who knew the pattern and could figure out the codes.

He looked down at his body and took stock of what parts still worked. He could see, he could hear, and he could think. He could walk, but barely. Blood and sweat caused his clothes to stick to him. It didn't help that it was late July and the heat was already building. Batterson tried to take a deep breath, but it was like breathing in steam. More than anything, he wanted to stand under a cold shower while drinking in as much water as he possibly could. He felt incredibly parched.

But for now, he sat outside a dirty, dusty parking garage down the street from his office. He'd been ushered out of the building by LEOs trying to secure the scene. Police and the FBI had cordoned off a large area around the blast site. The street had been blocked off too. He stared at all the people surrounding him. Some were being treated for injuries, others just standing around as if in shock. He understood. He prided himself on being prepared for anything, but he had to admit that being blown up was unexpected.

He couldn't take his eyes off the body bags. Seven so far. He wanted to ask who they were, but he just couldn't. Not yet. Right now he had to concentrate on getting Valerie Bennett to D.C. It was his top priority. After that, he'd find out who was dead and who was injured and contact the families. After that, every second he had would be spent finding the dirtbag who had planted the bomb that decimated their offices. And when he did, nothing would stop him from making sure justice was done. He had to choke back the rage that threatened to consume him. Right now, out-of-control anger would only keep him off-balance, and he couldn't afford to give in to it.

He noticed the paramedic who had allowed him to use his phone was watching him closely, while still assisting other injured persons. Batterson knew the guy wanted to cart him off to the hospital, but Batterson wasn't ready to go yet. There were things he needed to take care of first.

"You could have internal injuries, sir," the paramedic had said when Batterson asked to use his phone. "I don't want you dying on me today."

Batterson got the feeling that the only reason the paramedic allowed him to use his phone was because a couple of cops stood near them and overheard Batterson's request. They'd encouraged the paramedic to let go of his phone for a few minutes. In fact, they'd insisted on it. Grudgingly, the paramedic handed the phone over without any further argument, but Batterson could see the tension in his expression.

Although Batterson had promised to get in the ambulance after a couple of calls, it was a promise he had no intention of keeping. Whoever had set the bomb wouldn't be tracking a random paramedic's phone, and he needed to make sure his people were safe. He lifted the phone and began punching in another number. The paramedic saw him and started walking his way, probably with the intention of forcing him to go to the hospital. Batterson had just hit the last number when a crying woman grabbed the arm of the paramedic and pulled him over to a man sitting on the ground, holding his head in his hands. Batterson didn't know these people and assumed they were innocent bystanders hit by flying debris. He was grateful to the woman for giving him time to make another call.

One of the ambulances started to pull away, its siren drowning out everything else. Batterson struggled to his feet and walked into the parking garage. His body screamed at him, and he slumped down behind a concrete parking barrier. When the person on the other end answered, Batterson quickly said what he needed to and was getting ready to hang up when the paramedic jogged up next to him.

"Just one more quick call and I'll give you back your phone," Batterson said. He clicked off the phone and stared

up at the man, who didn't look pleased by his proclamation. Batterson wasn't used to begging, but this next call was
terribly important. "Look, I've already explained that I'm
the Chief Deputy U.S. Marshal for this district. I'm going
to have to insist that you allow me to use this phone." He
noticed the paramedic's badge. *John Nelson.* "John, I really
appreciate your concern for me, but this is important. Lives
depend on it."

As Batterson stared at the man, he realized that there was
no one else near them. John suddenly smiled, then glanced
around. It was then Batterson knew he was in trouble. He
went to reach for his gun, but he wasn't fast enough. John
stuck the barrel of his own gun into Batterson's chest.

"Toss your gun and give me the phone," he said. "Now."

Batterson took out his weapon slowly and threw it to the
ground, out of reach. He handed John the phone. "You're
our bomber," he said matter-of-factly.

John gave him another sweet, almost sickening smile. When
he did, Batterson noticed the scar that stretched from the corner of his left eye and ended not far from the side of his mouth.
The skin tightened by the scar pulled on his eye, making it
look deformed. It seemed that John had made an attempt to
hide it, but sweat had caused his thick makeup to run.

"I saw you in our building. You were dressed as a maintenance man."

John laughed. "It was way too easy to get into your offices.
Just check in as a new agent, change clothes in the bathroom,
and become the person no one pays attention to." He shook
his head, his eyes drilling into Batterson's. "Too bad you
didn't recognize me sooner. It might have saved your life."

Batterson looked around. Was there someone who might be able to help him? Hope dissipated as he realized that all attention was on the injured and dead outside the parking garage. At that moment it wasn't losing his life that bothered him the most. It was not making that last phone call. He shouldn't have put it off. His failure had put his people's lives in danger.

Batterson prepared himself for the bullet that would end his life. What he didn't expect was that John, or whatever his real name was, would raise the barrel of the gun and slam it as hard as he could into the side of Batterson's head. As he drifted away, Batterson felt something else. Like a beesting on his thigh.

Then he slipped away into darkness.

CHAPTER
FIVE

Casey pushed the tote bag that held her clothes to the side so that all the other suitcases and bags would fit in the back of her Cruiser. She'd taught herself to pack efficiently. By interchanging certain pieces of clothing, she could come up with several different outfits. She looked down at her black slacks, small black pumps, white blouse, and black jacket. Proper clothing for accompanying a witness under normal circumstances, but things had changed. She wished she could get her jeans and sneakers out of her bag, but they needed to get out of town as quickly as possible.

When they got into the car, she noticed E.J. took the passenger seat before Doug had a chance to grab it. She pushed back a quick flash of irritation. Why did he have to sit in front? She didn't want to be that close to him.

As she put her key in the ignition, she glanced sideways. E.J. Queen didn't look like a law enforcement officer. Thirty years old, tall, lean, dark curly hair and dark eyes, he looked more like an aristocrat than a Deputy U.S. Marshal. There was a good reason for that. Although he was born in the U.S., he was raised in London. His father, a banker, moved his wife and only child back to the States when E.J. was sixteen. When E.J. expressed an interest in law enforcement, his wealthy parents were horrified. Casey had no idea how they got along now, but when they worked together in D.C., E.J. had mentioned some long-standing family tension.

E.J.'s smooth looks and English accent were deceptive. Anyone who thought he was weak would be in for a surprise. An ex-Marine, he had a tattoo on his right arm that said *Semper Fi*, and in a dangerous situation there wasn't anyone else she'd want to have her back. He was tougher than nails. At one time she actually found herself attracted to him, but then he introduced her to his friend, Jared. She took that as a sign E.J. wasn't interested. Even though she still had feelings for him while she dated Jared, she wasn't the kind of person who would ever come between friends. She'd struggled to fight her attraction to E.J. Now, however, all she felt was contempt.

Ignoring him, she turned around to address Doug, who was also wearing a suit. "Once we get out of town, I suggest we change clothes. This car may not look like a government vehicle, but we still look like Marshals."

"Good point," Doug said. "We need to come off like four people on a road trip." He looked over at Valerie. "Two couples. That should help us."

Casey met E.J.'s gaze. Two couples? Her stomach lurched at the thought. "We'll see," she said, glancing in her side mirror. She backed out of her parking space and pulled out onto the street. "Highway 70 or something else, Doug? My guess,

70's faster. More traffic. We might get lost in the crowd. But if we take an alternative route, we could throw them off."

Doug was silent for a moment. Then he said, "I say we take 70. Highway Patrol is pretty active on that stretch of road. And as you said, it's so busy, we could blend in."

"But if we take a less obvious way, maybe by the time they figure it out, we'll be so far ahead of them, they won't be able to catch up," E.J. interjected.

"No, I agree with Doug," Casey said quickly. As soon as the words left her mouth, she wondered if she really thought Doug was right or if she just didn't want to agree with E.J. She recognized that she wasn't relying on her training and was reacting out of emotion. She owed Valerie more than that, so she rethought her conclusion. But in the end, she really did believe Highway 70 was the safer way to go. It would be very difficult for anyone to put them in a compromising position if they were surrounded by traffic. She looked over at E.J. "If we take 70, we have a lot of eyes on us. I don't want to get too isolated. That could be dangerous."

E.J. was silent for a moment. "I think you're right," he said finally. "Good point."

Casey realized that, so far, E.J. had been more professional than she'd been. She had to get her emotions under control. Right now she needed to be at her best. "We'll need to stop at a gas station and get a couple of maps. Can't use our GPS."

"I can look it up on my phone," Valerie said, reaching into her purse.

"No," Doug said sharply. "We need you to keep your phone off." He frowned at her. "Do you have an iPhone?"

She shook her head. "No. Why?"

"They can be tracked even when they're turned off."

"I didn't know that," Valerie said. "You mentioned something about the phones earlier. Sorry. I just forgot. I use it for almost everything. It's just an automatic reaction, I guess."

"Maybe it would be best if I took it," Doug offered.

Casey glanced in her rearview mirror. At that same instant, Valerie looked up and caught Casey staring at her. She could see the apprehension in Valerie's eyes. They needed her to calm down. Transporting an unstable witness could make things even more difficult.

"Just make sure it stays off," Casey said, giving her a smile. "If you have a pocket inside your purse, put it there and fasten it. That will help you to remember you can't use it."

"Th . . . thanks, I'll do that." She reached down for her purse and fumbled around a bit. Casey heard the sound of a zipper.

"Speaking of phones," Casey said, "I've turned on the burner phone. We should be hearing from Batterson before long."

"Are you sure you should leave it on?" E.J. asked. "It can't be traced, but the signal could be triangulated. That could give someone an approximate idea where we are."

"Maybe, but there's no way anyone can tie this phone to me. I had a friend buy it with cash. Even if our perps tracked all my purchases and used facial-recognition software in every single store that sold burner phones in the St. Louis area over the past two years, they couldn't find me or this phone."

"I'm confused," E.J. said. "Is this your only phone?"

She shook her head. "No, of course not."

"So you keep this phone just in case you need an untraceable phone?" E.J. chuckled. "I don't think I've heard of any-one else doing that."

"Our chief is big on burners," Doug interjected. "Says we need to be prepared in case we ever need one. I have one, but I didn't bring it. Didn't think it was necessary for this as-signment." He tapped Casey on the shoulder. "When we get out of the city limits, you should probably turn it off, Casey. In the event someone's tracking all phones headed toward D.C. You have the number of the chief's secure line, right?"

"Of course," she said sharply. As soon as the words left her mouth, she realized she'd just snapped at Doug. She had to get herself together and quit thinking about E.J. "Thanks, Doug," she said, even though it wasn't necessary. She looked in the rearview mirror and saw him staring at her strangely.

"No problem," he said. He shot her a quick smile to show her he wasn't offended. She breathed an inward sigh of relief. Doug was a great guy, and she enjoyed working with him.

Silence settled in the car as Casey navigated the streets of St. Louis, heading toward the highway. They were on the outer edge of the cordoned-off area. Even though traffic was heavy with others fleeing downtown, at least they were mov-ing. It certainly could have been worse.

"So you two worked together in D.C.?" Doug said finally, directing his question to E.J.

"Sure did. In fact, we were a great team. It was almost like we could read each other's minds." He chuckled. "We even had code words and phrases, remember, Casey? We had this one phrase we were going to use if one of us got in trouble but couldn't speak freely. You know, like a way to communicate that we needed help."

"What was it?" Doug asked.

E.J. grinned. "Do you remember, Casey?"

"Sure. *Just keep your head down.*"

"That's pretty simple," Doug said.

E.J. nodded. "It's supposed to be. Something unusual might sound suspicious. Our chief loved the idea and suggested other teams come up with the same kind of thing."

"Always good to impress the boss."

E.J. looked away. "Yeah. He was great, only he's gone now. We've got a new guy named Claypool. He's good, but it takes time to get used to someone different."

"Oh, sorry. I can't imagine losing Batterson. We all really respect him."

Casey snuck a quick look at E.J. He'd left out the part where he'd felt they needed a code because a serial killer had threatened to kidnap and kill Casey. E.J. wanted her to have something that would tip him off if she ever felt she was in danger. Casey had remained out of the killer's grasp, but he'd gotten away from them. Because of their failure, their boss lost his job. At the time, they'd both felt responsible. Casey still did.

"Maybe we need a code phrase," Doug said, grinning.

E.J. laughed. "You can use ours. Let's just pray none of us ever need it."

"Amen," Doug said.

Ever since they'd left, Casey had been focusing her attention on looking for any cars that might be tailing them. She'd changed lanes several times, watching for vehicles that followed the same pattern. At one point she became wary of a black truck, but after a while it turned off on an exit and drove away.

E.J. must have noticed she was keeping an eye out for tails, because he said, "I'll help watch, Casey. That way you can keep your eyes on the road."

"Thanks, but I'm capable of doing two things at a time."

E.J. didn't respond, though Casey could feel his eyes on her. This was going to be harder than she'd thought. "On second thought," she added, willing herself to sound calm and controlled, "it really would help if you'd check the traffic behind us. Thanks."

"You're welcome."

They'd been driving for almost two hours when Valerie cleared her throat. "I'm sorry, but can we stop soon? I need to use the bathroom. Maybe get something to drink."

"Sure," Casey said. "I'm thirsty too. I'll pull off as soon as I can." She began to look for a busy convenience store that also sold gas. They couldn't risk standing out. She glanced at Doug in the rearview. "We can change clothes."

"And grab some lunch," E.J. said. "It's past noon and I'm starving."

Casey hadn't thought about food. When she was on assignment, she'd frequently forget to eat. "Sorry. Sure." She pointed to a sign on the side of the road. "There's a QuikTrip up ahead. How about that? They have good food."

E.J. chuckled. "You must not eat out much if you think a convenience store serves good food."

Casey felt the hair on the back of her neck stand up, a sign that her temper was getting ready to flare. She took a deep breath and steadied herself. "I meant for fast food. Something quick. They even have healthy choices."

"I know," he said with a smile. "I was just teasing you. Sorry."

She'd overreacted. She wished D.C. had sent anyone except E.J. Why did it have to be him? She said a silent prayer, asking God to give her patience and help them get their witness to safety. Doing her job professionally was more important than dealing with old grudges. She was disappointed in herself.

She moved over to take the exit off the highway that led to the QuikTrip. Suddenly another car cut in front of her, almost forcing her off the road. She fought to get her car under control and barely kept them from careening off the pavement and tumbling down the embankment.

CHAPTER
SIX

E.J. grabbed his gun from its holster as Casey sped up, following the car that had cut them off. Yet E.J. wasn't suspicious. No one with any brains would use a sporty red vehicle to follow a target.

Casey stayed behind the Mustang until it turned into the parking lot of a restaurant. Then she pulled in front of it, effectively blocking it.

"Everyone, stay cool," E.J. said before opening his door. "Back me up, Doug." He holstered his weapon, not wanting to confront the driver with a drawn weapon since he wasn't convinced it was necessary.

"Ready," Doug said, gun in hand but pointed at the ground. Nodding, E.J. approached the car, Doug right behind him. Making certain he could easily get his weapon if he needed to, he leaned down and peered in the window. Inside was a girl, sixteen, maybe seventeen, looking scared out of her mind. E.J. made a circular gesture with his hand, asking her to lower her window. Although she didn't look like she wanted to comply, she finally did.

"You want to tell me why you cut us off like that?" he asked in a stern voice.

"I . . . I'm sorry, mister. I almost missed my exit. I thought there was more room." She sniffed loudly. "I haven't been driving long. It was really dumb."

"You're right, it was." E.J. was torn between berating her and praying for her. In the end, he said, "You could have caused a serious accident. You might have hurt my friends and even killed yourself."

"I know." She shook her head. "I'll be more careful. I promise."

E.J. sighed as he studied her. He wasn't certain she really understood the seriousness of the situation. "You know, I had a friend in high school who thought he was invincible. Didn't wear his seat belt." He pointed to her unfastened seat belt. "One night he lost control of his car and slammed into a tree. Flew through the windshield. His body was so torn up, his parents couldn't even identify him. I'll never forget their faces. I suggest you latch that seat belt and drive more responsibly so your parents will never have to live through a night like that."

The look on her face made it clear he'd gotten through to her. Tears ran down her cheeks. "I will. You don't have to worry about me ever doing something like that again."

"Good." E.J. straightened and walked away from the car. When he and Doug got into the Cruiser, he shook his head. "Just a teenager who needs to learn how to drive. Let's get going."

Casey turned the car around and drove back to QuikTrip. It took about twenty minutes for them to gas up, use the bathroom, change clothes, and get something to eat. Casey was right about the food. He grabbed a turkey sandwich, fruit, and an iced tea. He had to laugh as he watched Casey pick out two hot dogs, a candy bar, and a soda.

He sidled up next to her at the register. "What happened to healthy choices?"

At first it seemed as if he'd angered her once again, but then the corner of her mouth twitched and turned into a smile. "I might give good advice, but it doesn't mean I always follow it." She nodded at the hot dogs. "They're great here. The candy and the pop keep me awake. Sometimes driving makes me sleepy."

He nodded. "Yeah, me too. Maybe I should grab a candy bar too."

"Maybe."

They paid for their food and left. As they walked toward the car, E.J. couldn't help but notice how different Casey looked in jeans and sneakers. She was still wearing the white blouse she'd had on under her jacket, but she'd taken her blond hair out of the ponytail she always wore. Her golden hair, streaked with strands that were almost white, lay soft and thick on her shoulders. He couldn't help but think she'd be perfect for a shampoo commercial. Jared had told him once that Casey truly had no idea how beautiful she really was. *"She thinks she's plain,"* he'd said. *"Guess her mother convinced her she wasn't attractive."*

E.J. couldn't understand how anyone could make Casey Sloane feel inferior. Not only was she gorgeous, she could

outshoot, outfight, and outthink a lot of the other deputies in D.C., including him. She had a natural talent for
the job. When she left the office in D.C., more than one
person commented that the department wasn't as strong
without her. Pretty good for someone as small and young
as Casey. Actually, it was pretty good for anyone in law
enforcement.

"Why don't you let me drive for a bit?" he offered.

"I'm fine. I'm used to the car."

"Casey, it will take almost eight hours to get to Ohio.
Closer to nine with stops. You can trust me with your car, you
know. Wouldn't you like to eat your lunch and relax a bit?"

He could see the inner struggle play out on her face. Finally
she said, "Okay. I guess I could use a break. Thanks, E.J."

He smiled. "Not a problem."

He noticed that she almost smiled back, but then she
turned away as if fighting the urge. Seemed that one smile
a day was her limit. They were almost to the car when he
stopped. "Doug, will you take our food to the car? I want
to talk to Casey for a minute."

"What are you doing?" Casey asked E.J., her voice tight.

He looked at Doug. "Please take Valerie back to the
car."

Nodding at him, Doug quietly took the bags and drinks
E.J. held out. He escorted Valerie toward the car, leaving E.J.
and Casey standing in the middle of the parking lot like two
fighters getting ready to duke it out.

"Let's step over here," E.J. said, gesturing toward a small
patch of grass near the exit. Though he wasn't certain she'd
follow him, she did. Now they stood toe-to-toe, Casey glaring

up at him. "Look, Casey," E.J. began, "something's wrong and I truly have no idea what it is. Our witness needs our full attention, and you're not giving it to her."

She crossed her arms and looked away.

"You've been angry ever since I showed up," he said, his voice louder than he meant it to be. He took a deep breath and forced himself to speak quieter. "You want to tell me why? I thought we worked well together. I don't remember doing anything to earn this kind of treatment."

"That's just it," she said quickly. "You never did anything at all. In fact, you disappeared completely. I thought we were friends, but then you just walked away."

E.J. shook his head, totally confused. "You mean when you and Jared were dating? You were dating my friend, Casey. Three's a crowd. I backed off to give you two some space."

"I don't believe you."

E.J. was shocked by the intensity of her gaze. "I honestly don't know what you're talking about. Besides, you're the one who left. You walked out on Jared. He was devastated, and I had to help him work through it. I think he left D.C. because he couldn't stand being in the same town where you two had been together. I lost my best friend because of you." He hadn't meant to allow that last comment to slip out, yet it was true.

"You . . . you had to help *him*? Are you the most clueless man in the world?"

E.J. just stared at her. "You're going to have to explain."

Casey took a deep breath. "How long have you known Jared?"

"Since I was sixteen. When we moved back to the States, he lived next door. We became friends immediately. We both wanted the same things out of life, even decided to join the Marshals at the same time."

Her expression was cold and emotionless as her brown eyes locked on his. Deep, dark pools he felt he could drown in. He found himself having to catch his breath.

"Tell me about his parents," she said.

He frowned, not sure why this was important. "Jared had it tough. His father was a drunk, and he beat up on his wife. My dad had to call the police more than once. Finally they got divorced, and his father took off. To this day, Jared has no idea where he is."

"So his dad beat his mom?"

"Yes," E.J. said. "So?"

"We see a lot of things in law enforcement. What did we learn in that seminar we took about kids with abusive parents?"

"Many times they follow the same pattern of abuse," E.J. said automatically, reciting something from a class everyone was forced to take in D.C. At the time, he'd thought it wasn't really applicable to his job. He wasn't a cop on the street. Suddenly the light clicked on and he realized what Casey was trying to tell him.

"Jared wasn't anything like his father," he said emphatically, trying to choke back feelings of resentment. "Jared hated him. He was determined not to follow in his footsteps. He would never put anyone through what he and his mother endured." All of a sudden, memories began to pop to the surface. Casey sporting a sling on her left arm, saying she'd

48

injured herself playing basketball with friends. The limp she blamed on pulling a muscle while running. The thick makeup she wore for a couple of weeks, saying she was trying a new look. One by one, the layers of lies began to peel away. If there'd been a place to sit, he'd have taken it. His knees felt weak. "Casey . . ."

"When things got really bad, you took off. You couldn't ignore it anymore so you left."

"That's not true. I . . . I had no idea. Jared hated men who hurt women. I just can't believe . . ."

"You're trying to convince me you didn't know? You two didn't laugh about it behind my back?"

He stared at her slack-jawed. "I would never do something like that. How could you believe that of me?" Something occurred to him then. "Wait a minute. Why didn't you walk away? You didn't have to put up with that."

He realized immediately that he'd made a mistake. The seminar they'd attended had emphasized the confusion that comes from being in an abusive situation. "I'm sorry, Casey. I'm not judging you. Really. I have no idea what you went through, but you have to believe me when I say I didn't know anything about it."

She was quiet for a moment. "It's all right. I can't explain why I didn't leave immediately. I just thought . . . well, I thought he'd change. But he didn't." She glanced toward the car. "We need to get going."

"I feel awful," E.J. said, shaking his head. "I wish I'd done something different. It just . . . I mean, it truly never occurred to me. I wasn't thinking, wasn't being observant." He grunted. "You always seemed so strong. In control. I never saw you as someone who needed anyone. Especially me."

"Forget it. I shouldn't have gotten upset with you. In fact, I shouldn't have told you about it. I really don't want to talk about this anymore. Not now, not while we're on assignment." She started walking toward the car.

"Wait a minute." He reached out and grabbed her arm. "Are you sure this doesn't have anything to do with Carlton Randolph?"

She twisted out of his grip, her face a tight mask of anger. "Of course not. How could it?" She inhaled sharply, then pushed the air out slowly. "Let's get back to work, okay?"

She strode away quickly, leaving him standing in the parking lot, bewildered. First, she was upset, almost out of control, and then she was the trained Marshal he expected her to be. He was confused. Angry at Jared . . . even angrier at Casey. He'd never seen her as the type of woman who couldn't or wouldn't defend herself. But as he stood there, he realized that no matter how strong and competent she was, Casey Sloane was still a human being. She'd needed help, and he hadn't been there for her.

He'd noticed her abrupt reaction to Randolph's name. She must still blame herself for what happened on the case. Could that have anything to do with what she'd gone through with Jared? Try as he might, he couldn't figure out a connection. What bothered him the most was that she hadn't kicked Jared to the curb sooner. Her actions didn't seem to match what he knew about her. Casey didn't need to hold on to a man like Jared. She didn't have to take abuse from anyone. She could have any man she wanted.

She could have had him.

He followed her back to the car, trying to focus on the witness they had to protect while dealing with emotions he wasn't sure how to control.

CHAPTER
SEVEN

Deputy Marshal Tony DeLuca searched through all the people gathered outside the bombed building, trying to find his boss. It had been hours since anyone had seen Batterson. Tony had been in the far side of the building when the bomb went off. Except for some things falling off shelves, everyone in that part of the facility was okay.

Tony had called the hospital to see if Batterson had been transported there, but they didn't have any record of him. Then he did the unthinkable. He made the medical examiner unzip all the body bags. Seeing friends and colleagues dead, their sightless eyes staring back at him, made his stomach churn, but he had to keep looking. He was just starting to go back through the crowd once again when he noticed a boot peeking out from behind the wall of the parking garage across the street. Tony ran over there, brushing past a police officer who wanted to know where he was going.

As he rounded the wall, he discovered Richard Batterson's

body. Tony knelt down next to him, praying. He put his fingers on Batterson's neck and was relieved to feel a pulse, although it was weak and incredibly fast. He jumped up and yelled at a pair of paramedics who were treating a woman sitting on the back bumper of their ambulance. They grabbed their kits and ran over.

"Sorry, we didn't see him," they said as they knelt down beside Batterson.

"Is he going to be okay?" Tony asked while they worked on the chief.

"Not sure. He's got a pretty bad head injury, and his heart-beat is uneven. We need to get him to the hospital right away. Can you tell us who he is?"

"Yeah. Can I come with you?"

"Sure. We've already transported everyone else who needs to go. You can give us his information on the way."

The other guy, a tall man with red hair, frowned and seemed to be scanning the area.

"Is something wrong?" Tony asked.

"We've lost someone. Another paramedic."

"Could he have left with a different crew?"

"Maybe, but it would be highly unusual." He shrugged and turned his attention back to Batterson. "Let's get going. We'll look for him later. Situations like this cause a lot of confusion."

While the tall one went to get a gurney from the ambulance, and the other paramedic worked on Batterson, Tony pulled out his phone. His fiancée, Kate, answered immediately. He'd already called her to tell her he was okay, but she was still worried.

"I found Batterson. He's hurt pretty badly, Kate. I'm going with him to the hospital."

"Okay. I'll meet you there."

He started to tell her it wasn't necessary, but the faces of the dead floated in front of him and he knew he needed her. "See you there," he said quickly before hanging up. He couldn't lose it now. Not in front of the paramedics. Right now, getting Batterson to the hospital was all that mattered.

"Shouldn't the chief have phoned by now?" Doug asked.

Casey checked her watch. He'd had almost four hours to contact them. Still nothing. "Maybe it's taking a long time to get back into the building."

"No, something's not right," E.J. said. "If this guy is as stubborn as you say, he would have found a way to call us."

Although Casey didn't want to agree with him, she was worried too. "Let's stop. I'll call a friend of mine. See if she knows what's going on. I could use some coffee anyway."

"Who's your friend?" E.J. asked. "Someone you can trust?"

She felt a flash of resentment at his question, but she fought back the biting remark that popped into her head. He was just trying to be careful. "Yes," she said evenly. "She's a deputy, but she's on maternity leave. She should be at home. I'll call her landline with the burner. No one will trace it."

"But if all the deputies are compromised . . ."

"It's a landline, E.J. We've got to get some information. We can't keep flying blind."

She noticed the knuckles on his hands turn white as he gripped the steering wheel. She wasn't trying to upset him, but they had to talk to Batterson. They were out of communication with the Marshals, and it wasn't safe. Casey trusted Mercy to get a message to the chief. She waited until E.J. turned off the highway and pulled into another convenience store. Casey turned around to look at Doug and Valerie. "If you need anything, get it now. We probably won't stop again for a while."

"I could use something cold," Doug said. "How about you, Valerie?"

"That sounds great. Thanks."

She'd been quiet ever since she got into the car. Except for some occasional small talk, Valerie spent almost all her time staring out the window, ignoring them. Casey found it odd that a reporter would have so little to say.

"I'm staying here," E.J. said. "Can you grab me a bottle of water, Doug?"

Doug nodded and got out of the car. Casey stared into her side mirror as he and Valerie walked toward the store's entrance.

"I'm going to make that call," she told E.J. as she opened her door. She didn't want to talk in front of him. She felt him judging everything she did, and it bugged her. He'd changed clothes at their last stop and was wearing jeans, black boots, and a short-sleeved black shirt. He looked great, and for some reason, that irritated her even more. At least she was able to be civil to him. She felt she'd finally gotten herself under control, and she was determined to stay that way.

She walked a few feet away from the car. As she dialed Mercy's number, she reassured herself that she wasn't putting Valerie in danger. Not contacting Batterson was riskier than placing this phone call. So far, they appeared to be safe. Their trip had been uneventful. They'd all watched for cars that might be following them. Every time they thought a vehicle might be suspicious, it would turn off the highway or pass them.

The phone rang about four times before Mercy St. Laurent answered. Casey was so glad to hear Mercy's voice, she fought back tears. Mercy was a top-notch deputy, as was her husband, Mark. They were awaiting the birth of their first child, a girl they'd already named Rose.

"Mercy, it's me. Casey."

"Oh, thank God, Casey. I still don't know who was hurt in the explosion. They're keeping the identifications quiet for now."

"But Mark's okay?"

"Yes. He wasn't near the blast. It mainly hit the area around the chief's office."

"Actually, that's why I'm calling. We're transporting a witness. Batterson told me this morning that he thinks the explosion was meant for us. He ordered us to take off with the witness and meet up with the FBI at a safe location. He was going to get his secure phone out of the building and call hours ago, but we haven't heard from him. I'm getting concerned."

"You . . . talked to him this morning?" Mercy asked, a note of incredulity in her voice. "After the explosion?"

"Yeah. Why?"

"Because he's in the hospital, Casey. Mark's with him now. He was found not far from the office. He's badly injured."

Casey didn't know how to respond. It didn't make any

sense. "But . . . but he talked to us. Well, I mean he talked to Doug. How could he do that if he was in such bad shape?"

"And how could he get to the parking garage across the street?" Mercy added. "I guess he was able to hold on for a bit before he succumbed to his injuries. You know how stubborn he can be."

Although it made sense, Casey could hear the doubt in Mercy's voice. "You said Mark's at the hospital now?"

"Yeah. He's going to stay there for a while. Until they know for sure if . . . if the chief's going to make it."

"It's that bad?"

"It's pretty serious. A severe head injury, cuts and bruises, a couple of broken ribs. He's in intensive care."

"Okay. I'm going to call Mark at the hospital. I'll use the main hospital number. It should be safe. Mercy, please don't tell anyone except Mark that I contacted you. I didn't know what else to do."

"Where are you going?"

"Some place out of town. It's not one of our normal safe houses. Doug has the address. Batterson chose it. Better if I don't tell you over the phone. Just in case."

"Okay, but keep in touch with us, Casey. I don't like this. It sounds dangerous."

"Seriously, we're fine. Batterson already talked to the FBI. They're going to meet us at the location and take our witness to D.C. since we can't be sure how vulnerable we are right now."

"All right."

"Hey, how's Rose?"

Mercy chuckled. "She's fine. Getting more and more active. The doctor said it could be any day now. I'm ready. I thought being a Deputy Marshal was tough, but being pregnant takes some real guts."

Casey laughed. "I can't wait to hold that little girl."

"I'm sure she'll be excited to meet her Aunt Casey." Mercy was quiet for a moment. "Please be careful, okay?"

"Will do. And thanks, Mercy."

"You're welcome. See you soon."

Casey hung up, feeling slightly confused. How could Batterson have been in good enough shape to talk to Doug and then go so far downhill? Her gut told her something was wrong. Was she just being paranoid? Maybe she was still rattled by the bombing.

She rummaged in the trunk for her briefcase. She kept an emergency contact list and numbers for all the major hospitals in St. Louis, just in case a situation went sideways. She found the number to the hospital where they'd taken Batterson and called and requested intensive care. When they answered, she asked to speak to Deputy Mark St. Laurent, telling the nurse he was there visiting Richard Batterson. After a few minutes, she heard Mark's voice over the phone. She told him she'd just spoken to Mercy and that she knew about Batterson. "How's he doing?" she asked.

"Not good," Mark said. "He has a bad head injury and developed a subdural hematoma. It's like a pocket of blood pressing on his brain. They're getting ready to operate, Casey."

Casey could hear the concern in his voice. "What's the prognosis?"

"They don't know. It's a serious surgery."

"Doug talked to him this morning, Mark, before we took off with our witness."

There was a long pause. "I don't see how that could possibly be true," he said slowly. "He was unconscious when Tony found him and got him to the hospital. Tony's here too."

"Batterson was found across the street, right? So he had to have walked there himself. He must have collapsed after he talked to Doug."

"I guess," Mark responded, "but with his injuries it's hard to believe. Besides he didn't have a phone when he was found."

"Doug said he borrowed it from a paramedic."

"Well, that concerns me."

"What do you mean?"

"About thirty minutes ago, someone found the body of a paramedic under a car in the same parking garage where Batterson was found." Mark sighed deeply. "There's something very strange going on here, Casey. I'm worried that it might involve you and your witness in some way. You need to be really careful. Maybe you should turn around and come back here where we can protect you."

"I can't do that, Mark. The chief told me to keep going. To get Miss Bennett to D.C., and that's what I intend to do."

"I understand. Just be extra careful. Please."

Casey acknowledged his warning and told Mark she'd try her best to keep in touch. After she hung up, she stared toward her car for several seconds. Did they have reason to worry? Was there more going on than they realized?

CHAPTER
EIGHT

"Another two hours and we should be there," Doug said.

He'd taken over the driving for the last leg. Casey was in the back seat with Valerie, who still wasn't talking much. Casey noticed that she kept clenching and unclenching her fists. She was obviously worried. Casey decided to try a more direct approach to get her to open up. Maybe if she could get Valerie to talk, it would help her relax some.

"Valerie, this will be your first time testifying in front of a grand jury," Casey said. "Are you nervous?"

Valerie looked over at her, as if surprised Casey had mentioned the jury. "Uh, yeah. Some."

"I understand you were writing a story about an environmentalist when you stumbled into all this?"

Valerie nodded. "Martin Avery. Actually, I went to school with him. He made quite a name for himself. He was always really into saving the environment, you know, that kind of thing. I decided to call him one day and ask for an interview.

He was happy to do it." Her voice caught, and she turned to look out the window again. Casey could see Valerie's reflection in the glass. The stark expression on her face made it clear talking about her friend was difficult.

"He disappeared a while back, is that right?"

She nodded and slowly turned until her eyes met Casey's. "Martin was protesting the completion of a new oil pipeline. He and his group believed it would hurt the environment. After I wrote the article, we kept in touch. Then he started sending me strange texts. He was worried about Senator Dell Warren, one of Martin's big supporters. The senator financed quite a bit of Martin's work."

"And you became concerned as well?" Casey asked.

"Yeah. Martin was convinced the senator was involved with some scary people. He began to suspect Senator Warren was only helping him because someone else didn't want the pipeline to go through. Someone who didn't want to see America lose its dependence on foreign oil."

"Someone?" E.J. asked. "Did he know who?"

Valerie nodded. "I . . . I don't want to say."

Casey caught Doug looking at her in the rearview mirror. He frowned and shook his head slightly, and she gave him a little nod. This information wasn't secret. The news media already had the story after Valerie wrote about Martin's disappearance and his concerns about the senator's possible ties to terrorism. It seemed odd that Valerie didn't want to say the name Ali Al-Saud. Al-Saud was a businessman from Saudi Arabia who had huge investments in oil. He'd been very vocal in claiming he didn't know Senator Warren and certainly wasn't trying to stop the pipeline.

Al-Saud was reputed to have ties to ISIS, but it had never been proven.

"Martin went missing shortly after you wrote that article?" E.J. asked.

Valerie nodded. "The texts suddenly stopped. When I didn't hear from him for several days, I called the police. They looked for Martin, but they never found him. I told them everything I knew, and then the FBI contacted me, asked me to speak to a grand jury investigating the senator. I agreed. I'm not sure what they think I can tell them. Martin never gave me any proof."

From the tone of her voice, Casey wondered if Valerie regretted writing the article. This situation seemed to have taken over her life. "I'm sorry you've been put through all this," she said gently. "I can't imagine how hard it must be. At least once you testify, you should be able to get your life back."

Casey saw a tremor move slowly through Valerie's body. The woman was frightened. Really frightened.

"Look, I realize the bomb at the Marshals Office worries you," Casey said, "but like we said, it might not have anything to do with you. We handle a lot of sensitive cases. As for the precautions we're taking, it's just the way we do things. Don't judge your circumstances by our response. I'm sure everything will be fine." She reached over and lightly touched Valerie's arm. The reporter jumped like she'd been stabbed.

"I'm sorry," she said immediately. "I know you're trying to help. I'm just . . ." She sighed and shook her head. "This isn't me. I've always been pretty fearless. This has really rattled me." She gave Casey a tenuous smile. "Thanks for being so kind. Sorry I'm such a mess."

"It's understandable," Casey reassured, but she was surprised by Valerie's jumpiness. She was in the protection of the U.S. Marshals and was going to be turned over to the FBI. What was she so afraid of?

CHAPTER
NINE

Although the warm shades of salmon and blue in the ICU's waiting room were obviously meant to be calming, there was no way to chase away the reality of death that hovered over the muted elevator music and the soft, pale carpet. Tony had been here for hours, waiting. Praying. Mark had stayed for a while, but Tony finally told him to go home. His pregnant wife needed him.

He'd tried to take up watch right inside the door to the ICU, but the nurses had made him move to this room just outside the unit. He could see anyone who approached, however, and they assured him no unauthorized visitors would be admitted.

Tony rubbed his hands up and down the arms of the overstuffed chair in which he sat. A conversation he'd had with Mark had him on edge. Besides worrying about Batterson, now he was concerned about Casey and Doug—and their witness. There wasn't much he could do to help them now.

He didn't even know for sure where they were, and Batterson couldn't tell him where he'd sent them.

Next to him on a table were magazines and brochures. A lot of them about death and grieving. He tried to ignore them. Their presence stoked the fear slithering through him like a snake seeking its next victim.

"How long has it been since the doctor was here?"

Tony checked his watch and looked over at Dr. Karen Abbot. "About an hour and a half."

"Seems much longer."

He nodded. Karen's crimson fingernails tapped out a rhythm on the wooden arm of her chair. Tony wanted to ask her to stop, but he was afraid it might cause her to fall apart. He'd heard the chief was dating Karen, but still, it felt odd to see her here. Observe her fragility. She was the therapist on call when the chief was afraid one of them might "go squirrely," as he liked to call it. She was certainly attractive, with wavy chestnut-brown hair cut just above her shoulders, deep green eyes, a delicate face with full lips, and a trim body that never seemed to stay still. Even as her fingernails drummed out whatever song she heard in her head, her right leg, which was crossed over her left, bounced up and down to the beat of silent music she used in an attempt to calm herself.

Tony had seen her around the office, but she'd always seemed so cool and collected. This was something new. This was a woman in love. Funny how he'd never seen the chief as a man who could evoke this kind of response from a woman. He was . . . the chief. Not a man. Not a normal man, anyway. Except now he knew Richard Batterson really was human.

He lay in a hospital bed fighting for his life. Turned out he was vulnerable after all.

Batterson's adopted son, Marlon, sat next to Karen, his head hanging down. Tony had tried to talk to him, but Marlon only answered in grunts or one-syllable words. He might have seemed insolent to others looking on, but Tony knew he was just worried about Batterson. The chief had adopted Marlon after his mother, Carol Marchand, who was also Batterson's former administrative assistant, was arrested and put in prison. She'd colluded with the head of a drug cartel in an attempt to stop law enforcement from bringing an end to his operations. People had died because of her actions. Batterson cared about the boy and wanted to raise him. Eventually, Carol agreed to the adoption because she didn't want Marlon to go into the foster care system.

Right now, all Tony really wanted to do was sit here and wait for his fiancée, Kate, to return with something to eat. He was starving, hadn't eaten since this morning. But he felt the need to talk to Dr. Abbot and Marlon, to help them in some way.

He cleared his throat. "How did you find out he was here?"

"Mark called me. I . . . I couldn't believe it. I mean, Richard said he was okay when I spoke to him this morning."

Tony's ears perked up. "You heard from the chief this morning?"

She nodded. "Not long after the explosion. He called me to tell me he was all right. He was outside—in the parking garage across the street from the building."

This was the second person who said they'd talked to Batterson before Tony found him unconscious.

"Dr. Abbot . . ."

"Karen. Please."

"Okay. Karen, can you tell me exactly what the chief said to you?"

She blinked her long black lashes several times. "He didn't say much. Like I said, he wanted me to know he was okay. He said he'd talk to me again later, but first he needed to make another call. Said it was really important. I told him I loved him, and he hung up. That was it."

"I know this sounds like a weird question, but did you hear anything else? Background noise? Anyone else talking to him?"

"Yeah, there was something." Her forehead wrinkled as she tried to remember. "Right before the call disconnected, he was asking someone if he could use their phone one more time before he gave it back to them. Something like that." She looked at him through narrowed eyes. "Why? Is it important?"

"It might be. Would you excuse me?"

Tony got up and stepped outside the door, walking down the hall to another waiting room that was empty. Using the hospital phone, he dialed Mark's secure number.

"Just talked to Dr. Abbot," he said when Mark answered. "The chief said something else before he hung up from talking to her. Asked this person if he could use his phone one more time."

Mark's sigh drifted through the receiver. "I'm not sure what all this means. He called Doug. Said he was going to contact the FBI. Seems he also talked to Dr. Abbot. Who else was he planning to call? And whose phone did he use?

Karen said the number showed up as *unavailable*. The only reason she answered was because of the explosion. She didn't want to take a chance she'd miss a call from Batterson. The chief didn't have a phone on him when we found him, and his gun was found several feet away. Not sure why it was out of its holster."

"That does seem odd." Tony paused, trying to think through this latest information. "Mark, did the dead paramedic have a phone?"

"I have no idea, but I'll find out. Let me get back to you."

"Okay."

"Any change in the chief?"

"No. The doctor was here a little while ago. He said they're watching him closely, hoping he'll wake up. But nothing so far. The doctor seems very concerned. Any new leads on the bombing yet?"

"Well, they cleared the building. Only the one bomb. The bomb squad is looking at it. I have no idea what they've found. They're being pretty tight-lipped. Tom Monnier is in charge until the chief returns."

"You need to talk to him, Mark. Tell him about the chief's phone calls. I seriously doubt that whoever planted that bomb is through. I mean, why do something so obvious unless you're trying to make a point? But what is it? We haven't heard from anyone. No one's claimed responsibility. I'm worried they might be after the witness Casey and Doug are transporting."

"I'm not sure how all this ties together, but we can't take the chance that you're right. I'll get in touch with Tom right away. Maybe we need to call Doug and Casey."

"Let's leave that decision to Tom," Tony said. "Give him the number of the burner phone. Of course, if it's turned off, it won't do him much good."

Mark grunted. "I don't know. Maybe it's best if we don't know exactly where they are in case someone else is looking for them, though not having their location makes it impossible to provide backup. It makes me nervous."

"Wherever they are, they're supposed to meet the FBI at the secure location Batterson gave them. I'm sure we'll hear from them then. Hopefully it won't take much longer. Once the Feds take over, everything should be all right." Even as he said the words, Tony felt uneasy. Would someone who went to all this trouble just allow Casey and Doug to turn over their witness so easily?

"Okay. I'll get back to you as soon as I find out something."

"Same here. If anything changes with the chief, I'll call you."

"Thanks, Tony."

When Mark hung up, Tony stared at the phone. His Italian mother used to tell him that God put warning bells in our heads to tell us when we're in danger. *"You listen to God's bells, Tony,"* she'd say. *"When they go off, you stop what you're doing until you know everything's okay."*

Well, God's bells were ringing like crazy. The problem was, he didn't know what the danger was or how to protect their people from it.

Ben Mattan picked up the newspaper lying on the senator's porch, staying behind the thick bushes that lined the outside of the house. He used them as a shield until he made it around to the back. Then he unlocked the door to the senator's office and slipped inside. He quickly turned off the alarm, careful not to step in the blood that had sprayed onto the floor. The senator had only been dead about an hour. Not long enough to cause concern with the time of death. The police would assume the senator picked up his daily newspaper and took it to his office, where he looked at it and decided to end his life. Ben was certain they wouldn't look past the obvious. American police were sloppy, just like the doctors who would never find the real reason Richard Batterson was dead.

Light reflected off a large framed picture of Warren's ex-wife that sat on his desk. Divorced, but he still kept her picture. How stupid to let a woman—any woman—become that important. Women were placed on earth to serve men. And that was it. Still, it was lucky for them the senator had been willing to die to protect a woman who no longer cared for him.

Ben had been married once, and he'd never make that mistake again. He touched the scar on his face. The makeup was useless. He needed to get off the streets. The scar was too noticeable. People might remember, and he couldn't allow them to tie him to the bombing at the Marshals Office. He cursed the woman who'd cut him. His ex-wife. It was the last time that ignorant cow ever touched him—or anyone else.

Ben unfolded the newspaper and put it on the senator's desk. As had been the case for the past several days, an article about Warren's ties to terrorism splashed across the front page. Perfect. All that was left was the witness, and they had nothing to fear from her. True, their plan hadn't gone perfectly. Ben had been shocked by what he'd found on his phone after he took it back from Richard Batterson, but he'd come up with a plan that should fix everything. He had no intention of telling his boss what he'd done. Ali Al-Saud didn't like changes. Especially changes he didn't approve. It wasn't the only secret Ben kept from Al-Saud. Ben told Al-Saud only what he had to.

Ben picked up the two letters on the desk with his gloved hands and opened them. The letter to his ex-wife was fine. No problem. But the other letter was certainly troublesome. Ben almost admired Warren's forthrightness—his willingness to admit to his failures. Unfortunately, no one except him and Al-Saud would ever read these words. The senator had written it in longhand. If he'd used his computer, getting rid of the letter would have been much more difficult.

Ben refolded the paper, put it back into the envelope, and slipped it into a pocket in his jacket. His gloved hand touched the pill bottle he always carried with him. He pulled out the bottle, took off the cap, and put the bottle to his lips. He shook a couple of capsules into his mouth and then put the cap back and returned the bottle to his pocket. He waited a few seconds before chewing the bitter pills. Then he paused to enjoy the rush he knew would come. When it did, he smiled. His father didn't know about the pills—and he never would. Al-Saud didn't believe in relying on alcohol or drugs, but Ben needed them. They made him the man his father wanted him to be. Strong, decisive, confident. He didn't check his every move with his father anymore. He didn't need anyone telling him what to do. Not even Ali Al-Saud.

Ben grabbed a padded footstool next to an overstuffed leather chair in the corner and pushed it over to the bookshelves behind the senator's desk. It only took a few seconds for him to find and remove the hidden camera that had allowed him to watch the senator take his life. He put the footstool back, checked the desk and the senator carefully, making sure he hadn't disturbed anything. Then he hurried to two other rooms where he removed additional cameras and bugs. Once he was finished, he prepared to leave. It had been a long day. Flying from St. Louis to D.C. was tiring. He hadn't planned on the senator ending his life today. Would have been nice if he could have waited a day or two until Ben could get some rest. But these people rarely thought about anything except themselves.

Ben smiled as he slipped out the back door. Although he'd been thrown a few curveballs, he felt as if everything was finally under control.

CHAPTER
TEN

E.J. stared down at the map he held in his hands. He'd come to rely on GPS. Even though this was a new map, he couldn't find the turnoff he'd been looking for. For some reason, making mistakes in front of Casey irritated him. He hated the way he responded to her. Since he prided himself on his self-control, he was especially aggravated right now. He sighed and fought to refocus his attention on the stupid map.

"I think our turn is coming up soon," he said to Doug.

"Okay."

"We're looking for a town called Port Clinton?"

"Yeah. I guess it's on Lake Erie."

"Who does the house belong to?" Casey asked.

"Believe it or not, it's Batterson's," Doug said. "His second or third wife . . . can't remember, lived there after the divorce. All he said was that they stayed friends, and when she died, she left it to him. You know the chief. For him, that was a lot of information. I got the feeling he hadn't been here since she passed away."

"Was she sick?" Casey asked.

Doug nodded. "Cancer, I think."

"That's sad," Casey said. "He never shares personal things."

"You're right about that," Doug said. After a brief pause, he added, "You know, I can't believe the chief was in such bad shape when we talked. He sounded just like himself. The way he always does. A little worried, but fine."

"That's just the way he is," Casey said. "There was no way you could have known. It's just a good thing Tony found him before it was too late."

E.J. was surprised when Casey told him Batterson had been badly injured. It seemed almost impossible he could have sustained such serious trauma and talked to Doug on the phone not long after it happened. "It's just so hard to believe," E.J. had said. "I don't know anyone who can simply power through a severe head injury."

Although Casey had dismissed his concerns, citing Batterson's tough constitution, she'd had to admit it seemed unusual. Since there wasn't any way for them to know what was going on in St. Louis, they'd let it drop.

"I wonder if one of the reasons Batterson tends to stay away from women has to do with the ex-wife who died," Casey said. "Maybe it messed him up."

"Yeah, maybe," Doug said. "I guess something like that could make you gun-shy."

"Except he's not," Casey said. "Not now, anyway."

E.J. saw Doug glance into the rearview mirror, obviously looking at Casey. He wished Doug would keep his eyes on the road. "Our turn's coming up," he said sharply.

"Don't worry, I won't miss it." Doug checked the road

and then once again sought Casey in the mirror. "What do you mean? Is he dating someone?"

"Dr. Abbot."

Doug's eyebrows shot up. "The therapist? Are you serious?"

"Yep. I guess it's pretty serious. I hope she knows he's in the hospital."

"I wouldn't worry about that," Doug said. "All of St. Louis is aware of the bombing. I'm sure she's been notified."

Casey was quiet, staring out the window. E.J. could tell she was worried about her boss. A sign on the road brought his attention back to the matter at hand. "Hey, our turnoff is up here. On your right." Sure enough, about half a mile later they found the sign that would finally lead them to their destination. "Once we find this place, how do we get inside?" E.J. asked Doug.

"There's a key hidden in a fake rock in the front garden."

"Are you kidding?" E.J. couldn't help but laugh. "Someone whose husband is in law enforcement all these years hides a key in a fake rock? Wow. I assumed she'd have some real high-tech alarm system."

Doug shrugged. "I know. Weird, right?"

"So we're not going to walk in on anyone?" Casey asked.

"No. The chief said no one has lived here for years. He has a lady who cleans occasionally, but she's not scheduled to show up for another two weeks."

"Wonder why he kept the house," Casey mused. "And why his ex-wife would leave it to him."

Doug grunted. "You're asking me questions like I have some kind of answers. The chief told me next to nothing. Just that they were still friends when she died."

"Batterson's number one concern has always been for the job," Casey said. "And for his deputies. Not much room for a personal life."

Doug nodded but didn't say anything.

E.J. really hoped Richard Batterson recovered fully from his injuries. If he didn't, the people he worked with would obviously be devastated. For just a brief moment, he felt jealous of the relationship they had with their boss. It wasn't like that in D.C. The Marshals respected their leader, but they didn't socialize together. And E.J. would never call him unless it was for official business. That was okay with him. He didn't need to admire the people he worked for. He just needed them to help him get the job done. Whatever it was.

"How much farther?" Doug asked.

"Not much."

Doug slowed down. "Look, there's a burger place. Let's grab some food. We can't assume there's anything to eat in the house."

E.J. checked the rearview again. No cars behind them at all. "Okay. I think we're good."

Doug swung into the parking lot of the small carryout. It was a throwback from the 1950s. The paint job needed an update, and the neon sign out front had several letters out. "We'll go inside," E.J. told Casey and Valerie. "You stay here. What do you want?"

The women both ordered cheeseburgers, fries, and Cokes. When E.J. opened the door to the restaurant, the aroma of cooked beef and fried onions filled his nostrils. If the burgers tasted as good as the smells wafting from the kitchen, they were going to enjoy this meal.

"Whatcha need, honey?" An older woman sidled up to the old-fashioned yellow linoleum counter. She gave E.J. the once-over, a sly smile on her face.

Doug made a snorting sound, but E.J. ignored him. He smiled at the woman and gave her their order.

"Have a seat, sweetie," she said, pointing to the red plastic-covered stools in front of the counter. E.J. slid onto one as she winked at him and left for the kitchen.

"I'm gonna check out the jukebox," Doug said. "This place is cool."

E.J. nodded and perused the menu written on a nearby chalkboard. Too bad they weren't staying a while. He loved really good cheeseburgers, something his parents couldn't stand. *"Why grind up good beef, fry it, and throw it between two pieces of bread?"* his mother had told him more than once. *"Steak is much better for you. More sophisticated."* He loved his mother to pieces, but he'd rather have a well-done burger than a steak any day.

Once the FBI arrived, he'd be on his way to D.C. with Valerie. Maybe if the Feds took their sweet time, the deputies could stay the night and head back tomorrow. Might be able to work in one more trip to this place. He smiled at the thought.

Bobby Darin's voice filled the small diner: "Oh, the shark, babe, has such teeth, dear, and it shows them pearly white. . . ." E.J.'s grandmother had loved Bobby Darin and played his music for her grandson whenever they were alone together. "Mack the Knife" was his favorite Darin song. When he lived with his parents, E.J. was only allowed to listen to classical music and opera. He grinned at Doug and gave him a thumbs-up. He was getting ready to suggest another song by Darin when a black SUV pulled into the parking lot, blocking their view of Casey's car. E.J.'s hand immediately went for his gun as he ran toward the front door, Doug right behind him.

CHAPTER
ELEVEN

Tony downed another cup of awful coffee from a nearby vending machine. The cafeteria downstairs was closed, and the thick, dark liquid was the only thing available. He couldn't really call it coffee, but at least it was hot.

Karen had taken Marlon back to the chief's place, and he'd sent Kate home. She'd wanted to stay, but she had class in the morning. She was on the fast track to get her diploma. Kate would soon be a teacher. When she was through with school, they planned to get married. He could hardly wait. Every moment without her felt like an eternity. He'd met her through the Witness Protection Program. Now he couldn't imagine his life without her.

He was the only person still here. Tom had decided to keep someone posted outside Batterson's room until further notice. With the bomb going off close to his office, and the dead paramedic, they weren't willing to take any chances. While more than one deputy had offered to relieve Tony, he couldn't leave just yet. Richard Batterson was one of the toughest men he knew, and when he woke up, Tony wanted to be there. He felt he had a little closer relationship with Batterson than most of the other deputies. He also wanted to make sure Batterson was safe. He didn't think the chief was in danger in a hospital, but who could tell for sure? For now, better to be cautious.

The doctor had visited earlier. The news wasn't good. The surgery on the hematoma was successful, though Batterson still wasn't responding. Although it could take a while for him to regain consciousness after that kind of surgery, Tony could tell the doctor was concerned about permanent brain damage.

"We'll keep trying to rouse him," he'd said. "If he doesn't respond in the next twenty-four hours, we may have a problem."

Except for ex-wives, as far as Tony knew, Batterson had no one except Karen and Marlon. His mother, his greatest supporter, passed away a couple of months earlier. His father had been gone for almost twenty years. Since he was an only child, there wasn't anyone else. To Batterson, his deputies were his family. Maybe that was why Tony couldn't leave.

He was taking another sip of coffee when another doctor came into the room. "Are you Tony DeLuca?" she asked.

He nodded. "Is . . . is everything okay?"

"Nothing's changed." She sat down across from him. "I'm the doctor on shift tonight. I'm Dr. Silver. Leah Silver."

Tony immediately liked the small, dark-haired physician. She had an intense expression, but there was kindness in her eyes. "Nice to meet you," he said, wondering why she was here. Was it just to let him know who was on Batterson's case while his other doctor was gone?

"I'd like to ask you a question," she said hesitantly, "but I don't want you to draw any conclusions from what I'm going to say."

"I'm not sure what you mean. Just ask your question."

Dr. Silver looked down at the clipboard she'd carried into the waiting room. "Does your friend—"

"He's not my friend," Tony interrupted. "He's my boss."

She looked surprised. He was too. Why had he said that?

"I'm sorry," she said quietly. "Your boss. I was here earlier when some of your colleagues were sitting with you. It's obvious you all respect him very much."

That was it. The doctor had hit the nail on the head. Tony wanted her to know Batterson was his boss because it was important to him that she see how much Batterson was esteemed by the people who served under him. Tony blinked away tears. He didn't cry in front of people. Ever. But at that moment, he was on the verge of losing his professional façade.

"You had a question?" he choked out.

She took a deep breath before saying, "I'd ask his girlfriend, but she's gone home. If you can't help me, I'll call her."

"What is it, Doc?"

"Can you think of any . . . drugs or medications that he might be taking? Something we might not know about?"

Tony blinked at her a couple of times. "Drugs? Are you asking me if he takes drugs?"

"No, not really. Not the way you think. We didn't find evidence of anything in his toxicology report that overly concerned us. But has he ever talked about any kind of medical condition? Severe allergies? Anything like that?"

Tony shook his head. "Not that I know of. He's not big on medicine of any kind. In fact, he gets stress headaches and won't take aspirin. He's very bullheaded. You could certainly ask Karen, his girlfriend, but we all know about his aversion to drugs. Medicine of almost any kind."

The doctor seemed to study him for a moment, but she didn't say anything.

"Can I ask the reason for your question?"

"Of course. Your . . . boss sustained quite a few injuries from flying glass and other debris that hit him during the explosion, but there's a mark on his hip that, well, looks like an injection site to me. I'm trying to figure out exactly what it might be. I hoped you'd be able to tell me." She frowned. "You say he has tension headaches? Are they frequent?"

Tony shrugged. "I guess. I mean, he mentions them once in a while, but frankly with his job, it's not that unusual. I've never felt he had a problem. Why?"

"When he was brought in, his heart rate was through the roof. We got him stabilized, but I'm wondering if he might have an issue with high blood pressure."

"I noticed how uneven his heartbeat was at the scene. But as far as his blood pressure . . . I don't know. You should ask his doctor."

Dr. Silver smiled. "I did. Your boss keeps canceling appointments. The last time he saw the doctor was over a year ago. No problem with blood pressure then, but things can change."

Tony grunted. "That's interesting. Especially since he insists we see the doctor regularly. For the sake of the job, he says."

"I find this a lot with men. Especially men in law enforcement. You all seem to think you're invincible."

"We have to think that, Doc. If we didn't, we wouldn't walk into half of the things we do."

She nodded. "I understand. I don't approve, but I understand." She wrote something on the papers on her clipboard. "So in your opinion he doesn't handle stress very well?"

Tony was surprised by her question and had to think a minute. "Actually, he does. I mean, he can blow his top from time to time, but I think it actually helps him, you know? He seems to feel better afterward."

"Okay. I put a call into the paramedics who treated and transported Mr. Batterson. I want to see if they might have injected him with something. Maybe . . ."

At that moment, Tony heard a buzzing sound. Dr. Silver reached into her pocket and pulled out a pager. "This might be the call I've been waiting for. Thanks for your help." She reached over and rested her hand on his arm. "Just keep praying for him. We're doing everything we can to help him."

Tony thanked her and watched as she walked away. He picked up his styrofoam coffee cup. His terrible coffee was cold now, making it even worse. He carried the cup to the bathroom, poured out the liquid, and dumped the cup in the trash. Then he walked back over to the coffee dispenser. He started to put his money into the machine when a nurse from the nearby station called his name. She was headed his way, carrying a ceramic cup. She smiled and handed it to him.

"We have our own pot of coffee in the break room. You let

us know when you need more and we'll get it. I think you'll like it better than the sludge out of this machine."

He looked at her nametag. *Rachel*. Tony was determined to remember her name. He wasn't usually good with names, but the nurses in ICU were all so helpful and kind, the least he could do was keep them straight. Rachel was young, probably early twenties, with short red hair and a sweet smile. "Thank you, Rachel, from the bottom of my heart. The lining of my stomach thanks you too."

She laughed and walked away.

He returned to the waiting room, only this time he sat down in a different chair. His backside needed a change. He was enjoying a really great cup of coffee when Dr. Silver came back into the room. The look on her face made Tony put his cup down and stand up. "What's wrong?"

"I just talked to one of the paramedics who treated your boss. They noticed that an EpiPen was missing from their truck."

"You mean the kind of thing people take for allergies?"

"Epinephrine is also used for someone having a heart attack. But that dose is much stronger than what's used for allergies."

"You think someone injected him with this stuff?"

"Yes, I do. It would explain the state his heart was in when he got to the hospital. He was close to death, Deputy DeLuca. We assumed it was because of the trauma his body sustained, but now I think—" she took a deep breath and looked him in the eye—"I believe someone tried to kill your boss."

CHAPTER
TWELVE

E.J. took the passenger-side door while Doug went around to check out the driver. It was difficult to see inside because the windows were tinted and the setting sun glared off the glass.

"Get out of the car with your hands up," E.J. said loudly.

From the other side, he heard Doug give a similar command. The passenger-side door clicked and started to open slowly. Smoke drifted out as if the truck were on fire. E.J. grabbed the door and flung it the rest of the way, his gun trained on whoever was in the passenger seat. Staring at him with eyes as wide as saucers was a teenage boy in jeans and a T-shirt, holding a bong. E.J. looked past him and saw another skinny teenager with his hands up. E.J. noticed a bag of marijuana sticking out from under the driver's seat. Obviously he'd tried to kick it out of sight. The door on his side was wide open, and Doug stood there with his gun pointed at the driver.

"Don't shoot!" the kid in the passenger seat said. "Please, mister. Don't kill us!"

E.J. sighed and holstered his gun. Doug shook his head and put his away too. E.J. took out his wallet and flashed his badge. "U.S. Marshals. That's a controlled substance, son. I take it you don't need it for medical reasons?"

Although for a moment the kid seemed to consider trying that as a way out, he backed away from it. "It's not my fault. Really." He jerked his head toward the boy in the other seat. "It's Ronnie's. I didn't want anything to do with it."

E.J. caught Doug's eye and winked. "I want you two to get out of the car. Bring your drugs and paraphernalia with you."

The boys climbed out. The one near E.J. held the bong, while the other boy had the bag of pot in his hand. Although possessing pot was a misdemeanor in Ohio, E.J. assumed the kids were more afraid of their parents than they were of the law. For whatever reason, they both looked terrified. Good. He and Doug couldn't risk their assignment by messing with these kids, but at least they could scare them to within an inch of their lives. He pointed at a large dumpster next to the diner. "Dump it. All of it."

The boys obeyed immediately. Then they came back over to where E.J. and Doug waited. "We're going to let you go this time, but we'll be keeping an eye on you. If we catch you again, we'll make sure you pay for it. Do you understand?"

The relief on their faces was palpable. "We won't do it anymore, Officer," the other kid said. "Thank you so much."

"Yes, sir, thank you," the boy standing in front of E.J. echoed.

E.J. glared at them. "Why don't you both go home and think about how close you came to getting into real trouble today?"

They both nodded like their necks were made out of springs. Then they jumped back in their vehicle and drove away quickly.

E.J. went over to Casey's car to check on the girls. "Just kids," he said when Casey lowered the window. "We're okay."

Casey nodded. "I had it covered. You really gave those two a hard time. They'll think twice about smoking pot again."

"Even if they do, they'll never completely enjoy it," Doug said, grinning. He pointed at the restaurant. "We'd better check on those burgers."

E.J. nodded and followed him back inside. Although he'd been concerned when the SUV first pulled up, the entire trip had been uneventful. A reckless teenage driver and two kids with pot. That was it. Maybe Batterson's concerns were groundless. They were almost to the house where they would meet the FBI. E.J. was relieved that everything had gone well, but he wasn't ready to say good-bye to Casey yet. There were things that needed to be said, and he had a distinct impression this might be his last chance to talk to her. Hopefully he'd find some time before he took off with Valerie and the Feds.

After picking up their food, he and Doug got into the car and headed back onto the road. They passed several large houses on the way that looked extremely expensive.

"Wow," Casey said. "This is a prestigious neighborhood. The chief's ex-wife must have been rich."

They rounded a turn in the road and found the street the house was on. The final turn came up quickly, and they began to search for their destination. Turned out the *street* they were on was actually the house's driveway. E.J. heard

Casey say "Wow" again under her breath when they finally spotted the home. It was huge and backed up to Lake Erie. Painted blue and white, there was a three-car garage and a walkway behind the house that led to the lake.

"You're right about his wife being wealthy," E.J. said. "I suspect the houses around here are upwards of a million dollars."

"Doesn't look like the FBI is here yet," Doug said. "Maybe we can stay for a while. I could get used to a place like this."

Casey grunted. "Not on our salary you won't."

Casey and Doug stood by the car while E.J. did a quick perimeter check. The house was even more impressive from the back. There was a large sunroom with huge windows that looked out on the lake. Stone steps led to the long pier that stretched out over the water. It was a beautiful location. Peaceful. E.J. wondered if this was where Batterson planned to retire someday.

If so, E.J. prayed he'd live long enough to see his dream come true.

CHAPTER
THIRTEEN

After checking the back, including the doors and windows, and finding them secure, E.J. walked to the front of the house, where the Marshals and their witness waited. "Everything looks good," he said. "Let's find that key."

He checked one flower bed as Doug looked through the other. Finally, he found a rock that looked a little odd. He picked it up and turned it over. Sure enough, there was a strip of metal that slid open when he applied pressure. Inside the plaster rock lay a key.

He went to the car and opened the door to the back seat. "Let's get Valerie inside," he said to Casey. "I want to pull the car into the garage. We don't want neighbors calling the police because they think someone's breaking in."

"What neighbors?" she asked as she and Valerie climbed out.

E.J. glanced around. The house was so isolated, there weren't any neighbors close enough to see them. "I still want to put the car away, but you've got a point. No wonder Batterson thought this would be a perfect place to hide Valerie."

Everyone followed him to the front door. E.J. unlocked the house, and they all filed inside. The interior was just as impressive as the exterior.

"Just who was Batterson's wife anyway?" Casey said. "Some kind of movie star or something?"

"No clue," Doug said. "And I don't care. I'm starving. Let's eat."

E.J. laughed. "Way to prioritize."

He and Doug strode back to the car and retrieved the food. Doug started to carry it toward a long mahogany dining room table with intricately carved chairs. The set was obviously antique and quite valuable. It sat on a large Oriental rug, a matching buffet nearby.

"Hey, maybe we better take this greasy food into the kitchen," E.J. said. "I don't want to get grease or drink stains on that nice table." His mother had a similar dining room set, and the idea of setting a bag of hamburgers on it would have horrified her.

Doug looked a little confused by E.J.'s suggestion, but he nodded in agreement. They walked through the wide living room decorated with brown suede chairs and a massive leather couch. The kitchen was incredible. A huge island with a gray-and-white granite top filled the center. The appliances were all stainless steel and high-tech. Doug grunted as he looked over the refrigerator. It not only had ice and water in the door, but it also had an LCD touch screen over the dispenser. "Look at this," he said, a touch of awe in his voice.

"Does it work?" Casey asked.

E.J. poked at it a few times. "Nah. It's not hooked up." He reached over and flipped a nearby switch a couple of times. The ceiling lights went on and off. "At least the electricity is on. That's something."

E.J. and Doug put the food down on a table in a cozy breakfast nook with windows that faced the lake. The table was oak, with chairs on one side and a built-in bench on the other. It was so big that at least twelve people could gather comfortably around it.

E.J. removed Valerie's drink from the carrying pack and then took her food out of the bag. "Sit down and eat," he told her. "When the FBI gets here, they'll probably want to leave right away. You might not get another chance to eat for a while."

"I might run to the bathroom first, if it's okay."

E.J. pointed at Casey. "Let's find a bathroom for Valerie. I was going to do a check of the house anyway."

Casey nodded. "Sure."

He glanced at Valerie. "Follow us. Your food will stay warm as long as you don't take too long."

"Okay."

While Doug tore into his cheeseburger, E.J. and Casey started their tour of the house, E.J. in front of Valerie and Casey following behind. They quickly found a bathroom in the hallway outside the kitchen. "You go on," E.J. told Valerie. "We want to look through the rest of the house. I'm sure we're secure, but it's best if we check it out. Just wait here until we come back for you."

"I understand." Valerie stepped into the bathroom and pulled the door shut behind her.

E.J. headed down the hall, making quick work of checking

the four bedrooms and two more bathrooms. Every room was opulent. The master bath had a large tub with jets.

"You could get at least four people in this thing," he mumbled as they cleared the room.

"It concerns me that your mind went there," Casey said. "Do you usually bathe with a group?"

E.J. shrugged. "Not under normal circumstances. I guess joining family members in the hot tub doesn't qualify, although when I was a kid I used to tell my mother that time spent in the hot tub should count as a bath. She didn't buy it."

Casey laughed.

They were on their way back down the carpeted hallway when Casey stopped and held her hand up, signaling E.J. to stop as well. He quietly followed her as she crept up next to the bathroom where they'd left Valerie. Casey's ear was next to the door. She waved him over, and he stepped up next to her. A familiar clicking sound was coming from the bathroom. E.J. was pretty sure he knew what it was. Valerie was texting someone on her phone.

Casey motioned for E.J. to move away, so he took several steps back. She knocked on the door. "Valerie, it's Casey. Are you all right in there?"

The noise stopped immediately. A few seconds later, Valerie said, "I'm fine. I was just waiting until you came back to get me."

Casey looked at E.J. and rolled her eyes. He was beyond upset. Their witness could be compromising their entire operation.

"Why don't you come out now? I'll escort you back to the kitchen."

The door slowly opened, and Valerie stepped out into the hallway. "Good. I'm really hungry," she said with a thin smile.

"Great," E.J. said as he came up from behind Casey. "But first you're going to give us that phone."

Valerie's face went completely white. Thankfully, Casey's quick reflexes kept her from hitting the floor when she passed out.

CHAPTER
FOURTEEN

Casey went through Valerie's phone while E.J. got her a glass of water. They were seated in the living room, Valerie and E.J. on the couch, Casey in a chair across from them. Doug was outside putting the car in the garage and watching for the FBI. Since Valerie had used her phone against their advice, it was possible she'd just put them all in danger.

Casey was shocked as she went through message after message. Valerie had kept someone abreast of every single move they'd made since before they left the hotel.

"I think we need to get out of here," she told E.J. "Dump this phone and find someplace safer."

"What's going on here, Valerie?" E.J. asked their witness. Although he kept his tone steady, it was obvious he was angry. "We put our lives on the line for you. Our boss almost lost his. Are you working with the people who blew up our offices?"

Valerie, who was still as white as a ghost, shook her head. "It's not like that. You don't understand."

"Well, enlighten us and quickly. We need to know what to do. Are they on their way here?"

"I . . . I don't think so. They want me in D.C. They need me in front of that grand jury."

"Why?" Casey asked. "Aren't you testifying against Senator Warren? Is he behind this?"

"No." Her voice quivered as she spoke. "He made money from his involvement with a terrorist. I certainly didn't. I was forced to work with them." Her eyes were wild with fear.

If Casey wasn't already furious with the woman's betrayal, she might almost feel sorry for her. She looked at her watch. "Ten minutes, Valerie. Then we're leaving. Spill it. All of it. Now."

"The FBI is still coming, right?" she asked.

Casey nodded. "If we leave here, we'll call them and tell them where we are." Easier to promise than to pull off. Casey had no idea who Batterson had talked to. Maybe she could call Tony. He might know more about it. Although originally Casey hadn't believed they needed the Feds to transport Valerie, now she couldn't wait for them to arrive. Right now they could use all the backup they could get.

"Can I see my phone?" Valerie asked.

Casey shook her head. "I think it's best if we hold on to it."

"Okay. Look under videos."

Casey brought up the videos and nodded.

"Play the last one."

When Casey pressed the arrow in the middle of the screen, the image of a young woman came up. She was tied to a chair and had duct tape over her mouth. A hand reached in and ripped the tape off. It was obviously painful. The woman cried out as a muffled voice came from somewhere behind her, and she began to cry.

"Please, Valerie," she said, her voice shaking, "do whatever they ask. They're going to kill me if you don't." Two hands then appeared, and another strip of tape was put over the woman's mouth. The video ended.

"That's my sister, Susan," Valerie said. "They have her."

"Who are *they*?" E.J. asked. "And what do they want you to do?"

"I'm supposed to tell them that I made up part of the story about Martin," Valerie said, tears dripping down her face. "About the senator and his connection to Ali Al-Saud. I have to testify that I created the entire scenario because I wanted to advance my career. It will work too. With Martin gone, no one can prove I'm not telling the truth."

"I don't get it," Casey said. "The senator denied the story, right? I'm sure Al-Saud will do the same. If the authorities have no other evidence, why does anyone need you to take the fall for your story?"

"I really don't know. I guess they don't want anyone looking too closely at Al-Saud. If I say I made it up, the whole thing goes away."

"And with it your career," E.J. said.

"I don't care about that," she said, her voice breaking. "I just want my sister back."

"So they ordered you to stay in contact with them?" Casey said. "Tell them what was going on? Give them our location?"

She nodded. "Yeah, but I could only share what I actually knew. I never heard you mention this address. I assume they've been tracking us some other way." Her eyes sought Casey's.

"They can't find out I told you the truth. We have to proceed just like everything is okay. If we don't, Susan could die."

Casey held up the phone. "So unless they're tracking your phone, they only know the general vicinity we're in, right?"

"Right. But they have ways." She gulped. "You should probably check your car for some kind of tracking device. Before we left St. Louis, I told them we were taking your car. They wanted to know exactly where it was parked."

Casey looked over at Doug. "Would you look at my car?" she asked.

"Sure." Doug hurried over to the door in the kitchen that led to the garage. Casey heard him open the door and then close it.

"Did they blow up our offices?" Casey asked harshly.

Valerie sobbed, putting her head in her hands. Obviously the answer was yes. Casey fought back rage.

"I asked you a question," she said loudly, trying to be heard over Valerie's wailing.

Finally, Valerie looked up. Her voice shook so much it was hard to understand her. "I . . . I had no idea they were going to do that. I swear." She took several deep gulps, trying to control her crying. "You saw the text after it happened?"

Casey scrolled back through the texts. *Now you know we're serious*, she read. *These people can't keep you safe. We can infiltrate anyone. We're everywhere. If you want to save your sister, you know what you must do.*

"Are you telling me they killed our people just to scare you?" Casey couldn't keep the indignation out of her voice. She was seething with anger.

Valerie wrapped her arms around herself as if she needed

a hug. "Yes," she said softly. "And they'll kill us too if it becomes a more convenient way to reach their goals."

Doug came back into the living room. He held a round metal object in his hand. "Tracking device," he said.

Casey and E.J. stared at him. Casey was pretty sure E.J. was thinking the same thing she was. They needed to get out of there. Fast.

CHAPTER
FIFTEEN

Tony hung up the phone and went back to the waiting room after talking to Tom Monnier, who was the Acting Chief Deputy while Batterson was out. He reminded Tony that there were deputies waiting in line to provide security for the chief. Tony volunteered to stay overnight since it would take time to set up a schedule, but he was still hoping the chief would wake up while he was here. Tom had decided to move Karen and Marlon to a secure location, so they probably wouldn't be able to visit for a while, not until Tom was certain they'd be safe.

More than anything, Tony wished he could talk to the chief. There was so much information he needed, and Batterson was the only one with the answers. He was lost in thought when Rachel walked into the room. He was startled at the sound of her voice.

"Deputy DeLuca, there's a call for you."

"Thanks," he said. "Sorry to use your phone this way."

"It's okay. We were told you'd need to have access. It's fine."

As Tony followed her to the nurses' station, he wondered if they were going too far by staying off their own cellphones. What would anyone learn from him? His location? It wasn't a secret. Of course, if they were listening in to his calls, that could be dangerous for their witness and their deputies. In the end, using the hospital phone was the safest decision for now. But maybe it was time to switch to a secure phone. If the bomber found out Batterson was alive, he might try to breach hospital security. Hard but not impossible. He was certain if he could ask Batterson, he'd tell them to take every precaution. "We really appreciate it," he told Rachel. "I'm sure it's inconvenient."

She shook her head, her red hair falling in her eyes. "Don't worry about it."

He thanked her again and punched the line she indicated. After he said hello, he heard Mark's voice on the other end. Rachel left the station, heading for her patients. He appreciated her giving him some privacy.

"Sorry to call so late," Mark said.

"What time is it?"

"Almost ten."

"Wow. I thought it was later. It feels like this day just won't end."

"How's the chief?"

"The same. He's lucky to be alive." He told Mark about the injection of epinephrine.

"What are they going to do? Can they counteract it?"

"I think they already did. That stuff almost caused him to

have a heart attack. Somehow he managed to live through it. Someone tried to kill him, Mark."

"Keep me posted," Mark said. "No matter what time it is, okay? And if you need a break, I'd be happy to relieve you."

"Thanks. Just give Tom a call." He sighed. "Hey, Mark, can you get me a secure phone? I'm concerned about going through the hospital switchboard."

"I doubt anyone would try to hack their phone service. It would be pretty complicated."

"Seems to me these guys don't care much about complications. This appears to be a pretty well-oiled operation."

"I see what you mean. I'll do my best. If nothing else, I'll get you an old burner phone."

"Thanks."

"Speaking of phones, I wanted you to know as soon as possible that the dead paramedic had his phone on him, but there weren't any calls from Batterson on it. Whatever phone the chief used didn't belong to that guy."

"So does that mean the chief used a phone owned by the person who attacked him?"

"Looks like it."

"And this person murdered the real paramedic so he could assume his identity?"

"Yes."

Tony was silent for a few moments as he processed the information.

"We all thought the chief's injuries came from the explosion, but he was in good enough shape to get to the parking garage under his own power. Then something happened. For some reason this guy targeted the chief, but I have no idea why.

It doesn't make sense, Tony. I realize there are criminals out there who hate us, but usually they threaten deputies—the people who actually confront them. The chief is rarely out on the street."

"But the bomb was set off near his office."

"Yeah, but who knows? Maybe it's a coincidence."

"What happened in that parking garage wasn't coincidence."

"You're right about that," Mark said. "Oh, one other thing. A witness, a guy who saw the chief this morning, said he was outside the parking garage for a while, on the grass, but then he went inside, which is where you later found him. I'm not sure why he did that. If he'd stayed where he was, I don't think he could have been confronted without being seen."

Tony found this new information interesting, but there was no way to know why the chief changed locations without asking him. "So the bad guy was pretending to help Batterson, and then the chief asked to borrow his phone. Sometime after that, he convinced the chief to get out of public view so he could kill him?"

"Looks like it. I'm assuming Batterson's head injury came from our friend. But why not just shoot the chief? Get it over with."

Tony was finally beginning to see daylight. "Because he didn't want anyone to know Batterson died from anything besides the injuries he sustained in the blast. If he'd shot the chief, we'd realize he was a target. Even though he made it across the street, we'd probably just chalk it up to the chief's determination. Which is exactly what happened."

Tony rubbed his free hand over his face. Was Mark right? Was he reaching? "Regardless, Mark," he said finally, "our people are in trouble and we don't know their location. I'm afraid whoever bombed our building might know exactly where our witness is—and our friends. We need to figure this out before it's too late."

CHAPTER
SIXTEEN

Tony hung up, not bothering to tell Mark what he was doing. He quickly called the burner phone Casey had used when she'd contacted him earlier. Although he didn't expect her to answer, he was relieved when she did.

"Casey, there's a problem," he said when he heard her voice.

"Is it the chief?"

The fear in her voice made him feel guilty. He should have reassured her first. "No, it's not the chief. He's still the same, but the doctor is hopeful he'll wake up soon." It wasn't totally true, yet it wasn't a complete lie either. The doctor did hope Batterson would wake up. He just didn't tell Casey that the likelihood of that happening was getting less and less without some kind of miracle.

Tony told her about the phones and the paramedic. "I think whoever murdered that paramedic and hurt the chief wanted to know who Batterson called. My guess is he planned to kill the chief as soon as he had the information he needed." He paused for a moment. "He called you, Casey."

"Actually, he called Doug."

"Then he can track Doug's cell."

"No, we turned off Doug's phone. Now we're using only this burner phone. They can triangulate it if it's on, but since we left St. Louis I've kept it off."

"But you answered when I called."

"Because I was getting ready to call you. Not only has our witness compromised us, we found a tracking device on my car." She told him all about Valerie and what they'd discovered.

Tony got up and began pacing around the nurses' station as she talked. When she finished, he couldn't seem to make sense of what she'd shared. "I was afraid they might be able to find you, but this wasn't the way I thought it would happen. So . . . whoever bombed us knows your location?"

"I didn't think so at first since Valerie didn't have an actual address. But with the tracking device . . . I have to assume they know precisely where we are. Besides, she told them the house belonged to the chief. I doubt it would be too hard to find the connection between this house and Batterson, if they did any research. But here's the kicker. Valerie says they want her to make it to D.C. They need her to testify that her story wasn't true. If she's right, would they try to stop us? Seems to me they'd want us to meet up with the FBI and get Valerie to Washington safely."

"Casey, you can't take the chance. These people can't be trusted. They've killed some of our own. Tried to kill the chief. They're not playing."

"I'm sure you're right. I keep feeling like we're missing something."

"The Feds aren't there yet?"

"No, and that's a problem." Casey sighed. "Either we get out of here because whoever blew up our offices might know where we are, or we wait for the FBI. Once they arrive, we're handing Valerie over to them. She's their problem from then on. We'll fill them in on everything we know, but I'm confident they have a better chance of getting Valerie to D.C. than we do. We're just too compromised."

"Tom needs to contact the Feds and bring them up to speed," Tony said. "Find out where they are. We shouldn't be guessing about this."

"That's up to Tom. I wonder, though, if you should wait just a bit. Since we don't know who Batterson talked to, we might be giving away information best kept between us for now. I hate to sound paranoid, but we seem to be puppets in a show scripted by Ali Al-Saud. He has long strings, and I'm not sure how far they stretch. We'll watch ourselves. If the Feds don't show up soon, we'll get out. Go somewhere safe until we can figure out our next move."

"I think I'd rather see you head home."

"But we're closer to D.C. than we are to St. Louis. I think E.J. should call his chief. Get help from his office."

"That's a great idea. I'll run it past Tom and let you know what he wants you to do."

"So Valerie plans to tell the Feds what's been going on?"

"That's what she says. Frankly, she needs to give them a chance to find her sister. You know it's almost impossible they've kept her alive this long."

"Yeah. I take it she doesn't?"

"No, and we haven't told her."

"What if these guys find out Valerie spilled the beans?" Tony asked.

"That's the one thing we can't allow to happen. None of our lives would be worth a plug nickel."

"You need to shut Valerie up. She can't tell Al-Saud's people anything else that would put you in further danger."

"To be honest, Tony, I don't think that's going to be a problem. She's afraid they might hurt her sister because she betrayed them."

"I see your point. You've got to tell the FBI everything when they get there."

"Absolutely." A deep sigh came through the phone. "We'll wait here another hour. It's almost eleven o'clock. If they're not here by midnight, we'll take off."

"Seems to me they should have shown up hours ago."

"We have no idea what Batterson told them. Maybe he didn't think we'd get here this fast. I hate being in the dark like this."

"Me too. Well, if you decide to leave, let me know where you go," Tony said.

"Will do. Regardless, I'll check back with you in an hour or two. Where will you be?"

"Right here. Just call the hospital again. I'll let you know when I have a secure phone." He paused for a moment. "I just can't seem to leave, Casey. I want to be here when he opens his eyes."

There was silence on the other end of the line. Finally, Casey said, "I understand."

Tony heard the catch in her voice.

With that, she hung up. Tony went back into the waiting room and grabbed a magazine from a nearby table. He slumped back down in his chair. All this sitting was beginning to make his back tighten up.

He kept going over reasons someone would want Batterson dead. He even thought about recent cases, wondering if someone they'd put away might be involved. But no matter what, he couldn't come up with any solid answers. Just suspicions. He decided to read his magazine, hoping he could distract himself for a while. He was getting ready to open it when he noticed something on the wall-mounted TV screen. He'd turned off the sound earlier, but he found the remote and hit the mute button. His mouth dropped open as the news anchor said, "Repeating our top story this hour, the body of Colorado Senator Dell Warren was found by police about an hour ago. All the police are telling us is that they aren't looking for any suspects at this time."

They switched to an official picture of the senator as Tony sat there, stunned. Usually if the police weren't looking for suspects, it meant the death was either natural or a suicide. The senator had seemed to be in good health. What in the world was going on? He wondered what this turn of events meant for his friends. The situation was getting stranger by the hour. He felt as if it was made up of lots of little pieces of information, but he couldn't figure out how they all fit together. Right now, besides worrying about the chief, he was becoming more and more concerned about Casey and Doug. He wouldn't feel better until the FBI showed up.

Special Agent in Charge Alex Owens, in the Billings, Montana, office picked up the phone. He wondered who in the world could be calling so late. He was usually home by now, but the pile of paperwork on his desk had grown too large to ignore. He'd decided to stay until he could at least put a dent in it. A quickly cooling pizza sat on one side of his messy desk. The call had been transferred to him by an agent who warned him it could be a fake.

"Hello," he said. "This is Agent Owens."

He listened to the man on the other end of the line tell him a story that was hard to swallow.

"I'd need proof that you are who you say you are," Owens said. "I'm sure you can understand why it's hard to believe what you're telling me."

A few minutes later, he picked up a pen and wrote down the information the caller gave him. "Stay where you are and keep out of sight. We'll have someone there as soon as we can."

After hanging up the phone, he stared at the words he'd written on his notepad. He picked up the phone again. In the thirty years he'd worked at the bureau, this might be one of the most important phone calls he'd ever make. As he dialed the special number in Washington, he looked up another number. Once he finished with Washington, he needed to talk to someone connected to the U.S. Marshals Office in St. Louis.

CHAPTER
SEVENTEEN

"If the FBI doesn't arrive soon, we're out of here," Casey said to E.J. after she disconnected her call to Tony and turned off her phone. She told him about the paramedic and Batterson.

"So you think this guy, possibly the bomber, actually tried to kill your boss?" E.J. asked. "And he might know about Batterson's call to us? Then he'd also know about the call to the FBI, right? That should actually make us safer."

Casey shrugged and leaned back into the comfortable overstuffed chair where she sat. "I don't get it. They have Valerie under their thumb. Why would they need to know who the chief called?"

"You got me."

"Once I tell the FBI the truth," Valerie said, "they should be able to find Susan, right? If they can get her to safety, then I'm free to testify against the senator and Al-Saud."

"What proof do you have that Al-Saud was involved with the senator besides what Martin told you?" Casey asked.

"Well, right before Marty disappeared, his messages stopped and the intimidating ones began. They clearly threatened the life of my sister—and me. One of them says that Marty is dead. All the messages came from Marty's phone."

"That only proves they have his phone," E.J. said. "It doesn't prove they killed him. You need real evidence."

"I took screenshots of every single message. I can prove they were threatening me."

E.J. frowned. "That could come in handy, but it still isn't proof."

"I'm sure the Department of Justice has something else— something on the senator and Al-Saud—but I have no idea what it is." Valerie stared at Casey for a moment. "Of course, if the FBI finds my sister, she'll be able to tell them who kidnapped her."

Casey and E.J. looked at each other. "Maybe, but it's thin. A man like Al-Saud usually hires people to do his dirty work. He likes to keep his hands clean. Besides, he has enough money to retain the world's best lawyers. And he can buy off almost any jury. I really think you need something more solid. Frankly, I'm surprised you were asked to testify to the grand jury if you don't have more evidence than you seem to."

"But they don't know exactly what she has," E.J. interjected. "That's why they called her."

"Maybe, but you'd think they'd want something solid before calling for a grand jury."

"I do have another name," Valerie said. "A man Al-Saud uses to go after his enemies. He's the man who probably killed Marty."

Casey's ears perked up. "Do you think he's the one who bombed our offices?"

Valerie nodded. "I'd bet on it. Al-Saud has a lot of people under his control. Like the senator. He forces them to do what he wants by threatening them or their families. He might have used someone like that to plant the explosion, but Marty and I found he uses this man more than anyone else to carry out his most important plans."

"You know his name?" E.J. asked.

"Yeah. It's Benyamin Mattan. He's called Ali Al-Saud's shadow. Ruthless. Doesn't like to leave witnesses behind. Friends or enemies. I'm convinced he's the one sending these texts. The person I've been in contact with."

"This could be important, Valerie," Casey said. "If the FBI can find this guy and turn him, they might be able to bring Al-Saud and his whole network down."

"I doubt he would betray Al-Saud," Valerie said, uncertainty in her voice. "He seems beyond loyal. I did some research on him. I think he might be Al-Saud's illegitimate son."

E.J. grunted. "Well, that's interesting. Still, family members turn on each other all the time. We see it a lot. If we can offer them protection and keep them out of prison, they're pretty willing to turn on mommy, daddy, brother, or sister."

"Do you have Avery's testimony in writing?" Casey asked.

"Yeah. Everything's in my files." She gestured toward her phone on the table. "That's not my original phone. I was told to get rid of the other one."

"Can we recover it if we need to?"

"I'm sorry, but no. I threw it in a dumpster not long after Marty went missing. It's been gone for months."

"With the screenshots, her files, and her knowledge about this Mattan guy," Casey said to E.J., "it might be enough. The government could finally have a viable link to Al-Saud. Mattan might not even need to testify if the government turns their attention to him. Maybe through him they can uncover something that will give them what they need to bring Al-Saud's dynasty down."

"You've got a point. It could be enough to—"

The front door opened, and Doug poked his head inside. "Someone's here. I think it's the Feds, but you'd better get out here just in case."

E.J. jumped to his feet and pointed at Casey. "Take her in the back until we tell you it's clear."

Casey got up and grabbed Valerie's arm. "Come with me," she ordered. She pulled the frightened reporter toward the hallway and guided her to a back bedroom. Casey pointed at Valerie. "Go in the bathroom and lock the door. Stay there until I tell you to come out."

Valerie ran to the bathroom and closed the door. Casey heard the lock click. She held her gun out in front of her and slowly opened the bedroom door, trying to listen. No matter what happened, she was trained to protect their witness. Problem was, if her team was killed, she might not be able to hold off attackers by herself. Even so, she would give her life trying to keep Valerie safe. If that was the price that had to be paid, so be it.

She waited to hear something, but there wasn't any sound at all. Finally the front door opened, and she heard voices.

She saw E.J. coming down the hall. He gestured to her. "It's the FBI. You can bring Valerie out."

Casey breathed a deep sigh of relief. Now the Feds could take over. Their mission was completed. She put her gun back in its holster and went over to the bathroom. She rapped on the door. "It's okay, Valerie. The FBI is here. Come on out."

The doorknob turned slowly, and the lock clicked. The door opened a few inches, then part of Valerie's face appeared. "Are you sure it's them?"

"Yeah, we're sure," Casey said. "We check IDs very carefully."

The door opened all the way. Valerie stepped out. "I . . . I didn't used to be this timid," she said. "In fact, I considered myself courageous. A reporter's reporter, someone who would go after the truth no matter what." She wiped away a tear that slid down her cheek. "Now I'm afraid all the time. I hate the person I've become. You must think I'm the biggest wimp in the world."

"I can't judge you," Casey said. "I haven't been through what you have. To be honest, if someone was threatening a person I loved, I don't know how I'd respond."

Valerie leaned against the wall, her face pale. "Fear is . . . self-defeating. I've betrayed myself, and I betrayed you." She turned her face toward Casey. "I'm sorry. I really am."

"You were protecting your sister," Casey said softly. "Your fear wasn't just for yourself."

"I appreciate that, but maybe it's time I took my life back. Quit being scared." She grabbed Casey's arm. "I'm glad we're telling the FBI the truth. I should have come forward sooner.

Maybe they would have found Susan already. I never should have trusted Mattan to let her go."

"This is the right thing to do. The FBI is trained to deal with people like Al-Saud. If anyone can find your sister, it's them."

Valerie let go of Casey. "Well, let's get this over with. It's time Al-Saud paid for his crimes."

For the first time, Casey saw a flash of who Valerie must have been at one time. It made her feel a kinship with the woman. She'd had to stand up to Jared. Maybe it took longer than it should have, but she'd finally taken her life back. She wanted to help Valerie do the same. "Okay, let's go," she said with a smile. "Let's bring an end to this."

E.J. poked his head in the doorway. "Are you ladies coming out or not?"

"Yeah, we're on our way," Casey said. "Valerie is ready to talk to the Feds."

He nodded. "Okay, come on. I'll introduce you."

Casey and Valerie followed him down the hallway into the living room, where four men in dark suits stood waiting for them.

Casey was both relieved and concerned at the same time. She and Doug would be heading home soon. They'd gotten their witness safely to the location Batterson had sent them, but they still weren't out of the woods yet. She wouldn't relax completely until Valerie was sitting in front of the grand jury in D.C. Also, she wasn't ready to say good-bye to E.J. Whether it was pride or unresolved anger, Casey was concerned that once he walked out the door, she might never see him again. And she wasn't ready to let that happen. Not yet.

CHAPTER
EIGHTEEN

It was a little after midnight before Dr. Silver came back into the waiting room. Rachel had brought Tony a sandwich, claiming she'd made too much lunch for herself. Although he wasn't convinced she was telling the truth, he'd accepted her offer. He'd scarfed down her tuna salad sandwich like a man starving to death. While he was eating, Mark stopped by with the burner phone. Tony felt much more secure with it, but until he could give Casey the number, she would still call the hospital.

After he ate, he'd grabbed more coffee from the nurses' break room. It was not only good, but it also helped him to stay awake. He couldn't afford to nod off. He stood up when the doctor entered and prayed she had good news. When she smiled, his heart raced. Was the chief better?

"He's showing signs of consciousness. I even asked him a few questions, and he tried to answer me. Give him some time and I think you'll be able to talk to him."

Tony grabbed the doctor and hugged her, laughing with relief. He realized he was probably being inappropriate, but at that moment he didn't care. When he released her, he was happy to see her smile. "So he's going to be okay?" he asked, just making certain he'd heard her correctly.

"Barring any further complications, I believe he'll make a complete recovery."

"It's really important I talk to him. We've got some deputies in a dangerous situation, and he has information we need."

"I understand, but as I said, it will take a while. He may need an hour or so to be able to communicate clearly. And I'm being overly optimistic."

Tony took a big breath and let it out slowly. He needed to talk to Batterson now. He was about to ask the doctor another question when Rachel rushed into the room, her brown eyes wide with disbelief.

"Dr. Silver, your head trauma patient is awake and asking to speak to one of his deputies."

The doctor looked at Rachel with her mouth open. "Impossible."

"You don't know Richard Batterson," Tony said.

"I guess not," she said, shaking her head. "Let me examine him and then I'll come back."

"Then can I see him?"

"Only family is allowed in ICU."

"But I'm his brother. Didn't I tell you that?" Tony gave her the most innocent look he could manage and winked at Rachel.

"I guess I forgot," she said. "In that case you can go in

after I check him out. Wait here, please." She gave him a quick smile before walking out. Rachel winked back and trailed after her.

Tony took that moment to lower his head and thank God for saving his boss. He didn't care who saw or heard him. He was so thankful, what anyone else thought didn't matter. He thought about calling someone—Tom, Mark, Karen, Marlon—but he decided to wait until he spoke with Batterson face-to-face. Afterward he could tell them he'd actually seen the chief and spoken to him. It might go a long way to calm the fears of the people who loved him.

He paced the floor for what seemed like hours but was only minutes. Finally the doctor came back into the room.

"He wants to talk to you, Tony. I have to warn you that he seems very agitated. I'm not sure what he's upset about. Maybe you can figure it out."

"Sure. I'd be glad to try."

"He's still groggy and will be for some time. Don't expect too much, and don't be surprised if he falls asleep while he's talking. That will be normal for a while. His body and his brain have been through a lot."

"Okay. Got it."

"Come with me."

He followed her to the door that led to the ICU. She pushed it open, and Tony saw several beds, some empty, some with people, separated only by curtains. The nurses' station was situated across from the beds so they could keep an eye on their patients. The blinking and beeping of lights on the monitors in each room created a weird cacophony of sounds. It certainly wasn't relaxing. Life and death hung on each beep, on each flashing light. The realization gave Tony chills.

"He's right here," Dr. Silver said, pointing to a bed on their right.

Tony had to fight to keep his expression from showing the shock he felt when he saw Batterson. His face was swollen, his eyes almost shut. Part of his head was wrapped with gauze. He looked ten years older than he actually was. It was the first time Tony had ever seen him looking frail. It shook him to the core. Batterson pointed at him and then waved him over.

"Hey, Chief," Tony said quietly, feeling he shouldn't speak too loudly. There were really sick people around them. Some of them could even be dying. "You know, if you wanted time off, there are other ways to go about it."

Batterson mumbled something Tony couldn't make out. He moved closer. "I can't understand you. Can you say that again?"

"Casey . . . Doug."

"They're fine, Chief. I spoke to Casey earlier. They made it to the location you sent them to. Right now they're waiting for the FBI."

Batterson shook his head. "No . . . no."

Tony was bewildered. What was the chief thinking? He must be confused because of the head injury and his surgery. He looked at Dr. Silver, who only shook her head.

Batterson reached out and grabbed Tony's arm, pulling him closer. "FBI . . ." he said hoarsely. He pronounced each letter as if it were a separate sentence, slowly and emphatically.

"Sure, Chief. Everything's fine. Casey and Doug will hand Valerie Bennett over to them as soon as they show up." Tony cleared his throat. He hated to push the chief right now, yet he felt he had no choice. "It would help if you could tell me when the Feds are supposed to arrive and who is coordinating the pickup. We've been reluctant to contact them. We didn't want to compromise the operation."

Tony was shocked to see the look in Batterson's eyes. "No . . . no . . ." he said again.

Tony started to pull his arm out of Batterson's grip. He'd end up with a bruise where the chief's fingers dug into his skin.

"Tony, I . . . I . . ."

"Chief, please. Everything's going to be okay. Don't upset yourself. The FBI will get them safely to D.C. You don't need to worry."

"Tony . . . I never called them," Batterson whispered, the effort obviously taking everything out of him. "No time. Watch . . . for the man . . . scar on left . . . cheek. Maaaa . . . ma. . . . ten . . . man . . ." With that, his grip on Tony's arm relaxed, and Batterson passed out.

Tony couldn't believe what he was hearing. Casey and Doug were waiting for help that wasn't coming. They could be sitting ducks. They needed to get out, and get out now. The problem was, he couldn't get in touch with Casey until she turned her phone on. She said she'd call back in an hour or two. There was no other way to warn her—unless he could get someone to their location. If only Batterson had stayed conscious long enough to tell him. He should have insisted Casey give him their location. He'd have to call Tom to see if he had a way to figure out where their people were.

"Is something wrong?" Dr. Silver asked.

"I don't know. I hope not. We've got some deputies out there who think the cavalry is coming, but it's not. And I don't know how to let them know."

"You can't contact them?"

"I can try, except they're keeping their phones off. Probably won't answer. They're supposed to call here at some point. I really need to speak with them now, though. Right now."

Dr. Silver rested her hand on his arm. "I'm sure they'll be okay. Don't worry."

He smiled at her. Easier said than done, but she had a point. They weren't in immediate danger as far as he knew. When the FBI didn't show up, they'd move the witness and contact him or Tom—or someone. Casey and Doug were well-trained deputies. They wouldn't take any chances. He took a deep breath and tried to think. Then it occurred to him. Did the fake paramedic know Batterson planned to call the FBI? Was that why he tried to kill him? Because he didn't want him to make that call? But why give him the phone in the first place? Tony rubbed his temples. Nothing made sense.

"We need to let him sleep," Dr. Silver said after she checked Batterson over. She pointed to the exit of the ICU.

"Okay. When do you think he can talk to me again?"

"Not for a while. He needs rest if he's going to recover. Are you going to wait around?"

"Have to. We need to have someone here constantly."

"I'm aware of that, but does it have to be you . . . and only you? Can't someone else keep watch over him?"

"Sure, but not until I get that call."

Dr. Silver sighed. "Well, you're dedicated. I'll give you that."

She led him back to the waiting room. Then he went to the nurses' station and tried to call Casey, but she didn't pick up. He immediately called Tom.

CHAPTER
NINETEEN

Agent Owens shook his head at the man sitting across from him. "We all assumed you were dead. I'm sorry, but I can't understand your reasons for not coming forward before this."

"Maybe it's because one attempt to murder me was enough. I'm not a glutton for punishment."

Owens silently took stock of his guest. Tall, shaggy blond hair, short beard, round glasses. Exactly what he'd expected. "So why come in now?"

"When I heard the senator was dead, I knew it was now or never." Martin Avery took off his glasses and wiped them on his T-shirt. "Valerie is supposed to testify in D.C., right?"

Owens nodded.

"Even though Warren is gone?"

"Yes. We're trying to find out if there really was collusion between the senator and a man we suspect has ties to terrorism. Unfortunately, we've never been able to prove it."

"Oh, there was collusion all right, but one of two things is going to happen. Either Valerie will die before she reaches

Washington, or her testimony won't be what you're hoping for."

"I don't understand."

Martin put his glasses on and slid them back on his nose with his index finger.

The word *nerd* flashed through Owens' mind. He frowned at his reaction. This wasn't high school. Even if he thought a lot of these environmentalists were nut jobs, he needed to listen to Martin Avery. No one else had been as involved with Senator Warren and his connection to the oil pipeline. He'd looked over reports and talked to agents in Washington before Avery came in. He was the one who'd sent Valerie Bennett, a reporter for a newspaper in St. Louis, the information that led her to uncover a possible relationship between Senator Warren and Ali Al-Saud. If they could nail Al-Saud, a major terrorism cell would be exposed and destroyed.

"Al-Saud is smart," Avery said. "Either he has people eliminated by someone else—associates who usually don't live long after their assignments are completed—or he threatens people close to his targets. He's resorted to kidnapping quite a few times. If I were you, I'd do a quick check on Valerie's relatives. She was closest to her sister, Susan. Find out where Susan is. If she's missing, Al-Saud has her."

Owens made a note on the pad in front of him. "Okay. So what about Warren? He killed himself. And no, before you ask, it wasn't staged. He pulled the trigger. We're sure of that. Even left a note to his ex-wife."

"I'd love to see that note. If you read between the lines, I bet you'll find that the senator felt his wife was in danger. I'm certain he took his own life trying to keep her safe."

Owens' eyebrows arched. He'd seen a copy of the letter. Sure enough, the senator had made it clear it would be better for her if he was gone. That more than anything he wanted her to live a full, happy life. The way it was phrased, it was very possible Warren was trying to protect her.

"How did you get all this information about Warren and Al-Saud?"

"From the senator. He began to realize how far Al-Saud had pulled him in. When Dell Warren went to D.C., he had big plans. He wanted to make a difference. But the same thing happened to him that happens to many politicians who stay too long. Deals made under the table. Quid pro quo. And then someone like Al-Saud comes along. The senator found himself bought and paid for. One night, when we were out at a bar, he got drunk, and the whole story came out. He warned me that I couldn't tell anyone. That Al-Saud would kill me. But of course I thought I was immortal. That's when I started sharing some of this with Valerie. I was trying to get her to investigate—find the information I had. Before I could tell her everything, they came after me."

"And how did you know they were after *you*?"

"Men standing across the street from my apartment. Following me. So I took off. Thought I was being smart. But they found me and took me to a warehouse in Pennsylvania. They have a kind of headquarters there."

"And you got away?"

Avery nodded.

"So you've been hiding . . . where?"

Avery grinned. "Let's just say that Wyoming has a lot

of places in which to disappear. Beautiful state. I have no intention of telling you where I was. Just in case I need to go away again."

"Hopefully we can keep that from happening. We have some questions for you, Mr. Avery. Questions from Washington—and St. Louis."

Avery frowned. "Where is Valerie now?"

Owens bit his lip as he considered his answer. Finally he decided to tell the truth. "We're not sure."

"What do you mean you're *not sure*?"

Owens sighed. "There was an explosion at the Marshals Office in St. Louis. Assuming it might be connected to Bennett's testimony in D.C., the Marshals took off with her, headed to Washington. After hearing from you, I got a call from the acting chief deputy and he filled me in. Right now communication is sketchy." He didn't tell Avery that the lives of the deputies and their witness were in danger.

"Al-Saud," Avery said softly. He stared off into the distance for a moment. "My guess is, either they're all dead or Valerie will show in Washington to repeat the story Al-Saud has ordered her to tell." He shook his head. "The Marshals will never see their deputies again. If they know the truth, Al-Saud won't let them live. Their deaths won't look like an assassination. They will look like accidents. That's his trademark. Nothing that can be connected back to him."

"Still hard to believe you survived if Al-Saud is so smart."

Avery snorted. "It wasn't because I was brighter than Al-Saud, believe me. I simply turned down the wrong alley—or maybe it was the right one."

"What are you talking about?"

"At the warehouse. There was a man who seemed . . . different. I don't know. Anyway, he left a door open, and I escaped. I got the feeling he left it open on purpose, but I can't be sure. I was followed by another guy—someone I knew wanted to kill me. He's one of Al-Saud's men. Ben Mattan, Al-Saud's enforcer. When I saw him, I ran. I turned down an alley and figured he was right behind me. I thought I was dead. Tried to hide." He ran his hand through his hair. "Somehow I lost him. Someone found me, though. A homeless man who noticed my feet sticking out from beneath the garbage I was crouching under. Just wanted my shoes. I think I scared him almost as much as he frightened me. He had no idea a person was attached to those shoes. I got out of that alley and went into hiding. Until now."

Agent Owens considered everything Avery had told him. Could he be trusted? He wasn't sure and yet several lives were on the line. He really had no choice. "I want to bring Washington and St. Louis in on this," he said. "But we don't have time for them to come here."

"I agree."

"I'm going to get the interested parties on the phone. Are you willing to speak to them? Tell them what you told me, and also explain Al-Saud's involvement in Warren's life?"

"Absolutely. I'd like to save Valerie and these Marshals. It's my fault they're in this situation." He pointed at Owens. "I don't mean directly. I'm a victim too, but this all began because I made a mistake. Got involved with the wrong people. It's time to stop Al-Saud. He's a cancer that feeds on human lives—and he needs to be excised."

Owens nodded. "It will take me a few minutes to get set up. Can I get you something? Are you thirsty? Hungry?"

"Maybe just some water," Avery said. Owens could see exhaustion combined with determination in his expression. Were they really close to bringing Al-Saud down? But would it be in time to save all the lives that hung in the balance?

CHAPTER
TWENTY

When Casey and Valerie entered the living room where the FBI agents waited, Casey wondered why there weren't any female agents present, especially considering they were transporting a female witness. Must just be the luck of the draw. The bureau didn't discriminate.

"How do you do?" she said, shaking the hands of each agent. "Casey Sloane."

"Good to meet you," one of them said. "I'm Agent Palmer." He pointed at his colleagues. "This is Agent Barker, Agent Anderson, and Agent Tucker."

"We're really glad you're here." She turned to Valerie, whose face was set and determined. "This is Valerie Bennett. She's the person you'll be escorting to D.C."

"Thanks for the assistance," Valerie said.

Agent Palmer nodded at the others, prompting the agents to take out their badges and show them to Valerie.

"Thank you," she said.

Casey was pleased they'd taken the time to reassure Valerie, although she was certain E.J. had already checked their IDs.

"We want to get on the road right away," Agent Palmer said. "I know it's late, but we feel it's unwise to stay in one place for too long."

"We understand," E.J. said. He turned to Casey. "Maybe you should help Valerie get ready to leave."

Casey nodded. "Let's go, Valerie."

Valerie didn't say anything, just followed Casey back to the bedroom where she'd put her bags. As she started gathering her things, Casey quickly phoned the hospital. Someone answered from the nurses' station outside the ICU, a person she hadn't spoken to before.

"I'm sorry, I just came on duty. There's no one in the waiting room right now. Either Deputy DeLuca went home or he's somewhere else in the hospital."

Casey was certain Tony was still there. She knew he wouldn't leave the chief's side. "Could I leave him a message?"

"Sure."

"Tell him Casey called. The FBI has arrived and we're turning over our . . . package to them. We'll be home sometime tomorrow. Since it's so late, we may stay the night here before heading back."

There was a pause. Casey assumed the nurse was writing down the message. Sure enough, she read it back verbatim.

"Yes. Exactly. It's important he gets this message as soon as possible."

"Yes, ma'am. I'll watch for him. As soon as he shows up, I'll make sure he knows you called."

"Thanks." Casey ended the call and clicked off her phone.

She turned to see Valerie waiting for her. "Everything will be okay now," she said. "Don't worry. The FBI will get you safely to D.C."

"I wish you and Doug were coming with me."

"I do too, but it's the Feds' case now. We have to step away."

"I . . . I understand, but these guys don't look very friendly."

Valerie's comment made Casey chuckle. "The FBI tends to take themselves very seriously. It's par for the course. But it's also one of the reasons they're so good. You can trust them. I promise."

Valerie searched Casey's face. "If you say so."

"I do. Let's go."

They went back into the living room, where E.J. and Doug waited with the agents. Casey immediately noticed that something was wrong with E.J. He looked tense as his eyes locked on hers. What was going on?

"The deputies were telling us about your situation," Agent Palmer said to Valerie, "that your sister is in danger. Why don't we talk on the way to D.C.? We can certainly help you." He smiled at her. "You're doing the right thing, telling us the truth."

Valerie's eyes filled with tears. "Thank you. Thank you very much. I've been so frightened."

"Well, it's okay now. Are you ready to go?"

"Yes." She turned to smile through her tears at Casey, E.J., and Doug. "Thank you for everything. I don't know what I would have done without you."

"You're welcome," Casey said, her gut clenching and unclenching. What was wrong? Valerie put her suitcases down and hugged her.

Casey looked over Valerie's shoulder and saw E.J. staring at her. "You'll be fine," he said slowly. "Just keep your head down."

Immediately, Casey turned Valerie around so that her body was between her and the Feds. At the same time, she pulled her gun. E.J. did the same. Doug looked confused and hesitated a second before reaching for his weapon, but not before the man who called himself Barker pulled his gun and got a shot off. Doug immediately went down. In the next second, Casey took Barker out. The other three men scrambled behind the furniture. E.J. pulled Casey and Valerie through a nearby door that led outside to the dock. A yellow light fixture attached to the side of the house provided meager illumination, giving the area a strange eerie glow.

"Get to the car!" he yelled at Casey. "Get Valerie out of here. I'll keep them busy." He pulled the keys from his pocket and tossed them to Casey, who caught them with one hand while holding on to Valerie and her gun with the other.

"What's happening?" Valerie said, her voice high and her eyes wide.

"These men aren't with the FBI," Casey said. "We need to get you to safety."

The women ran along a walkway that circled the house. Though Casey was certain it would take them to the garage, she had to step carefully since it was so dark. The last thing she wanted was for either one of them to end up in the water because she missed a step. When they finally reached the front, she held Valerie back while she checked to make sure no one was between them and the door to the garage. She prayed Doug hadn't locked it. She'd just moved away from the house when the men calling themselves Agents Anderson and Tucker emerged from the shadows, their weapons pointed right at her.

"Drop it," Tucker said, a triumphant smile on his face.

Casey, E.J., and Valerie sat on the couch, guns pointed at them, their own weapons confiscated by the fake Feds. Casey couldn't help staring at Doug. He was lying on his stomach, his head turned away from them. No movement. No signs of breathing. He looked dead. How could this have happened? Batterson had arranged for the FBI to meet them here. So who were these guys?

As if reading her mind, E.J. said, "Who are you? What happened to the real FBI?"

Parker, or whatever his name was, shrugged. "We're just hired help. We were told to meet you here, pretend to be federal agents, and take you and Ms. Bennett with us. That was the plan, but then you got cute."

"How did you know?" Casey asked E.J.

He gestured at Parker. "His shoes"—he cocked his head toward Anderson—"and . . . that guy's watch."

Casey looked at both Parker and Anderson. "What do you mean?"

He nodded toward Parker. "Berluti shoes. Almost two thousand dollars." He pointed at Anderson. "His Rolex goes for around six thousand. Too much for any FBI agent. I should have become suspicious sooner, but their IDs looked authentic. Maybe if I hadn't been so slow, Doug would be alive."

Fighting tears, Casey tried not to look at Doug again. He was a friend. A good man with a wonderful family. A loving wife and two kids who didn't know their world had just been shattered to pieces.

"Shut up," Parker said. He pulled a phone out of his pocket and punched in a number. When someone answered, he said, "Things went badly here. I've lost a man, and one of the deputies is dead. You should know that your head Marshal, the one you thought you killed, is alive. In a hospital in St. Louis." He listened for a moment. "So what do you want us to do?" After a brief silence he said, "You paid us to transport two people to D.C. Not three." He listened for a little while but was shaking his head, as if the person on the other end of the line could see him. Finally he took a deep breath. "Look, I'm not gonna kill anyone for you. We already have two bodies here. You better clean this mess up real good and pray it doesn't come back to us. Either we transport these people the way we planned or we're outta here. This has gotten too complicated. I'm not interested in getting in any deeper." Another pause. "Okay. That will work." He took a small notepad and pen out of his pocket. "Give me the address." After writing it down, he abruptly ended the call.

"We gotta take them with us," he told Anderson. "He's gonna send someone to take care of them." He pointed at the two bodies lying on the floor.

Anderson swore under his breath. "I think we need to walk away. This has turned into something we didn't bargain for."

"I don't actually remember asking your opinion," Parker snapped. "We're going to Pennsylvania, dump these three, get the rest of our money, and take off." He turned to E.J.

and Casey. "You all get to meet the person who hired us." Then he pointed at Valerie. "And if you want to see your sister alive, you'd better go to D.C. and do whatever you're supposed to do."

The look on his face caused a tickle of fear to run up Casey's spine.

"All you had to do was let us take her," Anderson grumbled. "Your friend woulda lived. Then you had to tell us your boss was still alive. I doubt he'll stay that way much longer."

"You're blaming us for your mistakes?" E.J. said angrily. "If you'd have actually played your part, we'd be on the way to D.C. now and your own man wouldn't be lying dead on the floor." He sighed with frustration. "FBI agents don't wear expensive shoes and jewelry. Maybe whoever's paying you will be interested in learning how you blew your assignment."

"Look, dude," Parker said, "we don't really know anything except what we were hired to do and the little bit we were told. We don't even know the name of the guy who hired us. He uses a fake name. We got a boatload of money with the promise of even more once we deliver you and her." He nodded toward Valerie. "Your friends were supposed to be sent home. Clueless until it was too late." He shrugged. "I think the guy who hired us planned to take you out somehow. An accident or something. But we only care about our part of the operation. After we deliver you, we don't need to do anything but retire to a beach somewhere."

"You're an idiot," E.J. said. "I suspect the man who hired you has no intention of letting you live."

"Sorry, that won't work," Anderson said with a grin. "Good try, though."

"So you think they're going to kill us and let you live? Your benefactor doesn't have a good track record for leaving people alive who could lead law enforcement right to him. You're getting ready to meet him face-to-face? I have lint in my pocket worth more than your pathetic lives right now."

Anderson blinked a few times as E.J.'s words sunk in, but then his expression hardened again. "Let's go," he demanded, waving his gun.

"And how is your boss going to explain away a dead Deputy U.S. Marshal?" E.J. asked him.

Anderson shrugged. "Not my problem. He's had a lot of experience dealing with death. I'm sure he'll come up with something."

E.J. stood. "I'm going to check on my friend before we leave. I guess if you want to shoot me, you can, but it might ruin your boss's plan to make it look like we died in some *accident*." He walked slowly toward Doug's body. Anderson kept his gun trained on him, but thankfully he didn't fire. E.J. knelt down and put his fingers on Doug's neck. After a few seconds, his shoulders slumped and he stood again. He looked at Casey and shook his head.

Casey blinked away tears and tried to calm herself. Right now she had to concentrate on their witness, yet walking away and leaving Doug lying on the floor tore her to pieces inside. She nodded at E.J., then rose to her feet, pulling Valerie with her. "It'll be okay," she said softly to the frightened reporter.

But was she telling her the truth? Casey wasn't so certain.

CHAPTER
TWENTY-ONE

"Is everyone on?" Agent Owens asked.

"I'm here," Arthur Watson said. The FBI in D.C. had suggested that the Assistant to the Attorney General of the United States be in on the call. So now there were three hookups: Special Agent Norman Huddleston from D.C., Arthur Watson from the Attorney General's Office, and Acting Chief Deputy U.S. Marshal for the District of Missouri's U.S. Marshals Office, Tom Monnier. It was one o'clock in the morning, but a situation like this wouldn't wait for office hours.

"I'm here," Monnier said.

Special Agent Huddleston also acknowledged that he was ready to listen to Martin Avery.

"Let's do it this way, gentlemen," Agent Owens suggested. "Mr. Avery will tell us how he first became involved with Senator Warren, and then with Ali Al-Saud. After that, we'll take turns with questions. Will that work for all of you?"

The other three men acknowledged their agreement with the setup. Owens turned to look at Avery, who seemed fairly relaxed. Maybe finally getting the truth out was a relief to a man who'd spent the last several months running for his life.

"Go ahead, Mr. Avery," Owens said. "Will you please state your name and confirm that you're the Martin Avery involved with Champions for the Earth?"

"Yes," Avery said clearly. "I helped found the organization ten years ago. Recently we'd been focused on stopping the development of a new oil pipeline in the eastern part of the United States."

"Will you tell us how you became involved with Senator Warren?" Owens asked. "And then just bring us up to today—why you turned yourself in."

"Sure." Avery took a deep breath and slowly let it out. "We were targeting plans for the pipeline. Not only did we feel it was detrimental to the earth, there were also concerns about how water in the area would be affected. I was contacted by Senator Warren, who supported our cause and wanted to help. Being the senator from Colorado, it made perfect sense. The pipeline was slated to run through his state. He told me he had financial backers who were willing to donate to support our efforts."

"How much money are we talking?" Owens asked.

"Millions. We were able to buy advertising, send out mailers, keep our people out there protesting. We provided food and lodging, but that was it. No one was getting rich, believe me, but we were receiving a lot of valuable help. And then . . . things got weird." He paused. "I want to make one thing clear. I still believe the pipeline should be stopped, but—"

"Maybe you should explain what you mean by *things got weird*," Owens interrupted, trying to keep Avery on track.

"Some of the protestors who showed up had a different agenda. They didn't want anything to do with us, even though they were supposedly on our side. And they had money. Lots of money. I caught one guy handing out envelopes. I think they were being paid to protest. Then one day a group supporting the pipeline appeared with signs. We had that happen before, and even though we didn't agree with them, we respected their right to have a different opinion. They always protested peacefully, and we gave them their space."

"I remember something about this," Owens said. "Didn't a fight break out? Weren't a lot of people hurt?"

"Yeah," Martin said with a sigh. "My group got blamed for it, except it wasn't us. These new people went nuts. They beat up some of the people who were supporting the pipeline. And when we tried to step in and stop the violence, they went after us. A guy pulled me aside after it was all over and told me if I ever went up against him and his friends again, I'd regret it. And he wasn't kidding. Afterward, I went to Senator Warren and told him I was concerned about this group, that they weren't part of us and they needed to go. Violence wasn't going to help our cause, only hurt it. I told him about the money exchanging hands and asked him if he knew what was going on." Avery shook his head slowly. "It's an understatement to say that his reaction surprised me."

"And what was his reaction?" Owens prompted.

"Anger. Rage. He acted as if I was somehow planning to

destroy the environment singlehandedly. I tried to tell him I was just questioning this new group and their tactics. Trying to figure out where they came from. Why someone was giving them money. He told me in no uncertain terms that if I didn't drop my questions and get back to fighting the pipeline, all funds would be cut off for our efforts and that I would be sorry. Really sorry."

"What does that mean?"

"I had no idea at the time, but I do now. It was a threat against my life. I didn't feel it was coming from the senator. There was obviously someone else working behind the scenes. Someone scary."

"So what happened next?" Owens asked.

"That's when Valerie Bennett, a reporter for a newspaper in St. Louis, contacted me. We were friends in high school, and she wanted to interview me about the pipeline. I gave her the story she requested, the one her paper wanted, but then I started sharing some of my other concerns off the record. I thought maybe together we could figure out what was going on behind the scenes. She began to research some of the donations coming to us through the senator. That's when the name Ali Al-Saud came up. I had no idea who he was, but Valerie did. He's a Saudi businessman who makes his money through oil. We're talking billions of dollars. Some suspect him of funding ISIS, but that's never been proven. If it turned out to be true, he'd lose all his valuable oil contracts with America. But unfortunately, Al-Saud seems to be coated with Teflon. Accusations thrown at him just slide right off. People with information either won't talk or simply disappear."

"So America pursuing its own oil pipelines would put a crimp in his livelihood?"

"More than a crimp. It could decimate him. Right now we have a president who is fully behind making America energy independent, and he's moving quickly. You can see why Al-Saud felt the need to come up with a plan to help people like me delay or stop any and all pipelines."

"This is interesting, but where's your proof?" Owens asked, frowning.

Avery cleared his throat. Owens could see that he was starting to get nervous. "Valerie tried to get into Al-Saud's and Warren's financial records. She believed we could find evidence of collusion. But we never had time to search as thoroughly as we wanted to. Maybe there's something there, but I can't be certain. I haven't talked to her in months."

Even though Owens had asked that the others on the line hold their questions until the end, he heard the agent in Washington swear loudly.

"If Al-Saud had any suspicions you looked at those records," he said, "they're probably gone by now."

Owens saw the color fade from Martin's face. "I'm sure you're right. That means the only things we have left are our phones—and our word. You can certainly read the texts on my phone. I've got it with me, and I kept every exchange we ever had."

"That's not enough to put Al-Saud away," Owens said. "Frankly, I don't quite understand why Washington called Ms. Bennett to testify before the grand jury."

"She is being asked to testify so we can determine if she has any evidence," Arthur Watson replied. "There's really no way to know that ahead of time. Now with the death of Senator Warren . . . well, I'm not sure that grand jury will be called after all."

There was silence for several seconds. Owens suspected they were each wondering if Valerie Bennett was still alive. And if she was, how much longer that would hold true.

CHAPTER
TWENTY-TWO

It took a while for them to prepare to leave. Casey, Valerie, and E.J. were thoroughly searched. All phones were taken from them and turned off, then tossed into a tote bag. They forced everyone to use the bathroom, warning them that once they were in the car, there wouldn't be any stopping. E.J. couldn't shake how weird it felt, almost like they were getting ready to take a family vacation. But their final destination wasn't going to be fun, he was certain of that.

When they finally got ready to leave the house, it was almost three in the morning. E.J. kept turning over scenarios in his mind, trying to find a way to escape from their kidnappers. He knew they had to break free, otherwise he and Casey would probably die.

Once they were outside, the man calling himself Anderson led Valerie over to their SUV and pushed her inside. He got behind the wheel while Palmer climbed into the front passenger seat. E.J. and Casey watched as Valerie buckled her seat belt, her eyes fixed on them. E.J. gave her a quick nod, hoping to reassure her, but he wasn't sure how much it helped. At that moment, unless backup arrived pretty quick, they were all in a lot of trouble.

"You two get in the other car," Tucker ordered. He pointed his gun at Casey. "You drive. And you," he said, gesturing toward E.J., "get in the back. I'll have this gun on her the entire time. Either one of you tries something, I'll shoot her. We don't want to kill anyone, but if you don't behave, we won't have a choice. No matter what, we intend to get the rest of our money."

"But you won't kill Valerie . . . Ms. Bennett," Casey said. "That would make it tough for her to testify, wouldn't it? You wouldn't get paid."

He grinned. "You're right. But we can do other things to her. Things that won't keep her from the courtroom. Things that will make her wish we'd shoot her. You got it?"

Casey glared at him, but she nodded.

E.J. wanted nothing more than a few minutes alone with Tucker. He had a few ideas of his own that would have *him* wishing for death.

They both got in the car, Casey behind the wheel. Casey fastened her seat belt while Tucker kept his promise, his gun trained on her. E.J. could see her fingers tremble. It was hard to shake Casey Sloane, but this dirtbag had done it. E.J. knew her well, though. He knew she'd rally, control her anger, and do everything she could to find a way out of this mess.

The door next to him swung open, and Palmer stood there, holding a pair of handcuffs. "Just for insurance," he said. "But first buckle your seat belt."

With his seat belt fastened and his hands in cuffs, it would be difficult for him to overtake Tucker—but not impossible. Reluctantly he fastened the belt. Palmer reached over and pulled it tight, then told E.J. to hold his hands out. If Tucker didn't have his gun pointing at Casey, he would have taken that moment to go for Palmer's gun. But it was too risky, so he stuck his hands out and the cuffs were slapped on his wrists.

"Now, you be a good boy," Palmer said, his smile more of a sneer. "If you're nice, maybe you'll make it to your destination with all your bones intact. You can hope for that anyway."

He and Tucker laughed. E.J. found their lack of empathy for others especially chilling. How did human beings get this cold-blooded? It was something he would probably never understand.

Palmer slammed the door shut. Tucker hit the lock button next to him. As E.J. listened to the locks click, he hoped they didn't signal the end of the line for him and Casey. He had one ace in the hole. One hope of getting help, but he had no idea if it would work out. Time would tell.

"Okay, let's get back to your story," Owens said to Martin. "What happened next?"

"Well, Valerie and I had been texting each other. Talking about Al-Saud and trying to decide what to do. Then one day I came home to find my apartment ransacked. Whoever broke in was looking for something. I have no idea what they wanted."

Owens grunted. "Maybe they were afraid you'd found the records you were looking for. They were probably ordered to make certain those records never saw the light of day. I suspect your phone was tapped."

"Not only that," Martin went on, "I believe they cloned it. One day I was in my favorite coffee shop near the protest site. I left my phone on the table next to my backpack when I went to get my coffee from the barista counter. When I got back, the phone had been moved. Just a little, but I knew it wasn't in the same spot. I asked several people if they'd seen anyone hanging around my table, but no one had. Everyone was so busy looking at their own phones and laptops, they didn't notice anything unusual. I think someone downloaded my information. I know there are devices that can do that."

"What happened next?" Owens asked.

"Right after I left the coffee shop I noticed two men following me. It certainly made me nervous. One man in particular turned up almost every place I went. I took his picture once and sent it to Valerie. She had a friend in law enforcement who investigated. Maybe he used facial recognition software, I don't know. Anyway, this is the first time Ms. Bennett uncovered the identity of a man named Benyamin Mattan. The story is that his father was a longtime Al-Saud operative. But Valerie discovered something else very interesting about Ben. She believes he is actually Al-Saud's son. Al-Saud certainly treats Mattan like the next in line. He's involved in almost every aspect of Al-Saud's dealings. They call him Al-Saud's shadow."

"Excuse me, Agent Owens. It's Tom Monnier in St. Louis. Mr. Avery, can you describe this guy?"

"Well, he's got black hair. Dark eyes. Medium build. The most recognizable thing about him is the large scar across one side of his face. The story is that he got it when his wife attacked him with a knife. Needless to say, she hasn't been seen in years. Mattan and Al-Saud have little respect for women."

"I want to make sure I heard you correctly," Tom said. "Did you say he has a scar across his face?"

"Can't you hold your questions until Mr. Avery is finished, Mr. Monnier?"

"Not this one. Chief Batterson was attacked by someone with a scarred face. I think it's the same guy."

"Can you tell me a little more about what happened?" Martin asked.

"Someone using an ID belonging to one of our deputies got inside our building. By the time we realized that deputy wasn't in town, the intruder was gone. We started evacuating the building, but before everyone got out, a bomb went off. Several people were killed, and our boss, Richard Batterson, was injured. Suspecting the explosion might be connected to Ms. Bennett, he told two of his deputies to go off the grid and get her to D.C. as quickly as possible. We assumed he'd called the FBI to pick up our witness. We found out later he never got the chance to contact the Feds. Someone hit him over the head and injected him with epinephrine. We're certain his intention was to kill Batterson but make it look as if he died from his injuries from the blast. It almost worked, only our boss is a little too stubborn for that. As I said, when he woke up from surgery, he mentioned that the man who attacked him had a large scar on his face."

"I'm certain it was Ben Mattan," Martin said. There was a short pause. "Do you have any idea where your people are?"

"Not yet," Tom said slowly. "We're looking for them, but we still don't have a confirmed location. However, we do know how Mattan and Al-Saud have been getting their information. Valerie Bennett has been in contact with them this entire time."

Avery shook his head. "I'd tell you I'm surprised, but I'm not. As I told you, he probably has her sister—or someone in her family. Threatening loved ones is his M.O."

"We're investigating that now," Agent Owens said. "We're checking to see if the sister is missing."

"I hope you find her," Martin said. "Mattan has a lot of operatives—everywhere. Most of them have never had direct contact with Mattan, and they don't know each other. It's why they're so hard to find. He's got a perfect network behind him. No one knows anyone else, and when any of his operatives learn too much, he has them killed."

"All right," Owens said. "Let's hold any further questions for a while and let Mr. Avery continue his testimony." He cleared his throat. "So, what happened after your phone was tampered with?"

"Valerie started getting threatening messages from my number. That confirmed my suspicion about someone accessing it. She was told to get away from me, that I wouldn't live long, and if Valerie wanted to survive, she'd shut up about what we'd learned. Then one night when I got home, Mattan was waiting for me. He grabbed me and threw me into the trunk of his car. We ended up in Pennsylvania, where I managed to get away. Mattan followed me with a gun. I thought I was dead. But then like I told you, a homeless guy found me hiding under some trash next to a dumpster.

I could hardly believe I'd lost Mattan. I still have no idea what happened, but I was smart enough to know that the next time I might not be so lucky. That's when I knew I had to take off. I'd already packed some things and left them with a friend. I went to retrieve my stuff, and then I left the state. Never contacted Valerie again. I didn't want to risk it. Not long after that, she called the authorities. They asked her to testify. I suspect her sister was taken shortly after she made that call. Mattan has probably been terrorizing her ever since."

"And you came out of hiding because Senator Warren took his life?"

"Yes."

"How much do you think the senator actually knew?" Tom asked.

"Everything. Remember all the money Al-Saud funneled through him? I'm sure not all of it went to environmental causes. I'll bet a lot of that money found its way into the senator's pockets. Between that and the threats toward his ex-wife, Al-Saud owned him. Warren would have sacrificed me in a minute to keep his money and his ex-wife."

"So you think you're safer now? With Warren dead?"

"I assume so. Having a U.S. senator call me a liar pretty well stripped me of my chance to get anyone to believe me. Now it's just me and Al-Saud. I would hope that gives me a better chance of being taken seriously."

Owens asked if anyone else had questions for Mr. Avery. As Martin tried to respond to every query, mostly to points he'd already covered, Agent Owens was already looking for Susan Bennett.

CHAPTER
TWENTY-THREE

Tom Monnier walked into the ICU waiting room. He looked frazzled, his hair sticking up and his eyes red. Tony had a feeling that if he caught his own image in a mirror, he and Tom would be twins.

Tom came over and slumped down in a chair next to him. "Well, this has been quite a night." He frowned at Tony. "One thing I don't understand—the chief calling his girlfriend before the FBI. That doesn't sound like the Richard Batterson I know."

Tony shook his head slowly. "I know, but that's what he told me. He never made that call to the FBI. I've never known him to put people before his job, but for some reason he felt calling Karen was . . . something he had to do. I'm sure he was worried about Marlon too and knew Karen would make sure to tell him Batterson had survived. He's never been a father before. I think he was trying to do the right thing. The responsible thing. To be fair, he had no idea he wouldn't get the chance to make that next call." Tony studied Tom for a moment. "If you'd been in the building when it blew, who would you call first? Your wife and kids? Or would you jump on tracking the bomber?"

Tom hesitated for a moment before saying, "I'd call Vickie and my boys to let them know I was okay. To think they'd spend even a minute thinking I might be dead . . ."

Tony shrugged. "Seems our boss was in the same mind-set, Tom. I'm sure the call was quick, and I'm certain his next call was going to be to the Feds. He just didn't get the chance to make it."

"So the paramedic who gave him the phone in the first place was the one who tried to kill him?"

"Yeah. My guess is he wanted the chief to make the first call so he'd know how to track our people. But maybe the last thing he wanted was for Batterson to reach the FBI. He made sure that didn't happen."

"Actually, I don't think that had anything to do with it. I just spent time talking with the FBI and Martin Avery."

"Martin Avery?" Tony was shocked to hear Avery's name. "I thought he was missing. Presumed dead."

"You're right. But he's not dead. He was kidnapped by one of Al-Saud's henchmen, Benyamin Mattan. Somehow Avery got away. Went into hiding. After talking to him, my gut tells me that Batterson was a definite target."

"But why? What did they think that would accomplish?"

"I'm not exactly sure, but I found out something that helps to explain things a little. Mattan has a large scar on his face."

Tony's mouth dropped open. "So he *was* the person who attacked the chief." He turned to stare at Tom. "Maintenance man. I've got it."

"What are you talking about?"

"Remember I told you that Batterson said something about a maintenance man?"

"No. I remember you said he mumbled something you couldn't understand."

"He said maintenance man, Tom. I'm sure of it."

"And?"

Tony sighed. Tom must be tired. "This guy, Mattan, he was dressed like a paramedic. He hit the chief and gave him a shot of epinephrine, tried to kill him."

"We already know that."

"But I know why now. He's the one who planted the bomb. Batterson saw him. That's why Mattan decided he had to die."

"How do you know Mattan set the bomb?"

"Because Batterson said the bomber had a big scar on his face. Mattan got into our building by checking in as one of our new deputies. Then he changed clothes, became the maintenance man. He was getting ready to set the bomb when somehow he ran into Batterson. Maybe Mattan was afraid he'd remember him. That's why he followed the chief and tried to kill him. Maybe he never intended to put the bomb by the chief's office. Who knows? But once he realized that Batterson could identify him, Mattan decided to get rid of him. When the bomb didn't get him, Mattan took things into his own hands."

"He killed a paramedic so he could get his uniform and gear . . ."

"Right. Then he approached Batterson, planning to make sure he died this time."

"But why go through all that? The chief was behind a wall. No one would have seen Mattan kill him."

Tony shook his head. "Mark talked to an officer who said the chief was out in plain sight. This is before the attack. Mattan had to do something, but he couldn't draw attention to himself. I have no idea how the chief ended up behind the wall, yet it's exactly what Mattan was waiting for. Then shortly after that, our witness and our deputies take off for D.C. Batterson wanted to keep them safe, although they actually became more vulnerable without backup."

"But they were going anyway." Tom pressed his temples with his index fingers. "Something still isn't adding up."

"Well, they were going to fly. That would have narrowed Mattan's window of opportunity." Tony slapped his forehead. "Of course. Mattan let the chief use his phone. He knew he didn't call the FBI, so he set up the fake FBI. It had to be him."

"Why?"

"Maybe he didn't want Bennett and our deputies to get too chummy. It's possible she might have told them everything. Al-Saud . . . or Mattan couldn't afford to let anyone unmask their schemes. He needed to make sure Valerie Bennett stuck to the plan. People respect the FBI. Assume they can help them, trust them."

"Could be." Tom ran his hands over his face. "So now fake FBI agents have our witness and our deputies, and we still don't know where they are." He leaned back in his chair. "I wonder if our people know these guys aren't the real deal. Casey and Doug are sharp. I can't imagine they'd be fooled for very long."

Tony shrugged. "All I have is Casey's message that the

Feds showed up. At that point, she thought she was dealing with the real FBI."

"I worry that Mattan doesn't need our deputies anymore. They're a liability for him. Now that Bennett's spilled her guts, he can't allow them to live."

Tom got to his feet and paced the floor a couple of times. "I'm afraid you might be right. Al-Saud is known as a businessman, but in reality he's a particularly bloodthirsty terrorist."

Tony frowned. "I don't understand why Valerie Bennett isn't already dead. Al-Saud doesn't want her to testify. It would shine a light on his actions. America would stop all transactions if his terrorist ties were proven."

"Martin Avery says Mattan probably ordered her to lie. Tell the grand jury she made everything up."

"But why would she do that?"

"I guess Al-Saud routinely threatens and even kidnaps family members as a way to control people. Avery thinks he may have snatched Bennett's sister, Susan. The FBI is checking into that now. If she's missing, they'll start looking for her immediately."

Tony turned all this over in his head. "But why plant a bomb at our office in the first place? Wouldn't it have been better just to let her go to D.C. with our deputies? This could have been so simple."

"I can only guess, but there was an incident in Turkey about a year ago where an explosion rocked a police station. The government suspects Al-Saud was behind it. The point of the bomb was to show the Turkish government they would never be safe from him. It was done as a warning."

"Like our bomb," Tony said, nodding slowly. "Planned by Mattan to show Ms. Bennett he could get to the Marshals if he wanted to. It was a warning—that no one is safe from him." Tony swallowed hard. "Wow, this guy is bold. And insane."

"Exactly."

"We need to find our deputies. Now."

Tom didn't respond right away, and Tony knew it was because he was wondering, just like him, if they were already too late.

"No leads at all on the place Batterson sent them?" Tony asked.

"Not really. I did call Karen Abbott. She said Batterson mentioned a house once. She thinks it might have been in Ohio, but she just wasn't sure. We're running a check on the ex-wives' names, looking for property. Hopefully—" His words were cut off by the ringing of his phone. He fished it out of his pocket and answered it. "Yes?" As he listened, an odd look came over his face. Finally he said, "Can you repeat that last part?" After a few seconds, he blew out the breath he'd been holding. "Okay, thanks for calling." He listened a few more seconds before ending the call. "They found the house. Our witness and two of our deputies are gone."

"Two of our deputies?" Tony asked. "But there were three of them, including the guy from D.C."

"I'm aware of that. Casey and Queen are gone. Doug was left behind. He's been shot. I—" Tom's phone rang again, and he quickly answered it.

Tony felt as if his heart had leapt into his throat. As Tom talked to their contact at the FBI, Tony walked out of the waiting room and past the nurses' station. He took out his phone and tried Casey again. His call went straight to voice-mail. Having no other options, he decided to leave a message. Since he knew Casey was being held by dangerous people, he was taking a chance, but at this point she was in more danger without the truth. Using as few words as possible, he told her everything. What Batterson had said and that the Feds they were with were probably Al-Saud's men. "We need to know where you are, Casey," he added. "Do something to let us know your location. I don't care what you do, just help us find you." Afterward he wondered if he'd made a mistake in leaving the voicemail. He had no idea who had her phone, but one thing he was certain of. There really wasn't any other option. Chances were his message could either kill Casey—or save her.

CHAPTER
TWENTY-FOUR

Batterson felt like he was swimming through oil, trying to break through to the surface to where he could breathe again. The harder he fought, the thicker the oil became. Finally, with one violent push, he broke free. His eyes fluttered open, and he looked around. He was in the hospital. Little by little he began to remember talking to Tony. But where was he now?

Batterson turned his head to see if anyone else was in the room, but mind-numbing pain shot through his skull. He tried to touch his head, but he couldn't lift his hand all the way up to do so. Then he realized there was a needle in his arm. He noticed the bag hanging on a metal pole next to his bed. He was hooked up to an IV. He was thinking about pulling the needle out when a nurse approached his bedside. She looked to be in her forties. Black, frizzy hair. He didn't remember seeing her before.

"Can I get something for you, Mr. Batterson?"

"Tony DeLuca. I need to see him." His voice came out

hoarse and scratchy. His throat was dry and it hurt, but he had to talk to Tony again.

"Is that the blond man who's been here since you came in?"

Tony had been here the whole time? "Yeah. . . . I mean, I suppose that's him."

The nurse smiled. "I'd be happy to find him, but first I need to give you something." She took a syringe out of her pocket.

"I don't . . . Please don't give me anything that will make me sleepy," Batterson said. "I need to stay awake."

"Sorry, but I have my orders."

Without meaning to, Batterson let loose with a string of profanity. When he saw the nurse's face, he was embarrassed. "I'm sorry. . . ." He tried to read her nametag, but everything was blurry still and he couldn't quite make it out.

"Rachel," she said.

"I'm sorry, Rachel. It's not your fault. I shouldn't have unloaded on you."

"It's all right." She smiled again, but this time Batterson saw something in her bright green eyes that caused a frisson of alarm.

"Where's my doctor?" he croaked out. "I want to see him before you give me anything."

"This is something special." The nurse leaned down closer to him. "This is from Ben Mattan. He says to tell you hello. And good-bye."

As she took his IV line in one hand and moved the syringe closer to it, Batterson reached over and swiped at the things on his tray. One of them, a metal bedpan, hit the floor with a loud crash. He tried to call out but was unable to.

Just as the so-called nurse started to inject whatever was in the syringe into his IV, Tony rushed into the room. He grabbed the phony nurse and pulled her back. "What are you doing?"

She twisted away and ran back to Batterson, holding the syringe out in front of her as if she planned to stab him any way she could. Tony seized her again and pushed her into a chair. Then he pulled his gun and pointed it at her.

Behind him, Dr. Silver came into the room. "What on earth is going on here?"

Tony gestured to the nurse with his gun. "*She* was trying to give him something. Is she one of yours?"

"No, I've never seen her before and I didn't order any new meds." The doctor picked up the phone next to Batterson's bed and punched in a number. "Send security to ICU now," she ordered.

Before Tony could stop her, the woman jabbed the syringe into her own leg. Tony tried to pull it out before all the liquid was injected, but by the time he grabbed it, the woman had stopped breathing.

Tony straightened and turned to look at Batterson, who could hardly believe what had just happened.

"Is she . . . dead?" he asked in a ragged whisper.

Dr. Silver went over and put her fingers on the woman's neck. She looked at Tony. "Whatever she gave herself was incredibly fast-acting. I can't bring her back."

Tony walked up next to Batterson's bed. "What happened, Chief?"

"I . . . I don't know. She said she was sent by someone named . . . Mattan. I think that was it. I'm a little fuzzy, Tony."

"Benyamin Mattan?" Tony asked.

"She . . . she mentioned Ben Mattan." Batterson reached over and grabbed Tony's arm. "She said he wanted to say hello. I think he might have been the man in the garage. The one who tried to kill me."

"I believe you're right," Tony said. "Tom Monnier was here just a little while ago. He mentioned this Mattan guy. He works for Ali Al-Saud."

Just then two security guards ran into the room. "Is everything okay?" one of them asked.

Dr. Silver shook her head. "Hardly. This woman tried to murder my patient. When she failed, she killed herself."

The guards looked stunned. "What do you want us to do?"

"Well, let's get this woman out of here," Dr. Silver said. She leaned in closer to read the deceased's nametag. She gasped. "This is Rachel Tipton's badge. And her uniform." She spun around to face the security guards. "We need to find the real Rachel. I pray she's okay." She looked over at Tony. "What happens next?"

"Call the police first," Tony said. "I'll let the FBI know what's going on. They'll probably take over the investigation, but let's do this by the book."

Dr. Silver nodded. "Notify the police," she told the guards, "and tell them what happened here. And let them know Rachel Tipton may be missing. Start a search for her. Then tell the nurses at the station to get a gurney in here right away so we can remove this body."

One of the guards frowned. "The police won't want the crime scene disturbed. . . ."

Dr. Silver put one hand on her hip and glared at her. "This is the ICU. We're not going to leave a dead body in one of our rooms, nor are we going to allow the police to disturb our critically ill patients. We saw exactly what happened so we can give them all the testimony they'll need. I'll take full responsibility."

"Yes, ma'am," the guard said. She hurried out of the room, the other guard following close behind her.

"Actually, they might be right," Tony said.

"I don't care." Dr. Silver pressed the nurse's call button on Batterson's bed. She smiled at him. "I'm guessing you'd like something for your throat?"

Batterson tried to return her smile, but even that made him tired. "Yeah, I'm really thirsty. Could I have a glass of water?"

The doctor shook her head. "Not yet. How about some ice chips?"

He nodded. At that moment, ice chips sounded like heaven. He guessed the doctors must have put something down his throat. He looked up at a clock on the wall, which said 3:40. So it was 3:40 on Tuesday morning? His deputies and the deputy from D.C. had been out there for over twelve hours. Were they safe?

Another nurse stepped into the room. The doctor directed her to get a cup of ice chips. As she turned and left the room, Batterson motioned for Tony to come closer to his bed. His body felt so weak, and his eyes wanted to close, but he fought the urge to nod off.

"Hey, Chief," Tony said. "How are you doing?"

"What's wrong?" Batterson asked.

"I . . . I don't know what you mean."

"Yeah, you do."

Tony cleared his throat. "I know the missing nurse. I'm just worried about her."

"Oh. I'm sorry. I hope she's all right."

"I do too."

"Tony . . . where are my deputies? Where are Casey and Doug?"

"They're escorting our witness to D.C., Chief. You know that."

Though Tony's expression didn't reveal anything, he sniffed. His eyes widened as soon as it happened. Tony's tell. Whenever he wasn't being completely honest, he sniffed. Batterson had never told him about it, but by Tony's reaction, it was obvious someone else must have pointed it out.

"You want to try that again?" Batterson asked.

"Look, Chief, you need to concentrate on getting better. We're taking care of things. It'll be fine. Really."

"Yeah, I noticed how well you're taking care of things. That nut almost killed me."

"It won't happen again. We've had someone watching you since you got here. I was on assignment tonight. I'm sorry— somehow she slipped past me. I have no idea how she did it."

Batterson grunted. The last thing he wanted to do was to criticize Tony. If he wasn't so drugged up, he'd be able to control himself better.

"I'm not dead, DeLuca," he growled. "You did a great job, and as long as I'm alive, I'm still in charge. Quit trying to protect me."

At that moment, the nurse entered with a cup of ice chips in her hand, which she gave to the doctor. Dr. Silver walked over to the bed and scooped out some of the chips with a spoon, carefully lowering them to Batterson's lips. When the chips hit his throat, Batterson felt like shouting hallelujah. After a few more spoonfuls, he pushed the doctor's hand away.

"Thanks, Doc," he said, "but now I need to talk to my deputy."

Before she could reply, one of the guards came back into the room. Batterson knew by his expression the news wasn't good. He looked over at Tony. He was stoic, yet the look in his eyes made Batterson's heart drop.

"I'm sorry, Dr. Silver," the guard said. "We just found Rachel's body in a supply room. She's . . . dead."

CHAPTER
TWENTY-FIVE

A few minutes later, two nurses arrived with a gurney. They covered the phony nurse's body with a sheet and rolled her out.

"I'm sorry for your loss, Doc," Batterson said, straining his voice by speaking as loudly as he could. "I'd like some time alone with Deputy DeLuca. It's very important. More important than I can stress right now."

Dr. Silver leaned over the bed. "You're getting a little rambunctious. I think there's been enough drama in here for a while, don't you? This is the ICU. We have people here who are very, very ill."

Batterson didn't want to make things difficult for her, but if he had to . . . well, he'd do whatever it took to protect his deputies. "Sorry, Doc, but I need to know what's going on with my people. You're gonna have to let me do my job. Lives depend on it."

He saw the hesitation on her face. "I'll give you ten minutes," she said finally. "Then I'm throwing your *brother* out."

She locked eyes with him. "You may be in charge at the Marshals Office, but I'm the law around here."

Batterson started to argue, but he recognized that look. It was like staring into a mirror. Arguing with her wasn't going to result in anything good. Especially now. "Okay," he agreed. "Ten minutes. Now, would you excuse us, Nurse Ratched?"

"That's *Dr.* Ratched to you, Mr. Batterson." The doctor glared at Tony. "Ten minutes," she repeated before leaving the room.

"Maybe you should let up on her a bit," Tony said. "One of her colleagues was just murdered."

"I understand that, Tony, but she's a professional. She needs to stay focused, and she needs someone like me to challenge her. Trust me, it will help her more than pity. Besides, I don't want to experience the same thing she's going through. Now quit stalling—tell me what's going on. All of it."

With a sigh, Tony pulled a chair up to the bedside and sat down. "Like I said, we think the man who attacked you was working for Ali Al-Saud. His name is Benyamin Mattan."

"But Ms. Bennett is testifying against Senator Warren. How do you know he's not behind this?"

"Because he's dead. He killed himself."

Batterson tried to shift his position a little. His back hurt. "Are you sure it was suicide?"

"Yeah. There's no evidence of anyone else being there. A note was left for his wife. Although he didn't mention Al-Saud, it was obvious she was in danger. He died to take the heat off her, I guess."

"Okay, so why did they come after us . . . after me?"

Tony shook his head. "You're asking me things I'm not

sure about, but Tom and I think it was done as a warning to Ms. Bennett. They wanted to prove they could get to us, that no one could keep her safe. I don't think they planned to kill you at the outset."

Batterson grunted. "I know exactly why they wanted me dead."

Tony scooted his chair a little closer. "You do?"

Batterson nodded. "Did you happen to notice the maintenance man in the building not long before the blast?"

"No, but it sounds like you did."

"I practically ran into him. I realize now he was trying not to be seen. Our encounter was an accident."

"The maintenance man was Mattan, and he planted the bomb."

"Right," Batterson said. "He was also the paramedic who tried to kill me. He might not have cared originally if I lived or died, but once he realized I recognized him, he decided he couldn't risk it."

"He had to get rid of you."

"Yeah, I'm sure that's it."

"If you were able to identify him, it could have exposed Al-Saud. That's something he couldn't afford." Tony frowned. "Do you remember him hitting you?"

Batterson nodded. "And there was something else . . ." He tried to pull up a memory that evaded him.

"He injected you."

"That's it. I felt a sting in my hip." Batterson studied Tony. "What was it?"

"Epinephrine."

"For allergies?"

Tony nodded. "Only Mattan used a larger dose on you, Chief, like for cardiac patients. It should have killed you, should have stopped your heart. When you came into the hospital, your heartbeat was incredibly fast and uneven, but no one knew why. They assumed it was because of your injuries."

Batterson's eyebrows knit together as he stared at Tony. "The doctors told you all this?"

"Not completely. I . . . I found you and called for an ambulance. Then I went with you to the hospital."

"Now, why in the world would you do that?"

Tony snorted. "I don't know. Had nothing else to do yesterday morning."

"I'm sure you could have spent your time looking for our deputies. Wasn't that more important?"

"Don't be an idiot. And don't make me tell you how important you are to all of us. It's embarrassing."

Although Batterson's first reaction was to chew Tony out, he couldn't do it. Maybe it was the meds they had him on, but the loyalty Tony had shown made him feel emotional—too much so. He quickly changed the subject.

"I . . . I used his phone," Batterson said.

"We know. We initially thought he gave you his phone because he wanted to know who you'd call."

Batterson's mind was moving slower than normal, but fear suddenly gripped him. "I don't think that was his first thought, but I'm sure he checked his phone after he took it back. I-I called Doug . . . and Karen."

"I know that too. We've got Karen and Marlon somewhere safe. Don't worry."

Batterson sighed with relief. "Thank you, Tony. So when's the last time you heard from Howard and Sloane?"

"I talked to Casey just a few hours ago."

Batterson frowned at him. "Wanna tell me what she said?"

Tony glanced around. Batterson got the feeling he was looking for the doctor. "Tell me now, Tony. I mean it." He tried to sound tough, but the truth was, he was pretty sure he couldn't stand up by himself even if he managed to get out of bed.

"She . . . she said the FBI had arrived and that they were handing Valerie Bennett over to them."

"What?" Batterson felt faint. He fought to stay conscious. "I told you I didn't call them."

"I know, Chief. Look, I didn't tell you the whole story earlier. The FBI located the house. Our people were gone. We're doing everything we can to find them."

Batterson was silent for a moment. He'd called Karen first so she'd let Marlon know he was okay. He wanted to let the boy know he was alive. He'd lost his mother and had nightmares about being left alone. Batterson's reaction was pure instinct. He'd always put his job first . . . even through his three marriages. The one time in his life he'd made another human being his priority, it may have cost his deputies their lives.

"We know you talked to Doug and Karen," Tony said. "Was there anyone else?"

Batterson shook his head. "It's my fault. I should have called the FBI first."

"Don't be ridiculous," Tony said, his voice stern. "I would have called Kate first. It's the way love works, Chief. And again, you had no idea you wouldn't be able to make another call. Don't crucify yourself with some kind of false guilt."

"It's not false guilt. It's—"

"So there wasn't anyone else, Chief?" Tony said, interrupting him.

"No. That was it."

"Here's something else you're not going to like," Tony said. "Valerie Bennett's been in contact with Mattan for a while, feeding him information about us. She heard the phone call to Doug and shared with him that you planned to call the FBI."

Batterson couldn't believe what he was hearing. "Our witness betrayed us? Why? Is she working with this Mattan guy?"

"No. We believe he has Ms. Bennett's sister and has been threatening to kill her."

Batterson leaned back against his pillow and swore. "She's the reason he bombed our office. She's responsible for the people we lost."

"No, Chief. Mattan and Al-Saud are responsible. Ms. Bennett was only trying to protect her sister."

Batterson waved his hand at Tony. "Maybe. Go on."

"We believe when Mattan checked your phone, he saw there wasn't a call to the FBI. That's when he got the idea of sending someone to show up pretending to be the Feds. He thought you were dead, so no one would know the difference. But when the men Mattan sent talked to Doug and Casey, I believe they found out you were still alive. I'm sure they told Mattan, and then he sent our fake nurse." Tony took a deep breath and let it out. "Of course, this is conjecture. We're really flying blind here."

Batterson heard footsteps coming down the hallway. Had ten minutes gone by already? "Have you brought the real FBI in on this yet?"

"Tom's talked to them. They're working to help us now. They found the location of your ex-wife's house. Look, Casey and E.J. Queen are highly trained deputies. They'll watch out for our witness and keep themselves safe. I'm sure of it."

Batterson studied Tony for a moment. "What about Doug? You didn't mention him."

"Sorry, Chief. Just forgot. It's been so crazy, and I haven't had much sleep."

Batterson started to question him again when Dr. Silver came up and put her hand on his shoulder. "That's it for now." She pointed her index finger at Tony. "He needs rest. Check with me in a few hours. If he's doing okay, I'll let you talk to him again."

"Thanks, Doc. Take care of yourself, Chief." Tony walked away quickly as if he were trying to escape.

Batterson half listened as the doctor talked to him about what would happen next in his recovery. Tony was keeping something back, and it worried him. What was it he was afraid to tell him?

CHAPTER
TWENTY-SIX

They'd been on the road for almost three hours. Casey was tired of having a gun pointed at her. She'd been watching Tucker closely. Was he getting tired? If he started to nod off, maybe she could get the gun away from him, but what would happen to Valerie? Would they really abuse her? Casey was pretty sure these guys would do whatever they had to in order to get their money. She couldn't take the chance that something she did might lead to Valerie getting hurt.

She reached over and switched on the radio. A country station came on, and Toby Keith's "Courtesy of the Red, White, and Blue" drifted through the speakers. One of her favorite songs.

"Turn that noise off," Tucker snapped. "I hate country."

"Well, I like it," she said. "I need something to keep me awake. Unless you want me to fall asleep and run into someone, we need to keep it on." She really didn't feel tired; she just needed the distraction. Her head was pounding from trying to figure a way out of their situation. If she and E.J.

didn't do something before they reached their destination, neither one of them would live past this day.

Tucker grunted and shrugged. "Whatever. I guess since this is probably the last music you'll ever hear, you may as well listen to what you want."

The argument she'd used to get him to let her play the country station replayed in her head. She glanced over at Tucker. No seat belt. What about Valerie? An image of her getting into the car flashed in Casey's memory. She'd definitely fastened her belt. What about their captors? She had no idea, and there simply wasn't any way for her to be sure.

She looked around at the traffic. The sun was up now, lots of people on their way to work. Was her plan too dangerous? More than anything, she wished she could talk to E.J. She looked in the rearview mirror and saw him staring at her, a half smile on his face. Was he thinking the same thing she was? She slowly reached up and tugged on her seat belt with her right hand. When she did, E.J. nodded. Still, she couldn't be sure they were on the same page. It might be crazy, and she didn't want to do it unless he was in agreement.

"Any way we can stop for coffee?" she said to Tucker. "I could use the caffeine boost."

"No stopping," he said emphatically.

"Okay, but isn't picking up some coffee better than me falling asleep and crashing into another car?"

Tucker stuck the gun in her side. "How's this for a shot of adrenaline? No stopping unless Jerry . . . uh, I mean *Palmer* says it's okay. Ya got that?"

"All right. Sorry. Guess I just need to keep my head down," she said. Once again she sought E.J.'s eyes in the rearview mirror. Sure enough, he nodded again. She was convinced he understood. Now she just had to wonder if she really had the courage to go through with her plan. Her heart raced in her chest, and she prayed God would protect them.

She kept the car at a steady pace and waited for the right moment. It took almost thirty minutes for her to find a semi-truck she could get behind without making it seem suspicious. She tried to pull back and get into position two different times. She needed some space between her car and the truck. Both times someone pulled into the gap, forcing her to abandon her plan. Casey also had to make certain the car Valerie was in was right behind them. Finally, with her third attempt, everything was lined up just right. With one more look at E.J., she began to speed up.

"Hey, what are you doing?" Tucker yelled. "Slow down!"

In response she punched the accelerator. The driver behind her increased speed just as she'd assumed he would. She saw E.J. raise his cuffed hands to cover his face. Then Casey closed her eyes and buried her face into her one free arm. She slammed into the back of the semi. Immediately the car holding Valerie hit them. Though she'd tried to prepare for it, when the airbag inflated, it punched her in the face like a heavyweight boxer putting all his strength behind his fist. She started to black out but fought against it with every ounce of determination she could muster.

She stomped on the brake and shifted the car into park. She looked to see where they were. Her car was about fifty feet behind the semitruck. Thankfully it hadn't ended up in another lane. No other cars had been hit. Trying to stay conscious, she unhooked her seat belt and looked to her right.

Even though the sight before her was what she'd expected, she quickly turned her head away, her stomach churning. Tucker had gone partially through the windshield. His body was torn and bloody. Without looking at him again, she reached over and grabbed his gun. Then she twisted around to check on E.J. His head was bent over, and for a moment she was afraid he was badly injured. But then he moaned, raised his head and blinked at her.

"Are you all right?" he mumbled, his words hard to understand.

"I'm fine. I've got the gun. We need to get out of here so you can rescue Valerie."

He nodded. "You'll have to help me."

Casey realized she needed the key to the cuffs. Pushing back the nausea threatening to overtake her, she reached into Tucker's pocket hoping the key was in the left side of his pants. Her hand closed around a key ring. She pulled it out of his pocket and then crawled out of the car, trying to stand to her feet. She could see the other car now. The front was crushed almost flat. Its windshield was spotted with blood, the glass cracked in several places.

Had the other men worn their seat belts? If so, would they be getting out of the car with their guns drawn? Casey pulled on the back car door. At first it wouldn't budge. She finally got it to open but not all the way. After fumbling with the keys for a few seconds, she found the right one. She leaned in, unlocked E.J.'s handcuffs, and unfastened his seat belt.

"You sure you're okay?" she asked.

"I'm just sore," E.J. said. She was thankful he wasn't badly injured. He slowly scooted out of the car. "Give me the gun," he told her.

"I'll take care of it," she insisted. "You look dazed."

"Please, Casey. Don't argue with me. We're not in competition. I'm bigger and stronger. And I want to see what's going on in the other car."

Reluctantly she handed him the gun. "I'm a better shot than you."

"I know that, but we may actually need brute strength. Besides, I'm a larger target than you." He gave her a crooked smile.

"Fine, but I'm coming with you." She knew he wanted to protect her, but she didn't need him to watch over her. She was every bit the deputy he was. Still, knowing he cared about her so much made her feel good.

As they approached the black SUV, Casey noticed other vehicles stopping around them, people staring. Many of them were taking video on their smartphones. A couple of people started to get out of their cars, probably wanting to help. But when they saw the gun in E.J.'s hand, they quickly retreated, some even speeding away from the scene. Casey couldn't blame them.

E.J. held the gun in front of him as he pulled the driver's door open. Anderson's head was bent forward. He was either dead or unconscious. Palmer hadn't fastened his seat belt. He hadn't been thrown through the windshield like Tucker had, but he'd struck it hard enough to crush part of his head. He was obviously dead.

Casey opened the back door. Valerie stared at her, panting, her eyes wide. "What . . . what happened?"

"We've had an accident," Casey said. "Come on. We need to get you out of here right away."

Valerie unhooked her seat belt and tried to push herself over to the door. "My body really hurts."

"It will for a while. You're going to have to fight through the pain."

From somewhere behind them came the shrill whine of a siren.

"Thank God," Casey said. "The police." She turned to E.J. "You'd better put that gun away. I'd hate to see you shot by the cops."

"Good point." E.J. gestured toward Casey's car. "Let's go over there and wait," he said to Valerie.

"Hold on a minute," Casey said. She noticed the tote bag of phones the men had collected lying on the floor and grabbed the bag. "I'm tired of not having a phone." She opened it and dumped everything onto the ground. Finding her burner phone, she snatched it up and put the phone in her pocket. She thought about getting Valerie's phone, but then decided to let the police secure it.

She was getting ready to follow E.J. and Valerie when Anderson grabbed her arm and pulled her back. She twisted away and ran toward E.J.

"He's conscious!" she cried out. "Be careful."

Before E.J. had a chance to respond, Anderson climbed out of the car and fired his weapon, barely missing E.J., who pulled his gun from his waistband and fired back. Anderson was hit but not stopped. He fired again. At first, Casey thought he'd missed. Then she felt an odd sting in her side. When she looked down, she saw blood seeping onto her white blouse.

Anderson had taken cover behind the open car door. E.J. fired two shots at him and then sprinted over to a man idling in a white sedan. He yanked the door open and ordered the man out. "I'm a Deputy U.S. Marshal and I need this vehicle."

Although the man looked as if he wanted to argue, his eyes never left E.J.'s gun. Finally he nodded and ran from his car. E.J. led Valerie into the back seat and ran back for Casey, who was crouched behind the back of her ruined Cruiser.

Anderson stepped out from behind cover and raised his weapon.

"Watch out, E.J.!" Casey shouted.

E.J. turned and fired at Anderson, who'd ducked down once again. E.J. grabbed Casey and ran with her to the white sedan. He shoved her into the back seat next to Valerie. Then, after firing one more shot at Anderson, he slid behind the wheel, stepped on the accelerator, and began to navigate between the two lanes of stopped traffic. Casey prayed as the sides of the car scraped against other vehicles. Motorists who'd exited their cars to see what was going on had to jump out of the way.

"Careful! Don't run into anyone," Casey said.

E.J.'s jaw was set with determination. "They're gonna have to take care of themselves."

"What about the police?" she asked.

"Can't wait for them. Not with Anderson shooting at us." He came to an open spot and took the exit.

"Pull over," Casey said. "We can call and get some help."

He shook his head. "We need to get someplace safe." He

looked at her in the rearview mirror. "What if Anderson did the same thing we did? He could be right behind us."

She hadn't thought of that. Casey wasn't certain how badly she was injured, but their witness was in trouble. It was her job to make sure Valerie stayed safe. Right now, nothing was more important than that. Not even her own life.

CHAPTER
TWENTY-SEVEN

Tony rushed into the temporary office set up for Tom Monnier while the rest of the building was being repaired. "Tom, have you seen the news?"

Tom shook his head. "No, Tony. I've been a little busy."

"You'll want to see this." Tony handed Tom his phone, then clicked on a story that had just aired on a national news channel.

They both listened as a reporter relayed the details of a frightening scene unfolding on a Pennsylvania highway. As Tom watched, he saw a man get out of a car that looked as if it had crashed into the back of a semitruck. The man rushed toward the car behind them while a woman from the first car followed him. The man reached into the second car and pulled out a passenger, a woman. He began to lead her away when a second man got out and began shooting at the other three. The first man ran over and pulled a bystander from his car, pushed him out of the line of fire, and ushered the women inside as he fired back at the shooter. Tom gasped. "That's Casey!"

"Yeah, and that's Valerie Bennett. The man there is E.J. Queen, the deputy from D.C."

"And where was this? How long ago?"

"Not too far from Pittsburgh on Highway 70. The video was taken about half an hour ago."

"Call law enforcement in the area. I'll contact the bureau. We need a chance to find our people and bring them in before Mattan goes after them."

Both men got on the phone, and Tony prayed they could get help to their deputies before Mattan ordered their executions.

E.J. drove until he found a road that didn't look well traveled. He turned and kept going until he arrived at a small town that looked deserted. He wasn't sure just where they were. Somewhere in Pennsylvania. The last sign he'd seen on the highway was Cranberry. That didn't mean anything to him.

He pulled behind an abandoned service station. When he turned around to say something to Casey, he noticed the blood on her blouse.

"Are you all right?" Not waiting for an answer, he jumped out of the car and ran around to where she sat.

She waved him away. "I'm okay. The bullet just grazed me. Bled a lot at first, but it seems to have stopped."

"Are you sure?"

"Seriously, don't worry about me."

E.J. looked over at Valerie, who appeared to be in shock. "We'll be fine," he said to her, hoping she'd believe him. "Where's that bag of phones, Casey?"

"I didn't take the entire bag. Just my burner phone."

"Where is it?"

"In my pocket." She reached down and pulled it out. E.J. saw her wince.

"You're hurting."

She smiled. "Let's shoot a bullet through your side and see how great you feel."

"I thought you said it was a graze."

"It is. A deep graze. I'll be fine, though."

E.J. held the phone up so he could see it clearly. "We need help. Let the authorities know where we are. I'm betting we can get the cops here before anyone else is able to find us."

"I hope you're right."

E.J. walked a few yards from the car and turned the phone on. They were really out in the boonies. After a couple of attempts, he finally got a signal and quickly dialed 9-1-1. He told the dispatcher who he was and that they needed backup and an ambulance. Even though Casey had reassured him she'd be okay, he wasn't taking any chances.

"You're in Arbuckle," the dispatcher said. "That town folded after the coal mine closed. I'll get someone there as soon as I can, but it might take a while. You're a long way from us. You'll just have to be patient."

"We have some pretty bad people chasing us, and a woman who needs medical attention. Please hurry."

The dispatcher told him she'd do her best. Next, he thought about calling the office. With Batterson out of action, Tom Monnier was probably in charge. He'd just started to scroll through the contacts when Casey called out.

"I think someone's coming," she said.

He hurried back to the car. Casey was peering around the corner of the building. A pickup truck was barreling down the street, right for them. E.J. put the phone away and pulled out his gun. They waited until the truck drove past them.

"Help is on the way," he said to Casey with a sigh. "Someone should be here before too long."

They walked back to the car, where Valerie waited. "Thank you for getting us out of there," she said. "I thought we were all going to die."

"I don't think they would have killed you," E.J. said. "They were offered a great deal of money if they delivered you alive." He turned to Casey. "Of course, you could be referring to our *rescue*. Wow. Pretty gutsy."

Casey smiled weakly. "It was all I could come up with. Did you have a better idea?"

E.J. grunted. "No, but let's not use that maneuver again, okay? I don't think my heart could take it."

Casey chuckled. "I hear you."

"You two have put your lives on the line for me time after time," Valerie said, her voice shaking with emotion. "Deputy Howard is dead." Tears filled her eyes. "I'm really sorry I wrote that story. If I'd known how much trouble it would cause . . ."

"Don't be silly," Casey said. "None of this is your fault. You were trying to expose corruption. The blame rests on Ali Al-Saud and his lapdog, Mattan."

Valerie nodded slowly, wiping tears from her cheeks. "I know what you're saying is right, but I'm not sure I'd do the same thing again."

"Then men like Al-Saud will win," E.J. said firmly. "And we can't allow that to happen."

Valerie didn't respond, but it was obvious E.J.'s words had made an impact.

"I need to call Tom," E.J. said to Casey. "Do you have his number in here?"

She nodded. "I entered it as we were leaving St. Louis."

E.J. noticed that Casey looked a little pale. "Listen, even if you're not badly wounded, you lost some blood. Why don't you sit down? Take it easy? There's not much we can do now anyway. Just wait for help."

"Stop handling me," Casey said sharply, frowning at him.

"Okay, okay. Keep an eye on Valerie while I see if I can reach Tom."

Casey encouraged Valerie to get back in the car. "Let's sit down for a bit," she told her. "Help is on the way."

Valerie slid back into the car. Casey got in beside her.

E.J. found Tom's number and tried several times to get through. The reception was so poor, at first he was afraid he wouldn't be able to complete the call. When finally he got through, it went to voicemail.

E.J. left a detailed message about what was happening and where they were. "We're in some ghost town called Arbuckle, Tom, a few miles off the highway. We're behind an abandoned gas station. I've called the police and requested an ambulance. You can either call me back, or I'll call you again when we're someplace safe. You need to get to Batterson's house in Port Clinton, Ohio. Doug is there. He was shot. When we left, he was alive. I pray he still is." E. J. felt guilty about not telling Casey that Doug wasn't dead, but his pulse was so faint, he didn't want to give her false hope.

He started to say something else when he heard the wail of a siren coming up the road. He disconnected his call to Tom and sent up a silent prayer of thanks. It had taken a while, but at least they were finally about to be rescued. Within seconds, a police cruiser pulled up and an officer jumped out. Casey got out of the vehicle and waved him down.

"Are you the folks who called for help?" he asked as he approached.

"Yes," E.J. said, hurrying over to the officer. "Do you have an ambulance on the way?"

The officer pulled his gun from his holster. "No," he said with a smile. "But you won't need one. Get into my car. Now."

E.J. heard Valerie cry out.

"You're not with the police," Casey said.

"Good guess," the man said. "I work for Ali Al-Saud. Now *get* in the car. We don't have much time." The man strode over and grabbed Valerie, putting the gun to her head.

"Remove your gun from its holster slowly and toss it on the ground by me," he told E.J. "And toss that phone over here too."

E.J. hesitated a moment, but he had no idea what this guy might do. He took out the gun he'd taken from Tucker, set it on the ground, and kicked it over toward the man's feet. Then he threw the phone next to his gun. The man lifted his boot and brought it down hard on the phone, smashing it. He picked up the shattered device and hurled it into the bushes a few yards away.

"My job is to deliver you to Ben Mattan as soon as possible. Hopefully alive. I personally don't care which way it goes."

"How did you get here before the police?" Casey asked, her face tight with anger.

"Mattan sent me to follow you after you left Ohio. I've been watching you—and listening to a police scanner. They really come in handy." He shrugged. "All I had to do was intercept the police officer sent to assist you. It really wasn't that difficult." He waved his gun at them. "Let's go. Into the car. Now."

As E.J. helped Valerie and Casey into the back of the cruiser, he pulled off the dog tags he wore. He dropped them to the ground, partly under the car so that the man wouldn't notice them. He then scribbled something in the dirt before he slid into the back seat next to Casey.

Once everyone was inside, the man started the car and roared away. From somewhere behind them, E.J. could hear another siren. Probably the ambulance. He wanted to believe the police would realize they were in trouble and pursue them, but by the time they arrived, secured the scene, and searched the area, E. J., Casey, and Valerie would be long gone.

CHAPTER
TWENTY-EIGHT

E.J. sat silently next to Casey in the back seat with the man so close to Valerie, they couldn't do anything. His gun was still pointed straight at her. E.J. looked to see if Casey's wound was still bleeding, but it seemed to be under control. He could see the tension in her face and wondered if it came from the situation they were in or from the gunshot. He was concerned she was hurt more than she was letting on.

He managed to catch Valerie's eye. He smiled at her, trying to keep her calm. She seemed to be doing okay. He was thankful, but he wondered how much more she could take.

Finally, the man slowed the car, took a turnoff, and got on the highway. Though E.J. still wasn't sure where they were, ahead he saw what looked to be a large city. Just then he saw a road sign. They were headed to Pittsburgh. After several more turns, their driver pulled up in front of a large building. It appeared to be an abandoned warehouse. The man honked twice and a large door slid open, like a garage door but much bigger. They pulled inside, and two men came over to the car.

The driver got out, slamming the door behind him. "Remove them," he said, gesturing first to Valerie, then to E.J. and Casey.

A man built like a wrestler opened the door and started to grab Casey.

"Put your hands on her and she's the last thing you'll ever touch," E.J. said in a low voice.

The big brute looked surprised, but he backed up. Casey glared at E.J. and shook her head. She could certainly take care of herself. What was wrong with him? For some reason, he was feeling incredibly protective. Was it because she'd been injured?

Another man, dressed in fatigues, walked up next to them. "What's wrong with her?" he asked, nodding toward Casey.

"She's been shot," E.J. answered.

"Just a flesh wound," Casey said.

"I have some medical training. Bring her back here and let me have a look. Better safe than sorry." He pointed at Valerie. "She stays here." He gestured toward a nearby chair, and Valerie sat down, her eyes never leaving E.J.

"You wait here for me," he told her. "I'll be right back."

While E.J. didn't trust any of these guys, he followed the man through the large building to the back where there were several large rooms. One of them had cots. Were these men living here?

"This way," the man said, gesturing to his right. He didn't seem to fit in with the others. He was younger, his hair braided into cornrows.

He shut the door and went over to the closet, pulling out several bottles, along with some large pads, gauze, and a pair of scissors. He brought everything over to where Casey stood. "I'm going to raise your blouse so I can see your wound," he said.

Casey shook her head. "No thanks. I can do that myself." She lifted her blouse just enough to expose a long red gash in her side. It looked worse than E.J. had imagined.

"It's not deep enough to have hit any vital organs," the man said. "But I bet it hurts."

Casey shrugged but didn't say anything.

"I'm going to clean and dress the wound now. You need to stay as still as possible so you don't start bleeding again."

"I'll do my best," Casey said, "but since your friend probably plans to kill us, I'm not sure I need to worry about it too much."

"Look, I'm just trying to help. I can treat you or I can walk away. It's your choice."

Casey nodded at him while E.J. watched the man through narrowed eyes. He intended to let this guy help Casey, but then he planned to grab him around the neck. If he had a weapon, E.J. would take it. He had to get them out of here.

The man carefully cleaned the wound and then covered it with a large pad.

"Come over here," he told E.J. "Help me wrap this gauze around her."

E.J. stepped over, glad for the chance to get closer. He looked for a gun but didn't see one. However, there was a knife in a sheath on the man's belt and a pair of small scissors on the cot next to the gauze. One of those would have to do.

"Can you lift up your arms?" the man asked Casey.

She raised her right arm, but then brought up the left arm much more slowly.

As the man handed E.J. the end of the gauze strip so he could wrap it around Casey's waist, E.J. heard him whisper, "They're watching and listening to everything. I'm undercover, and I plan to get you out of here. Just be cool. You need to trust me." Then the man straightened and spoke in a normal tone of voice. "Keep your arms up until I'm done." He and E.J. wrapped the dressing around Casey four times. "Okay, put your arms down, but be careful." He secured the tape, and Casey let go of her blouse.

"Keep an eye on her," he said rather loudly to E.J. "And don't get cute. If you do, my boss will kill you both." He gathered the medical supplies he'd used on Casey, except for the scissors, and put everything back in a cabinet in the closet. "Stay here until I find out what my boss wants to do with you." With that, he left the room.

E.J. heard the door lock behind him and quickly grabbed the scissors. He was certain the man had left them there on purpose. E.J. cupped the scissors in his hand and twisted his body so he could slip them into his pocket without anyone seeing.

"Are you sure you're okay?" he asked Casey.

"I swear if you ask me that again, you'll be sorry."

"I just want to make sure."

"You're treating me like I'm weak," she insisted. "I'm a Deputy U.S. Marshal just like you are. Now knock it off."

E.J. sighed. "Point made. Sorry. So where do you think we are?"

"You're thinking about Jared, aren't you?" Casey asked, her tone accusatory. "Why can't you let that go?"

"I didn't bring it up, you did."

Casey just stared at him, slack-jawed.

"Look at you," E.J. spit out. "You just pulled off one of the most outrageous rescues I've ever seen. You're . . . invincible. Fearless." He ran his hands over his face, trying to steady his nerves. "For some reason it's driving me nuts."

He expected her to get angry, but instead she smiled sadly. "E.J., you're a knight in shining armor. A good guy. I was upset when you left and so I tried to make you feel guilty. That's something you can't handle." She shook her head. "It's not your fault. You didn't do anything wrong. I'm sorry I made you think you did." She came over and put her hand on his shoulder, her dark eyes boring into his. He realized instantly that she was right. He felt guilty . . . and something else. He had feelings for Casey Sloane, and it was making him crazy. "But I think we should table this for now and talk about it later."

He sighed. "According to you, there's never any time that's right to talk about it, yet we can't ignore this forever. It's a wall between us, and we need to be a team right now."

"Please, E.J."

"Okay. You're right. Later." He got up and walked a few feet away. When he turned around, he found her staring at him with an expression he'd never seen before. She looked almost . . . vulnerable. "I'll be fine," he said quickly. "Seeing you get shot scared me. I know it's part of the job, but I'm not ready to watch you die. I care about you, Casey. Maybe more than I realized. The thought that I might lose you seems to have unhinged me." He laughed softly. "Forgive me. I'm an idiot."

Her expression softened, and she nodded. "Yeah, you are. Now, let's figure out how to protect our witness and get out of this without dying, okay?"

CHAPTER
TWENTY-NINE

Lieutenant Tally Williams with the St. Louis PD sat across the desk from Assistant Special Agent in Charge Sarah Armstrong, who was with the FBI in St. Louis.

"So we're looking for a woman by the name of Susan Bennett?" Tally asked. "You have information that she's been kidnapped?"

Sarah nodded. "We believe she's being held in an attempt to coerce a witness."

"I take it that's all you can tell me?"

"Yeah. Sorry." Sarah liked the young lieutenant. She'd heard lots of great things about him. He worked closely with the local U.S. Marshals. Tom Monnier, the Acting Chief Deputy U.S. Marshal for the District of Missouri's U.S. Marshals Office, had recommended they contact him. Lieutenant Williams was an expert when it came to places criminals might hide out in Missouri. It took someone with knowledge of the area to uncover drug dealers and meth labs tucked away near the small towns that dotted the state. The FBI hoped that knowledge would help them find Susan Bennett.

The lieutenant rubbed the back of his neck, probably trying to release tension. "So what *can* you tell me?"

"Susan Bennett works at a coffee shop downtown. I asked and received surveillance videos from the shop and from two other businesses nearby on the day she disappeared and from a few days prior. I just got the videos and haven't looked at them yet. Do you want to go through them with me?"

"Sure. Do we know what time she went missing?"

Sarah nodded. "Right after she left work at three o'clock in the afternoon on Friday."

"She's been gone four days?"

Sarah acknowledged the look on the lieutenant's ebony face. "I know. Usually when someone's gone this long, we're searching for a body. But the guy who ordered her kidnapping isn't the one holding her. It's possible he hasn't ordered her execution yet, Lieutenant."

"All right. Let's take a look. But if we're going to be working together, why don't you call me Tally?"

She smiled. "So long as you call me Sarah."

"You've got a deal."

Sarah got up and pulled another chair up to her desk. Tally joined her in front of her computer monitor. "Here's the video from the coffee shop." Sarah checked the notes written by the coffee shop owner. "I guess this was recorded just as she was leaving."

They watched as a young woman with dark hair walked

toward the front door. She waved good-bye to her coworkers and headed to the left. That was it. Not much to go on.

"Does anyone walk out after her?" Tally asked.

"Not for several minutes, and it's a couple. They went the other way."

"Okay. Let's see the other videos."

"At around the same time?"

Tally nodded.

Sarah clicked on the first one. "This is from a security camera down the street. They've been having break-ins so they started recording the sidewalk outside their store. You can see Susan walk by there. She's alone."

They watched her stride past, and then Sarah turned the video off. "This is the last one. A traffic camera down the street at the intersection."

Although the coffee shop was halfway down the block, Sarah and Tally could see Susan walk out the door of the shop and head toward the intersection. At the end of the block, she turned left and disappeared from sight.

"I checked for cameras on that street, but there weren't any pointed in the right direction."

"Do you mind if I go over these again?" Tally asked.

"Of course not," Sarah said. "Do you want some coffee?"

"Sure."

Sarah left her office and went to the kitchen to get two cups of coffee. After pouring them, she realized she hadn't asked Tally what he took in his coffee. She stuffed some packets of sugar, artificial sweetener, and creamer in her pocket just in case he didn't like his coffee black.

She was almost back to her office when she saw Tally step out into the hallway, obviously looking for her.

"I found something," he said as she approached.

"Already?" Surprised, she followed him back to her desk, where she put down the steaming cups. She pulled all the extras out of her pocket and dropped them onto the desktop.

"I take it black, thanks," Tally said, reaching for the cup nearest him and taking a sip.

Sarah slipped into the chair next to him. "So what did you see?"

He clicked on the video from the coffee shop. "See this green truck that drives past Susan?" He pointed at a truck that headed down the street a few minutes before Valerie's sister left.

"Yeah, I see it."

"Now look at the day before she disappeared." Tally backed up the tape and showed her the feed from the camera pointed toward the front door. The entire front of the coffee shop was glass, making it easier to see the street. "There's a green truck parked in front of the shop."

"Can we see into the cab?"

He shook his head. "The windows are tinted. Always a bad sign."

"Okay, but maybe the driver likes this coffee shop."

"I rewound to the moment he first pulls up. Then I fast-forwarded to when he left. No one ever got out of the truck. Now, here's the video from the traffic cam."

Sarah watched as the truck they'd seen earlier drove past the shop. Then Susan walked out of the coffee shop. When she reached the end of the block and turned the corner, moving out of camera range, the same green truck drove slowly down the street again and turned after her.

"I think you've found the kidnappers," Sarah said. "Good work."

"We need to enlarge the license plate, get the number," Tally said, "and then locate an address."

Sarah picked up her phone and began to type furiously on her keyboard. "Bobby, I'm sending you a video. At three-thirteen on Friday, a green truck drives down the street and turns left. I need you to get that license number and run the plates. This is the highest priority, Bobby. Get back to me right away."

Sarah turned to Tally. "You and I need to assemble a team immediately."

Tally smiled and nodded.

E.J. had only seconds to react when he heard someone at the door. He started to put his hand into his pocket so he could pull out the scissors when he realized how ridiculous that was. He had no chance against several armed men with only with a small pair of scissors. He pulled his hand back just before the door swung open and a man they hadn't seen before walked into the room. He had slicked-back dark hair and a deep scar across his cheek. He also had a gun in his hand. The man who'd treated Casey's gunshot was right behind him.

The first man's face was scrunched together in a tight scowl as he pointed his gun right at them. "How do you do? I'm Ben Mattan. Sorry I missed you earlier. Good thing I

had someone in the area who was able to bring us together."
His smile reminded E.J. of a baby with gas. "It pays to have
operatives all over the country."

He walked over to Casey. "You look a little pale, my dear.
Seems one of my friends injured you." He turned around
to sneer at the man who'd helped Casey earlier. "I told you
patching her up was a waste of time, Ace." Mattan sighed
as he turned back to them. "I'm not sure what we're going
to do with you now. You've ruined my original plan, and
now we have a dead deputy on our hands. I'm going to have
to come up with a way to explain that." He swung his gun
toward E.J. "I may still need you to accompany our witness
to D.C. Until I make a final decision, you'll stay alive." He
made a clicking sound with his tongue and peered closely
at Casey. "You're not that important to me," he told her,
"but I'll keep you for now. Maybe I can use you to control
your boyfriend."

"He's not my boyfriend," Casey said.

Mattan laughed. "You may not think that, but he doesn't
know it, does he?" Mattan waved his gun toward the ceiling.
"We have cameras all over. It's clear this man cares about
you. Not sure why. I've never found that women are worth
very much."

E.J. could feel rage rise up in him, but with effort he pushed
it down. Unless they were being played, they had a friend
here. A chance to get out of this alive. He wouldn't risk that.
Still, he found himself saying, "This woman is a thousand
times the human being you are."

As Mattan laughed loudly, E.J. noticed the man's pupils
were dilated. Mattan was higher than a kite. He gestured to

the one he'd called Ace. "Bring them both into the warehouse and tie 'em up."

"Sure, boss," Ace said.

E.J. could tell Mattan was scared. Drugs were his way of coping. It was clear he was afraid of Al-Saud. Maybe Mattan's ruined plans had put him in hot water with Daddy. Good. The more frightened he was, the more off-balance he'd become. The more vulnerable. Of course, it could also mean he might grow even more unpredictable. And that could lead to rash decisions. Like killing him and Casey.

Ace motioned toward the door. As Casey and E.J. walked into the large warehouse, E.J. noticed Casey touch her side a couple of times. She was definitely in pain, but she'd never admit it. As they followed Ace, E.J. began to wonder if there really was any way for all of them to get out of this alive.

CHAPTER
THIRTY

Tally and Sarah sat in one of three black SWAT SUVs racing down Highway 55 for Pevely, Missouri. The green truck was registered to a couple named Brady. Darrell and Mary Sue Brady. Sarah wasn't sure they should be speeding with lights flashing and sirens blaring, but Tally was convinced it was the smart thing to do.

"They don't seem like seasoned kidnappers," he'd told Sarah. "I'm betting these folks are amateurs. I think they'll freeze when they hear the sirens. I believe it's our best bet to get Susan back alive."

Based on what she'd heard about Tally Williams, Sarah decided to do it his way.

As they rushed past traffic on the highway, Sarah was amazed once again by the people who paid little attention to emergency vehicles. Most people pulled over to the side of the road just as they should. But some kept driving as if they couldn't hear the sirens or see the flashing lights.

Agent Newport flipped on his blinker and took the Pevely

exit. The other two SUVs followed him. After several twists and turns, the last one on a dirt road, they finally saw the Bradys' house. It was set back from the road, with an ugly metal shed about five hundred yards from the main structure.

They roared into the driveway, gravel flying everywhere. As they approached, the front door swung open, and a tall, skinny man with long hair and a beard came out, a rifle in his hands. He wore torn jeans and a dirty, faded T-shirt. He was shouting something that Sarah couldn't understand.

Tally opened the car door even before they'd completely stopped. Sarah started to call after him, tell him to get back into the vehicle, but in the end she kept quiet. Instead, she got out, drew her weapon, and took a stance on the other side of the SUV. Tally already had his AK-15 pointed at the guy's head.

"Put it down, Darrell!" Tally shouted. "Right now. I don't want to have to shoot you."

"How'd you find us?" Darrell yelled back. "You shouldna found us."

"We'll talk about that later," Tally said, trying to calm him down. "Right now I need you to put down that rifle."

Several more agents climbed out of the other SUVs, their weapons drawn. Darrell's eyes were as big as saucers. He immediately dropped his rifle and stuck his grimy hands up in the air. At the same moment, the door to the large metal shed to their left opened, and a large woman with red frizzy hair ran out, screaming at the top of her lungs. She raised her rifle and fired at them, barely missing one of the agents. The agents returned fire, instantly killing the woman.

Darrell started shrieking, calling out his wife's name. Sarah ordered two agents to secure him. Then she sent the other agents inside the house while she and Tally ran toward the shed. She prayed silently for Susan. If she was still alive, it would be a miracle.

Casey fought a sharp stab of pain as some man tied her and E.J. up to a couple of metal folding chairs a few feet away from each other. Her hands were bound fairly tight, but at least the line they'd used wasn't cutting into her skin. Even though she wasn't seriously injured, she'd discovered that being shot hurt. A lot. She tried to distance herself from the pain. She noticed some old signs on the walls that indicated that the warehouse was once used to ship fishing equipment. That explained what they were using to truss them up. Nylon fishing line.

"Where's Valerie Bennett?" E.J. asked the man who'd posed as a cop.

"We're dealing with her," he responded. "She was ready to tell the FBI about our boss. There are consequences for her actions."

"If you hurt her, I'll make you pay," E.J. said emphatically.

"I don't think so. You're not going to be doing anything—except maybe dying." He laughed and walked away, his two companions following him. The large, muscular ape who didn't look too smart, and Ace, who'd cleaned and dressed Casey's wound. The men went into a back room in the large warehouse. The walls were glass halfway up, so she and E.J. were able to watch them.

"What do we do now?" she whispered to E.J. "I want to know where Valerie is. I don't like that they've separated us."

"I don't either. She was already traumatized. My guess is they're threatening her, making sure they can control her. Mattan still wants her to testify. Or maybe I should say it's probably what his daddy wants." E.J. took a quick breath and blew it out slowly. "I'm so sorry about this. I was certain we could get help before Mattan's people found us. I never would have called the police if I knew we were being tracked."

"It's not your fault. It was a good plan." Casey managed a small smile. "We just haven't had much luck today, have we?"

"Not so far."

"So you think all these men work for Mattan?"

"Or Ali Al-Saud. I can't quite figure out who's in charge." He caught Casey's eye and swung his gaze upward, mouthing the word *bugs*.

Casey's eyes darted around the room, looking for cameras and listening devices. Sure enough, she spotted several cameras at various spots around the room. But they weren't close, and even if they were wired for sound, they would have a tough time picking up any conversation kept at low levels. Still, they needed to be careful not to let these people overhear anything they wanted to keep private.

"Mattan acts . . . crazy," she said in a low voice.

"Drugs," he said under his breath. "He's high as a kite."

"That will only make him more unpredictable and violent."

Before E.J. could respond, the garage door opened, and a car drove into the warehouse. When the driver got out, she recognized him right away. Anderson. He rushed up to them, his face twisted with rage, blood on his sleeve where he'd been shot in the arm. He struck E.J. across the face and pulled his gun. Not knowing what else to do, Casey screamed as loud as she could, getting the attention of the men talking in the glass-walled office.

Mattan ran out and shouted, "Put down your gun, Ari! You kill him, I'm gonna have to shoot you. I might still need him."

It looked as if it took all of Anderson's self-control to lower his gun. Casey was pretty sure he wanted nothing more than to make E.J. pay for what had happened on the highway. She was relieved to discover Mattan really didn't want them dead. Not yet anyway.

"He killed everyone. Including Walli."

"I'm sorry about your brother," Mattan said, "but the assignment comes first."

The man they'd known as Anderson stepped away from E.J., whose cut lip was bleeding, and took several steps toward Mattan. "No *assignment* is worth more than my brother's life. I have to tell our mother. Are you telling me your plans mean more than the grief my mother will feel?"

"Can you do what you're told or not?" Mattan asked quietly.

"No. This man dies. Now." He turned and was walking back toward E.J. when a shot rang out. Anderson fell to the floor. Casey looked over at Mattan. He was slowly putting his gun back in its holster. He pointed at the big man. "Clean this up and get rid of him. You know what to do."

Casey felt sick to her stomach. Mattan was out of control. She looked over at E.J. The muscles in his face were taut. He was obviously worried too.

She watched as the large man grabbed Anderson by the feet and dragged him out of the room toward the back of the warehouse as if his body were nothing. A scrap of paper. The large man had long dark hair and a muscular build, but the most noticeable thing about him was his complete lack of expression. Like no one was home behind those blank eyes. He reminded Casey of a shark.

The other guy, Ace, came out with a pail and a mop. He cleaned up the blood and then put the equipment away, but blood wasn't so easily dispatched. CSIs would find traces of blood for a DNA test, and they'd know who Anderson, or Ari, really was. But right now, Casey and E.J. needed to make sure their blood didn't end up on the floor as well.

Mattan watched over the proceedings. Though his expression was unreadable, a twitch underneath one eye spoke either to nervousness or the effect of the drugs he'd been pumping into his body. Ben Mattan was past caring about anyone except himself. It meant that her and E.J.'s lives were hanging by a thread.

CHAPTER
THIRTY-ONE

Once Ace finished cleaning up the mess caused by Mattan's heartless murder, the men went back into the glass-walled office. Casey turned to E.J. "Wow. That guy is cold."

"He's a psychopath. Like his boss. And now he's so drugged up he's completely lost it. We've got to hope our people find us in time."

"There were lots of phones taking video and pictures back on the highway," she said softly. "I'm sure they're looking for us, but I'm not sure how they'll ever find us."

"They'll find the car in Arbuckle," he said.

"But will they know we were there?" she whispered.

"Besides the blood you left behind, I gave them some clues. I can't guarantee it will help, but at least they'll know where we were before we were brought here. Every little bit helps."

"What kind of clues?"

"I tossed my dog tags on the ground. That way they won't have to wait to process your blood to match the car to us. And I wrote the plate number of the police cruiser in the dirt.

Hopefully someone noticed it. People remember police cars, and they're easier to spot on traffic cameras." He grunted as he tried to find a more comfortable position in the hard metal chair. "I'm hoping the police car they used to drive us here has GPS, but I'm not counting on it."

"What do you mean?"

"Well, look at it."

Casey glanced over at the car. *Cranberry Township Police Department*. "Right, small town. They might not have GPS tracking."

"Yeah, but hopefully there's a laptop inside. I didn't notice. If there is, and it's on—"

"They can find us that way."

He smiled at her. "At least it's a chance."

"Hey, it might be all we need." While she tried to sound positive, she wasn't sure it would be enough. "Back to my previous question—what do we do now?"

"We wait. And we pray."

Casey nodded. A bead of sweat rolled down her forehead. It was hot in the warehouse, and she was thirsty. She felt dehydrated. Her side was beginning to hurt even more than it had just after she'd been shot. Being tied to an uncomfortable chair wasn't helping.

"Do you think they'd give us something to drink?" she asked E.J. "I'm feeling a little woozy."

E.J. looked over toward the office where the men seemed to be involved in an intense conversation. He yelled out, and Ace looked his way. He said something to Mattan and left the room, headed toward them.

"She needs water," E.J. said as he approached.

"Are you feeling faint?" he asked Casey.

"What do you care?" she asked, trying to respond to him in a way that wouldn't arouse suspicion.

"I don't." His eyes flicked toward a nearby steel support beam. It was so fast, it looked like a blink. There was a camera attached to the beam that she hadn't noticed. She gave Ace an almost imperceptible nod. Could he really be on their side or was he playing them? They needed to be careful. Not only for their own protection, but also for Ace's, if he was really who he claimed to be. If Mattan found out Ace was trying to help them, he'd kill him on the spot—just like he had Anderson.

Ace went over to a pop machine. He pulled the front door open and took out a bottle of water. He carried it back to her, unscrewed the cap, and held it to her mouth. Casey tried to drink slowly, but it tasted so good, she found herself gulping the cold liquid. As it went down, she began to feel better. Finally, Ace took it away.

"Not too much at once," he said rather loudly. "It can make you sick, and I don't want to have to clean up your puke."

"What if I need to use the bathroom?" she asked, trying to look frightened, which didn't take a lot of acting. "Will someone help me?"

"Not right now," Ace snapped. "Look, that's enough. We bandaged you up. Gave you water. Now quit bothering us." He walked around behind her. "I wanna make sure you haven't loosened these bonds." He pulled at them, and Casey felt them give some. He leaned in close. "I'm going to sabotage their cameras and listening devices. Can't take a chance they'll hear something to make them suspicious.

Mattan is popping pills so fast he's liable to go over the edge any minute." He straightened up. "Yeah, nice and tight," he said loudly enough to be overheard. "You're not going anywhere." Then he walked over to E.J., seemingly checking his bonds as well. Although E.J. didn't react, Casey was pretty sure Ace loosened the ties.

She watched as Ace went back to Mattan and the other guys. But even with Ace's help, the odds were still against them. The only weapon they had was a small pair of scissors, and they couldn't even get to them. It sure wasn't enough to take down Mattan and his henchmen. She suspected there were more of Al-Saud's goons in the building since Valerie wasn't anywhere to be seen. She wondered how many of them there were. No matter which scenario Casey ran through her head, it didn't look good for them.

"I don't believe you can keep me here against my wishes."

Tony watched helplessly as Batterson argued with Dr. Jackson. The chief was worried about his people, but he wasn't in any shape to check out of the hospital. "Please, Chief," he said, "you just had brain surgery. This wasn't some kind of light injury. You've got to stay in the hospital until you get better. You can't help us by killing yourself."

"I know how I feel," Batterson grumbled. "I assure you I'm just fine."

Dr. Jackson sighed. "Mr. Batterson, you're on a morphine drip. Of course you feel fine. Trust me, if we remove it, you won't feel *fine* at all. I'm telling you that if you try to leave that bed too soon, you could die."

NANCY MEHL

Batterson frowned at Tony as if trying to send him some kind of message. Tony knew what he wanted, but he had no intention of supplying it. He shook his head. "No, Chief. There's no way. You've got to stay where you are." He looked over at the doctor, who nodded at him. "I promise to keep you updated on everything that's going on. And if you have orders, I'll make sure your deputies get them, okay?"

Although he continued to scowl at Tony, Batterson's body relaxed some, and he sank back against his pillows. Tony breathed a sigh of relief. He'd been afraid that Batterson was going to pull out his IV and try to get out of bed.

Tony was tired and had planned to go home. Mark was coming to the hospital to provide security for their boss, yet if the chief wanted him to stay and keep him updated on his witness and his deputies, Tony would do it.

Before Batterson had a chance to say anything else, he closed his eyes and fell asleep.

"He'll keep doing that as long as he's on morphine," Dr. Jackson said. "His reasoning is affected by his medication. I would advise you to keep him happy. Don't give him bad news. Right now he can't handle it. It could spike his blood pressure and his heart rate. He may think he wants to know everything that's going on, but trust me, keeping him in the dark about things that might upset him will actually help him to heal."

Tony nodded and thanked the doctor. As Dr. Jackson left the room, Tony shook his head. Yeah, and keeping Richard Batterson in the dark about anything could also get him fired.

CHAPTER
THIRTY-TWO

Except for the men in the office behind them, Casey and E.J. seemed to be alone in the warehouse. E.J. scanned the large room slowly, searching for ways out. The clues he'd left behind might not be enough to lead the police to this location. So far, Ace was their best chance for rescue, but E.J. had no idea who he worked for or what he was investigating. Would he risk his operation to save two Deputy Marshals and a witness? He couldn't be sure.

He looked at Casey. "We could be here a while. We can just sit here, or we can try to figure a way out." E.J. cocked his head toward a row of windows near the ceiling. "We might be able to get out through those windows, but first we'll have to find a way up there. Unless one of us can turn into Plastic Man or jump really high, we don't stand much of a chance." He scooted his chair closer to Casey, keeping an eye on the men in the office. No one seemed to notice. "I think Ace is our best chance," he said softly.

Casey sighed. "Our Ace in the hole, so to speak?"

"Maybe. Depends on who he's working for, and why. You know some law enforcement agencies put their operations before . . . collateral interests."

"I know," she said. "But would he just stand by and watch them kill us?"

"No, I don't think he wants to do that."

"But we can't count on it—or him. We've got to take control of things."

Once again, it was like they could read each other's minds. E.J. took a deep breath. "I know you don't want to hear this, but I have to say something. Just in case—"

"We don't make it out of here?"

E.J. nodded. "I'm sorry I left you with Jared. I really didn't know. I just didn't want to be a third wheel. That's why I quit hanging around you two."

"I know," Casey said. "Forget it."

"I wish I could." He was quiet for a moment. "Look at me, Casey."

After a few seconds, she turned her face toward his. He gazed directly into her eyes. "I'm going to do everything I can to get us out of here, but if I can't . . . there are things I need to say. Please, Casey. It's not like we're too busy right now."

Casey hung her head down, her hair covering her face. She was silent for several seconds. Finally she raised her head and looked him in the eye. "Okay. But I'm not giving up. We're going to get out of here alive. With our witness."

"Amen." He cleared his throat. "Casey, can you tell me why you stayed with Jared if he was hurting you? I just don't get it. It's not like you. I just can't wrap my head around it."

"I . . . I can't explain it," she said. "Don't you think I've tried to understand it myself? I thought I loved Jared, and he kept promising to change. I don't know. For some reason I believed him. He had a way of making it seem as if he was the victim. You know, because of his dad. I should have kicked him to the curb after it happened the first time, but I thought I could help him. Does that sound nuts?"

"No, I guess not. So somehow he made himself the victim and you were his deliverer?"

She nodded. "I guess it was a challenge. I wanted to *save* him." She struggled to sit up a little straighter. He saw her cringe in pain.

"You're hurting more?"

"Yeah, it seems to be getting worse."

E.J. nodded, then paused before continuing. "Please don't get angry at me, but are you sure you stayed because you wanted to help Jared? Could you have been trying to punish yourself?"

Instantly, Casey's face became a mask of fury. "Punish myself?" she hissed. "Punish myself for what?" She looked away from him. Then, without warning, she began to cry.

He wanted to take her in his arms, but he couldn't. He waited for her to say something else. When she didn't, he finally said, "Casey . . ." as gently as he could.

She slumped in her chair. "I can't get their faces out of my head, E.J. Three young women. Slaughtered." Tears ran down her face. "I heard once that when you look into the eyes of the dead, you're responsible for them. But that really happened when I let Carlton Randolph get away. I own that, E.J."

"Randolph made a deal, Casey. Telling the authorities

where all the bodies were buried in exchange for life in prison. No one thought he was going to escape. Besides, we were with him all the time. Right outside his door. He had assistance from the outside. Someone who helped him get out of that room. We did everything we could with the information we had. It was just . . . one of those things."

"Was it *one of those things* for the women who died? Is that excuse good enough?" She groaned, and E.J. couldn't tell if the pain was physical or emotional. "I see them, E.J. In my dreams. Almost every night. Some nights I try to stay awake so I don't have to look into their empty eyes."

E.J. sighed. "So when Jared hit you, you felt better?"

She lowered her head, her hair hiding her face again. "I don't know," she said, her voice cracked and hoarse. "Maybe." She took a big gulp of air. "It only happened three times. After the third time I stopped it. Told him we were done."

"But why did he do it? Was he angry? Drunk?"

"The truth?" She sighed so deeply it seemed to seep through her entire being and leave her deflated. "I'd go after him, E.J. Push his buttons. Make him mad. I tried to stop, but it was like someone else took over my body. I taunted him until he lost his temper."

"You pushed him until he hit you?"

She looked into his eyes and nodded. "He was fighting his own demons. I purposely agitated him, and he was too weak to fight them. I'm sure that's why he left. Like you said, he didn't want to be that man. I . . . I'm not excusing him. There's no justification for hitting a woman. For hitting anyone. But I goaded him, E.J."

E.J. wanted to be furious at Jared, but he also knew how

hard Jared fought against his father's evil legacy. Part of him felt sorry for his old friend. Even so, Jared could have come to him. Asked for help. And he didn't.

"We were both at fault," Casey said so softly he could barely hear her. "Maybe I didn't really love him. I guess I just wanted to stop feeling guilty."

"Casey, you're not responsible for Carlton Randolph. Honestly. You want to blame yourself, but the only person to blame is Randolph. He's the one who killed those women. He's the one who gave in to his violent desires. Not you."

She started to say something, but E.J. shook his head.

"Look," he said, "if you could have stopped him, would you have done it?"

"Of course," she said, a look of horror on her face. "I would have given my life to protect those women. To stop him. Why would you ask something like that?"

Instead of answering her, he just stared into her eyes until recognition dawned.

"It's ridiculous to blame yourself, Casey. He got past both of us. Are Randolph's murders my fault?"

"Of course not."

"Then why are they yours? That doesn't make any sense."

She didn't answer him.

"It's time you forgave yourself. Randolph's dead. His reign of terror is over. I think it's time you moved on too, don't you?"

As Casey's tears flowed, E.J. wondered if she'd be embarrassed later about letting him see her vulnerability. Her reputation as tough and immovable was important to her. "When we get back, Casey—and we will—I . . . I think you need to see someone. I'm not a therapist or a pastor. I'm just a dumb deputy, but I know it's not God's will for you to carry this burden. It's self-destructive. Please promise me you'll get some help."

He was glad to see her laugh at his last comment. He was afraid suggesting she needed counseling would offend her.

"I think you're right, E.J. And I will. I promise." Before he realized what she was doing, Casey scooted her chair right up next to his. She leaned in and kissed him. Tenderly at first, and then with more passion. He gently pulled his head back.

"Don't do that now," he said quietly. "Not when you're upset."

At first, he thought she was going to get angry, but she didn't. Instead the corners of her mouth twitched.

"Does that mean when I'm not . . . emotional, I can do that again?"

He couldn't help but smile at her. "When you're feeling like yourself, and we're not being held captive by people who want to kill us . . . yes. I look forward to it." At that moment, more than anything, he wanted to wipe the tears from her face. "In fact, I'm counting on it," he whispered.

She smiled and scooted her chair back to where it had been. Then she looked behind her to see if Mattan was watching them. E.J. followed her gaze. The men seemed involved in some kind of argument. Mattan was waving his arms around, and although they couldn't make out what he was saying, they could hear him shouting. At least he wasn't interested in them right now.

"Okay, let's figure out how to get out of here," Casey

said. "After that, I suggest you call me and ask for a date. You know, do it the right way."

"You have my word." He felt overwhelmed by the nearness of her. The power of her incredible spirit. Not being able to hold her frustrated him beyond belief.

CHAPTER
THIRTY-THREE

Tony pulled his rental car behind the police cruiser he'd followed to the last place they knew Casey, E.J., and their witness had been. The flight to Pennsylvania wasn't too bad, but the change in Chicago added an extra hour to his travel time. He was grateful to have grabbed a little sleep on the plane. He was tired but determined to find their people. Calculating from the time of the confrontation on TV, law enforcement determined they'd been here around eight or nine that morning. Now it was almost four o'clock in the afternoon. A long time to be missing.

Batterson was doing better and didn't seem determined to escape the hospital any longer. He'd been fine with Tony flying to Pennsylvania, but he'd made his deputy promise to keep him apprised of any progress. Tom was taking everything in stride. While he was the acting chief, all of them knew Batterson was the real power behind the scenes, and no one was brave enough to try to usurp his authority.

It helped a lot that Karen and Marlon were with Batterson

now that he'd been moved out of ICU. He still had tight security, so they'd been transported to the hospital by Marshals dedicated to protecting them from any kind of threats. Keeping the three of them together guaranteed tighter security. So far, everything was quiet. Hopefully, the woman who'd tried to kill the chief was Al-Saud's last attempt. Although Batterson was still worried about his deputies, he was more relaxed and willing to follow his doctor's orders with Karen and Marlon by his side. And with Batterson stable, it was easier for Tony to concentrate on finding their missing witness and the deputies with her.

He got out of his car and went over to where the officer waited. "This is where we found the dog tags I showed you at the station," the officer said. "Not sure what you're looking for."

Since he didn't bother to introduce himself, Tony looked at his badge for the officer's name. Officer Holman seemed a little offended that the Marshals had sent someone to Pennsylvania. But nothing could keep them away. D.C. had wanted to send someone too, but Batterson convinced them to wait until they had more information.

"If there's nothing here, you've wasted a trip," Holman said.

Tony wanted to tell him it wasn't up to him to decide how the Marshals spent their time. Instead he decided it would be best to get this guy's cooperation. If putting ego aside would help his friends, he was willing to do it. "You might be right," Tony said, "but we still want to look things over. We can't stand by while two of our deputies go missing. I'm sure you feel the same way about your people."

The officer grudgingly agreed. Behind them, a tow truck

pulled into the almost vacant parking lot. Holman stepped away from Tony and waved the driver over. When the truck got closer, Holman raised his hand and gestured for it to stay where it was.

"We'll give you some time, but we gotta get this car back to the station as soon as possible. It hasn't been processed completely yet."

Tony nodded. "I get it. Thanks." He began to walk around the area, looking closely at everything. "Where did you find the dog tags?" he asked Holman. The officer came over and pointed at the area where the tags were picked up off the ground.

Tony got down on his hands and knees and looked over everything slowly, methodically. At first he didn't notice anything unusual, but not far from the spot where the dog tags had been left, he found something that looked like words scrawled into the dirt. Tony pulled a flashlight out of his pocket, along with a notepad and pen. He carefully wrote down what he saw. It was hard to make out. The top part of what appeared to be numbers was smudged, yet it looked like 651247. There was something else next to the numbers. Letters maybe? It was too hard to read. Was this a license number? How had the police missed this? He stood and called Holman over.

"Did you see this?" he asked. "Doesn't this look like a partial license plate number?"

Holman frowned. "No, not really. More like accidental markings made when we retrieved the dog tags."

Tony wanted to lambaste the patrolman for his casual attitude, though the man was partially right—the letters and numbers looked a bit like scratches in the dirt. Maybe it was because Tony was looking too hard for something—anything—that would give them a clue as to where their people were.

Tony tore out the top page from his notepad and handed it to Holman. "Please run this as soon as you can. Tell me whose plate it is."

"Our state plates don't read like that," he replied.

"Please. Just run what you have and let me know what you find."

Although he didn't look convinced, Holman nodded, went back to his car, and got on the radio.

Using a handkerchief from his pocket, Tony opened the car door. There were some things inside, but he had no idea if they belonged to the owner or if Casey and E.J. had left them behind. He didn't see anything that would help them. Some blood on the back seat. They would test it right away, find out whose blood it was. He was certain it was Cascy's. He'd watched the video from the highway and seen her get shot. He prayed she was okay. He shook his head and continued checking the car without touching anything. Finished, he turned to tell Holman what he'd found. The words died in his mouth as Holman walked toward him. The officer's face was ashen. He looked like someone had punched him in the gut.

"What's wrong?" Tony asked as Holman approached. Apprehension made it hard to speak. Were his friends okay? "Have you heard something?" he choked out.

Holman nodded. "The number . . . it's a vehicle used by one of our Highway Patrol officers. Jerry Reynard. They just found his body on a side road near here. His car's gone. It looks like whoever has your friends killed him—for his car and his uniform. It must have happened not long after he went off duty."

The two men stood there staring at each other. At that moment they didn't work for different departments. They were both bound together by a bond most people could never understand.

When Sarah and Tally stepped inside the metal building, the heat almost knocked Sarah over. She was immediately afraid for Susan. Weapons drawn, they rounded a large divider where they saw someone secured to a chair, her hands and feet bound with duct tape. Her head was bowed, and Sarah couldn't see her face as she and Tally hurried over to her. Sarah realized Tally was praying softly.

When she reached Susan, Sarah put her hand under the girl's chin and raised her face. She half expected to find her dead. Susan's eyes were closed, but Sarah heard her moan.

"She's alive!" Sarah shouted. A police officer who'd followed them into the shed immediately called for an ambulance while Tally and Sarah removed the duct tape from around Susan's wrists and ankles. She was unresponsive. Her skin was hot, but she wasn't sweating. A symptom of heat stroke.

Tally gently picked her up and carried her outside where it was cooler. "We need to get her out of the sun." He took her over to the SUV and placed her in the front seat. "Turn on the air conditioning," he told the agent who'd driven the vehicle. As the man got the car started, Tally asked if anyone had some fresh water. Several agents brought over water bottles.

Sarah watched as Tally poured the cool water on Susan's head and tried to get her to take a drink. Seeing that Tally had things under control until the paramedics arrived, she went over to the agents who had handcuffed Darrell Brady. When he saw her, he began to yell.

"You killed my wife! It's police brutality." He glared at Sarah with wild eyes. "I'm gonna sue you. Take you to court. You'll lose your badge!"

Sarah shook her head. "I'm sorry for your loss, Mr. Brady, but your wife took a shot at us. We have every right to defend ourselves. And as far as taking us to court, unfortunately I think you'll be a little too busy being charged with kidnapping . . . and murder, if Ms. Bennett doesn't survive."

At that moment, one of her agents, a man named McGee, came out of the house with a small dog in his arms. The dog was in bad physical shape—matted fur, dirty, and skinny. "Hey, Sarah," he said, "I work with an animal-rescue group. Can I take this little guy to them?"

Sarah nodded. "Please do." She walked over and looked into the pup's big brown eyes. Even in his poor condition, he leaned over and licked her hand. Sarah had to blink back tears, but not before McGee noticed.

"He'll be okay. I'll keep you updated."

"Thanks." Sarah went back to where Darrell waited, still grumbling about police brutality. "Has he been read his rights?" she asked the agents who'd cuffed him.

"Yes, ma'am," one of them answered.

"Mr. Brady . . ." Sarah began. The wind died down then,

and the man's body odor became apparent. Sarah almost gagged. It took everything she had to ignore it. "It's possible you could get a lighter sentence if you tell us why you kidnapped Ms. Bennett. Who put you up to it?"

Darrell shook his ratty head. "You wanna get me killed?" He looked around like someone might be listening. "I ain't gonna tell you nothin'."

"That's totally up to you," Sarah said. "But we can protect you. Get you a deal. Just think about it."

Again, Darrell shook his head. "Ain't gonna happen."

"If it makes you feel any better, Al-Saud's men aren't in Missouri right now. You're safe."

Darrell stared at Sarah, his eyes narrowed into slits. "Al . . . Al who? I don't know who you're talkin' about. I don't know anyone named Al."

Sarah could tell he was telling the truth. "What about Benyamin Mattan? Do you know him?"

"I got no idea what you're talkin' about, but I'll tell ya that the guy who paid us to take that lady is meaner than a rabid dog. And I ain't takin' no chances by squealin' on him."

Those were the last words Darrell Brady ever said. A hail of bullets rained down on the agents. The first casualty was Darrell. Then two of Sarah's agents went down. The rest of them hit the dirt, pulling out their weapons and trying to figure out where the bullets were coming from.

CHAPTER
THIRTY-FOUR

E.J. was finding it difficult to breathe in the large metal building. Although Mattan and his men had air conditioning, out here it was almost unbearable. Now he and Casey both needed water. They'd been sitting in one spot for hours. Casey seemed to be getting lethargic. He realized Ace was trying to keep his cover intact, but Casey was in serious trouble. Her head hung down, and the last time she'd said something, her words were mumbled.

He was just about to call her name when a door slammed behind them. E.J. saw Ace striding their way. When he reached them, he immediately put a new bottle of water to Casey's lips. She drank it down like someone dying of thirst.

"Thank you," she said softly.

"The cameras and listening devices are down," he said. "They'll stay down until we can get you out of here. You can say whatever you want." He nodded toward the back of the room. "Mattan is apoplectic. Not being able to listen to you has made him even more paranoid, but it had to be done. We need to be even more careful now."

"Thanks," E.J. said. He cocked his head toward Casey. "Something's wrong with her. What's going on?"

Ace glanced toward the back and then quickly pulled Casey's blouse up until he could see the spot they'd bandaged. He loosened the gauze and lifted the pad . . . then swore under his breath. "It's infected."

"Clean it again."

"I can't. Mattan won't let me. If I cross him when he's this crazy, he might kill her."

"But—"

"I'm sorry," Ace said, cutting him off. "Mattan is *psychotic*. He suspects everything we say or do as proof we're turning on him."

"Do you have a plan to get us out?"

"Working on it." He brought the water bottle to E.J. and held it up to his lips. "I can't compromise this operation, but I won't let you die either."

"Who are you with?"

"Pittsburgh PD. Mattan has been selling drugs and weapons out of this place. I don't think his father knows about that."

"Yeah, Valerie told us Mattan was Ali Al-Saud's son. Puts a whole new spin on this thing."

"Yep, but Daddy isn't too happy right now. In fact, he won't even take Junior's calls."

"What does that mean for us?" Casey mumbled.

"I don't know." He took a step back. "Don't get offended by what I'm getting ready to do. I think it will help you." He moved closer to Casey, turned the large bottle of cold water upside down, and poured some of it on her head. Then he laughed. After that he did the same to E.J. It felt wonderful, but to Mattan and his cronies, E.J. was pretty sure it looked as if Ace was taunting them.

"Thanks," E.J. said, shaking his head. Water flew everywhere.

"Listen," Ace said, "Mattan's not only scarfing down pills, he's snorting cocaine. I'm worried about what he might do next. If it looks like he's going to take you out, I'll stop him. But if he decides to move you, I won't do anything to keep that from happening. It could actually be the break we need. Getting out of here might give us more options. If that happens, I'll find a way to go with you."

"Will you still be able to protect your operation?" Casey asked. Her words were a little clearer, though her eyes were unfocused. E.J. could tell she was fighting to stay engaged.

"I'm trying. We still don't have what we need to shut Al-Saud down. If we don't get it, we'll have Mattan, but Al-Saud will continue funding terrorism. We want him. Badly." He glanced back toward the office and waved his hand, letting them know he was on his way back. "Mattan has some nasty stuff here. Bombs, guns, suicide vests, even chemical weapons. He might be planning something big, and we need to know what that is. I'm trying to keep track of where it's going, but even having it available is scary enough. Especially if it's being used to support terrorists already in the country."

Ace's words made E.J.'s blood run cold. "Is there any way you can sneak a look into that police car?" he asked. "We're wondering if there's a laptop inside. Someone might be able to track us that way."

"There was, but Mattan had it removed right after you two got here."

E.J. saw the disappointment on Casey's face, and he hated it.

Ace reached into his pocket and pulled out a pill. He took it over to Casey. "I don't know if you want this, but I took it from Mattan's stash. It's oxycodone. It will help with the pain."

Casey looked up at him. "Will it make me sleepy?"

"No. In fact, it will probably help you stay awake. It won't hurt you, I promise."

She nodded. "Please."

Ace put the pill in her mouth and then put the bottle to her lips. There was just enough water to help her swallow it.

"I grabbed a few more." Ace slid them into her jeans pocket. "If you need more, I'll get them for you. What you really need are antibiotics, but Mattan doesn't have any."

"It's okay. Thank you," Casey said, her voice breaking.

"Not a problem." He moved over to E.J. "Sorry about this, but I'm trying to keep you alive." He then slapped E.J. across the face.

"Wow," E.J. said, working his jaw around. "That hurt."

"Just trying to make it realistic."

"You get us out of here, and you can hit me whenever you want."

"I'll take that deal."

With that, Ace walked away, heading back to the office.

"I think he's genuine," Casey said.

"Yeah, me too. But now my jaw's sore."

"Sorry," Casey said with a small smile. As she stared down at the floor, a drop of water rolled down her face and landed on her shoe. Although Ace had helped them cool off some, it hadn't lasted long. E.J.'s eyes stung with the sweat that dripped into them.

Casey took a deep breath. "We can't just sit here and let these people decide our fate," she said. "I'm glad Ace is on our side, but I'm not willing to let him decide if we live or die. And we've got to rescue Valerie. I can't imagine what they're doing to her."

"I doubt they'll hurt her physically. She's supposed to testify tomorrow. They're not going to let her show up with bruises and broken bones. Mattan's so scared of his father, for now, he's afraid to get rid of us. We just need to pray he continues to feel that way."

"Frankly, Mattan's made one bad decision after another. His father may be a terrorist, but he's not stupid. He's built a well-oiled empire. How could he trust his son now when he's made so many mistakes?"

"True. Would Al-Saud go so far as to take out his son to protect himself?"

Casey snorted. "We can only hope."

"I'd think this FBI thing would be the final straw. I'll bet that was his own idea and it didn't go over well at all. In fact, this whole situation is a huge disaster. I think Mattan's desperate to find a way out of it. While he's contemplating his circumstances, I'm hopeful we'll be found."

"I wish I could believe that."

"Don't give up, Casey," E.J. said sharply. "Besides Ace, there are other things working for us."

She sighed. "If you say so."

E. J. still had hope that Doug had survived and could provide information that could lead to their rescue, but it was an outside chance at best.

A door opened from another room—around the corner from the one they could see. A man they hadn't noticed before led Valerie by the arm. He kept her in front of him, occasionally giving her a little push. E.J. didn't like the look on Valerie's face. She seemed . . . out of it. Her eyes stared straight ahead. Her complexion was pale and waxy.

After reaching Casey and E.J., the man grabbed an empty chair near the wall, pulled it up next to Casey, and plunked Valerie down onto it. Next, he secured her. He didn't say a word to them. When he was done, he walked away.

"Valerie, are you okay?" Casey asked.

No response.

"Valerie, can you hear me?"

"I think she's in shock," E.J. said. "I'm not sure she knows what you're saying."

"Great. Do they think she's going to make a good witness like this? She'll be useless."

E.J. didn't say anything, but his concern was for all three of them now. The only reason Valerie had been kept alive was because Al-Saud wanted her to destroy any suspicion that he had ties to ISIS. If she was useless, she would be expendable.

Just like he and Casey.

CHAPTER
THIRTY-FIVE

Sarah looked over at the SUV where Tally had carried Susan Bennett. She couldn't see either one of them.

Sarah yelled at her agents to find the shooter once the bullets stopped. As they took off, she ran over to the SUV. Crouching down, she flung the door open to find Tally lying over the top of Susan, protecting her.

"Are you okay?" Sarah asked breathlessly.

"We're fine," Tally said, pulling himself up. "Where did the shots come from?"

"I have no idea. Seems Al-Saud has people everywhere."

Sirens in the background signaled the arrival of the ambulance.

"Should you warn them?" Tally asked.

"Stay here," Sarah ordered. Still keeping herself hidden behind the vehicle, she made her way around to the back of the SUV. Sarah almost cried with relief to see the two agents who'd taken bullets sitting up and talking.

"Bullets hit their vests," McGee said as he came around

to where Sarah stood. "The shooting has stopped. I think he's gone."

"Where's the dog?"

He smiled. "He's fine. I put him in the other car."

"Well, looks like we came out okay, but I'm afraid Mr. and Mrs. Brady won't be testifying."

"Not our fault." McGee shook his head. "How many tentacles does Al-Saud have? I've never seen anything like this."

"I haven't either. This guy needs to be taken down. Now."

The ambulance pulled up next to them. Sarah ran over to the paramedics. She told them about Susan, then led them to the SUV. Tally carefully lifted her out of the car and carried her to the back of the ambulance where the paramedics took over.

He waited while they worked on her. Sarah joined him. "I think you saved her life," she told him. "My guess is that whoever killed Darrell planned to kill Susan too."

"Hopefully she'll live," Tally said, "and give us information that will lead back to Al-Saud."

"I pray you're right, but I have a feeling he's kept himself at a distance. He's extremely slippery. He's good at staying hidden behind the people he hires to carry out his dirty work. Honestly, I doubt we'll ever find the person who shot at us."

One of the paramedics came over to address them. "We need to get her to the hospital. I think she's going to be okay, but she needs treatment as soon as possible."

"Where are you taking her?" Sarah asked.

"Mercy Hospital in Festus. It's the closest."

"Okay." She looked at Tally. "Why don't you go with her?

I need to stay here and clean up. Wait to see if we have a lead on the shooter."

"Thanks, I'd like that," Tally said. "Is it okay with you?" he asked the paramedics.

"Sure," one of them said. "I recognize you, Lieutenant Williams. We'd be honored to have you along with us."

"Thanks." He turned back to Sarah. "I'll check in with you later."

Sarah smiled. "I appreciate your help. I don't believe we would have found Susan in time without it."

Nodding, Tally said, "I'm sure you would have located her eventually, but I'm glad you allowed me to be a part of this." He put his hand on her shoulder, a big grin on his face. "And you'd better let McGee know that the pup has a home after they get him cleaned up and checked out."

Sarah laughed. "How did you know what I was thinking?"

"I'm a dog lover. I can tell the signs."

"We gotta go," the paramedic said.

As they closed the ambulance doors, Sarah waved good-bye to Tally Williams. Then she went to check on her agents and let her boss know that they'd found Susan Bennett. And that, at least for now, she was alive.

"Valerie? Valerie," Casey hissed. She was uncomfortable, but thanks to the pain medication Ace gave her, she felt better. Her arms were sore from being twisted behind her, but she tried to ignore the discomfort. They had to find a way to reach Valerie. She had the best chance of getting out of this place alive.

Finally, Valerie blinked several times and seemed to focus on Casey and E.J. "I . . . I'm sorry. I think they gave me something . . ." Her words came out slurred and thick. "In a bottle of water."

Casey breathed a sigh of relief. If she'd been in shock, it might have been impossible for her to assist them in an escape. However, she should eventually recover from any kind of drug they might have given her.

"Where . . . where are we?" Valerie asked, looking around them.

"An old warehouse in Pennsylvania," E.J. said.

She glanced up. "I . . . I think we're being recorded. I heard them talking about it."

"Their equipment isn't working right now. We're okay."

Valerie nodded. "Good. Listen," she said, pronouncing each word carefully while fighting the effects of the drugs, "there's a guy in there, they call him Ace. He might be convinced to help us. He was . . . kind. The rest of them?" She shook her head. "If it's left up to them, I'm not so sure I'll make it to Washington alive."

Casey frowned at her. "What makes you say that?"

Valerie tried to lean forward a little but was bound so tightly she couldn't move much. "I overheard them talking. Senator Warren is dead. He killed himself. Why would the government want me to testify if he's dead? I mean, I was supposed to tell them about his connection to Al-Saud."

Casey and E.J. stared at her. Warren was dead? Did that change things? Casey wasn't sure just what that meant for them now.

"I assume these people still want you to testify that you

made up the story," E.J. said. "To stop any suspicions directed toward Al-Saud."

"Maybe. But Mattan is crazy," Valerie said. "I'm afraid of what he might do next. Do you have a plan? Some way to get us out of here?"

"E.J. left some clues behind when we were picked up by our fake cop," Casey said. "Also, the fiasco on the highway was recorded by a lot of people. I'm sure our people know we're alive. I'm confident they're trying to find us right now."

"And you're right about Ace," E.J. said. "He's an undercover cop. He promised to get us out safely."

Valerie sighed, and her shoulders relaxed. "Thank God. I can't stop thinking about Susan. I pray she's still alive."

"Did they say anything about her?"

"Just more threats. I'm afraid they're going to kill her now that Warren is dead." She took a deep gulping breath, and tears flooded her eyes.

Casey didn't say anything, but if Al-Saud decided to dispose of Valerie, Susan would cease to be valuable to them. They wouldn't want to take any chances she'd repeat something she'd seen or heard. Something that might lead back to Al-Saud. Of course, that would really ramp up the body count. How would they explain a bombing, the deaths of the senator, three Deputy U.S. Marshals, and a federal witness and her sister all within a day or two of each other? Casey didn't believe even Ali Al-Saud could spin that. So what would they do now? What options did they have?

"This is getting really complicated for them, isn't it?" E.J. said quietly, expressing exactly what Casey was thinking.

She'd forgotten how often this had happened when they worked together in D.C.

"They certainly seem to be discussing their options," Valerie said. "Mattan has some kind of plan. I was too out of it to understand what he was saying, but the other men weren't at all happy about it. I wouldn't be surprised to see a mutiny."

Casey glanced back at the office. Mattan and his cohorts were still involved in some kind of deep conversation.

"I'm not sure what their options are," E.J. said. "Even if you testify, once Susan is released, why wouldn't you tell the truth?"

"I was told they could get to her again or someone else I cared about whenever they wanted to."

"But if you came to us . . . or the FBI . . . you'd get protection," Casey said. "How long can anyone use that threat?"

"As long as there are people in my life who are important," Valerie said. "You'd be surprised how scary it is to think you could actually cause the death of someone you love."

"Okay, I get that," E.J. said to Casey, "but here's what doesn't make sense. Originally I think they expected us to turn Valerie over to their fake FBI, and then they planned to take her to D.C. Didn't Mattan realize we'd find out those guys weren't the FBI?"

"Maybe," Casey said, "but what could we do about it? Valerie would have testified. The deed would be done. Who would listen to three Deputy U.S. Marshals who said they'd handed a witness over to people who claimed they were FBI, but weren't? It would probably get pushed under the rug. Some people in government are more interested in protecting themselves than in telling the truth."

"That's it," Valerie said. "They figure you'd keep that to yourselves. It makes you look incompetent."

"My boss wouldn't go for it, Valerie," Casey said.

E.J. snorted. "It wouldn't be up to your boss."

Though Casey didn't want to agree with him, he was probably right. If Batterson was told by higher-ups to keep their mistake quiet, he'd have to do it.

"Regardless, we know Al-Saud is angry," Casey said. "My guess is most of it has to do with Mattan's FBI gambit. If it had worked, maybe his father would have approved. But it was a disaster."

"Maybe," E.J. said. He hesitated. "That's it," he said suddenly. "We need to get Mattan to turn on Al-Saud."

Casey turned his suggestion over in her mind. Then she nodded. "You're right. That's how we get out of this alive. We need to make Mattan feel insecure. Give him a deal. You know, to testify against Al-Saud. We offer him WITSEC. A new life."

"I don't think he'll turn against Al-Saud," Valerie said slowly. "No matter what you offer him. He doesn't want to betray his father. "

Casey shook her head. "I don't think family loyalty will buy Mattan much protection. Al-Saud's killed family before. He's a psychopath. Just like his son."

"I hate the idea of letting Mattan get away with everything he's done," Valerie said. "He's a murderer, and he's hurt a lot of people."

"But Al-Saud is a *mass* murderer," Casey said. "His ties to terrorism are strong. He's very dangerous. He believes that Islam should be the rule of law for the entire world, and he's willing to do whatever he has to do to bring that about. That's why he funds ISIS."

"I understand," Valerie said, "but still . . ."

"Trust me, Valerie," Casey said, "the Witness Protection Program has its benefits, but for someone like Mattan, it will be a nightmare. Living in a small town, his power gone? I know it's not real justice since he's free in the most literal sense, but he will still have to live the kind of life he never planned for. Never wanted. Besides, I've found that someone like Mattan will end up reaping what he's sown eventually. I'm confident somehow he'll end up paying for what he's done."

"We need to start planting the idea in his head," E.J. said. He gave Casey a half smile. "This could work. He's created a big mess, his father is angry with him, and we have the answer." He frowned, his eyebrows knit together in thought. "So the next phase begins. How do we convince him he needs to turn on his father?"

The three captives looked at each other, but no one had an answer. Yet.

CHAPTER
THIRTY-SIX

Martin Avery was surrounded by law enforcement officers: Pittsburgh Police, the FBI, two officers from the Cranberry Township Police Department, Tom Monnier, and Tony. They'd all gathered together in a conference room at the Pittsburgh FBI building.

"I . . . I just don't know if I can remember where the warehouse is," he said. "They put something over my head when they drove me there, and then they kept me drugged up. I was really out of it. I still can't believe I got out alive. I was able to get loose and find an unlocked door. After that homeless guy found me, I was so scared I grabbed the first local bus that came by. I didn't even bother to see which bus it was. I just rode it downtown and got on a Greyhound out of town. I never looked back."

One of the officers at the table cleared his throat. "I'm Captain Ramos," he began. "Pittsburgh PD. You were released on purpose, young man. When Al-Saud heard you'd escaped, he was furious. If he had any idea who'd left that door open, he would've had him killed." He let his gaze travel around the table. The captain was a large man with a receding hairline and a commanding presence. "We have an officer working undercover with Benyamin Mattan. Mattan's been selling drugs and weapons out of that warehouse without his father's knowledge. We believe he even has chemical weapons stored there." The captain sighed. "If we blow our man's cover, we might be able to shut down this warehouse, but we have good intel that Al-Saud will just open up another supply base. We could lose our ability to stop a major attack in the United States. I hesitate to allow that to happen."

"We have deputies in there," Tom said. "And a witness. We're not going to stand by and let them die."

"Actually, it's not your call, Mr. Monnier," Taggart, one of the FBI agents, said. "We have the lead on this, and we're not ready to go in yet."

"I don't care what you say. My witness and my deputies aren't going to be sacrificed for you or anyone else."

Taggart shrugged. "That's all we have to say right now. Until my boss gives the okay, we wait."

Tony was pretty sure the captain wasn't pleased with the FBI's proclamation either. Tom was livid.

"Isn't there some way we could go in without compromising this officer?" Tony asked.

Taggart shook his head. "Believe me, we've thought about it. Ran different scenarios." He looked Tony in the eye. "We don't want to lose your people. But Al-Saud could kill millions of Americans with the weapons he's bringing in. We just don't have enough to nail him yet."

"Our man undercover will do everything he can to get

your people out safely," the captain said to Tony. "He's a good officer."

"But if he feels your operation is at risk, then our people die?"

"Not if he can help it."

Tony turned to Taggart. "We need to do some brainstorming, see if we can come up with something. Leaving LEOs in danger is unacceptable."

Taggart nodded. "I'm game. Just remember, my boss won't take a chance of losing Al-Saud."

Tom checked his watch. "It's after nine o'clock. Let's get to work. I want those people out tonight if at all possible."

Tony stood. "We're going to need food and drink. I saw a pizza place down the street. I'll get us something."

The LEOs around the table started pulling money out of their wallets and tossing it at Tony. Tony repeated back the kinds of pizza they wanted—pepperoni, sausage, deluxe.

"Got it," he said. "You have coffee here?"

Taggart nodded. "And there's a pop machine down the hall. I think the pizza will be enough. Thanks for offering to pick it up."

"Sure." He looked over at Martin. "Do you mind coming with me? You could help carry the pizza."

Martin rose from the table and stretched. "Sounds good, but let's get back as soon as we can. I want to be in on this. Valerie's my friend."

"I'd go with you, Tony, but since I only have one hand right now, I'm afraid I wouldn't be much help."

Tony smiled at Doug Howard. He was grateful Doug had survived his gunshot wound. When E.J. had felt for a pulse at the house, he'd lied to Mattan's men. Told them Doug was dead. Once everyone left, Doug, who was playing possum, called for help. When law enforcement arrived, they found Doug, hurt but alive. The FBI got there not long after that. Mattan's cleanup crew had a surprise when they came to get rid of the bodies and any evidence that might link back to Mattan. The FBI cut them a deal, and they called Mattan to tell him the scene was secure. Mattan had no idea things had gone horribly wrong in Port Clinton. The FBI tried to trace the number Mattan's crew called, but it was impossible to track, and the crew had no idea where Mattan was.

Doug had been shot in the arm, and some of his bones had shattered, but he was going to be okay. Tom had ordered him to return to St. Louis, but Doug had begged to go to Pittsburgh. He was determined to finish his assignment and make sure his fellow deputies got home safely. He also wanted to personally thank E.J. for saving his life. In the end, Tom relented and let him go.

"Be back soon," Tony said.

Martin followed him as they checked out of the building. When they were outside, Martin turned to him with a smile. "Now we look for that warehouse."

Tony grinned. "Smart man. Let's get started."

Casey needed more pain medication, and they hadn't eaten all day. Of course, staying alive was more important than food, but E.J. was worried about Casey keeping her strength up. She was getting weaker by the hour.

A door slammed shut in the back of the warehouse. E.J.

was relieved to see Ace walking toward them, carrying fast-food bags. He put them on the floor and slid an old wooden table over to where they sat.

"Believe it or not, Mattan told me to feed you. He's afraid to let you die. He's terrified to do anything that might make his father angrier. I'm going to cut you loose, long enough for you to eat. When you're done, I have to tie you back up." He placed the bags of food on the table, then went to the pop machine and took out bottles of water. He put the bottles on the table and drew his gun. "It would help if you looked afraid." He glanced back toward the office and nodded.

"Are the cameras and microphones still out?" Casey whispered.

Ace winked at her. "Oh, yeah. They'll be out for a while. Good thing none of these numbskulls know anything about electronics. Except how to blow up bombs."

First he freed Valerie, then Casey, and finally E.J. As he bent down to cut the line restraining E.J.'s wrists, he said, "Mattan is getting worse. He's always played around with crack cocaine, but since his father cut off communication, he's overdoing it. It's getting really hard to control him."

"Can you get me a gun?" E.J. asked.

"I don't know. I had a knife, and he made me hand it over. He's convinced we're planning to kill him. I have to give this gun back after you eat. I'll do my best to get you a weapon, but I can't make any promises."

"Is it just the drugs?"

"No. Mattan knows he's fouled things up, and he wants to get back in his father's good graces. Problem is, he has no idea how to do that. Like I said, that actually works in your favor. For now anyway." He finished cutting E.J. free. "Pull your chair up and help yourself." Ace pulled a bag over near Casey and gave her a bottle of water. She reached into her pocket, grabbed a pain pill, and stuck one in her mouth. Ace walked over to the other side of the table and stood there, watching, his gun trained on them.

"We've been talking," E.J. said. "What if we offered him protection? You know, for his testimony about his father. We can put him into WITSEC."

"I honestly think he might go for it—if he wasn't so hopped up. Right now? I wouldn't bring it up. He's not stable enough to understand what you're talking about. He could see it as more proof of betrayal by everyone around him."

"It might be the only way we can all make it out of this alive."

"I hear you." Ace was quiet for a moment. "Keep that idea on the back burner. We actually thought about WITSEC early on, but Mattan was so dedicated to his father, we felt the offer would backfire. Might be time to revisit it, though. At this point, it could be his only option."

E.J. opened the paper bags and found roast beef sandwiches, chips, and fruit. The beef was thick and tender. "Wow, this looks awesome. Thanks," he said.

Ace nodded. "Just make it fast."

"So what's going to happen now?" Valerie asked.

"Some of the men are thinking about leaving. They're afraid Mattan's going to bring the law down on their heads. Or Al-Saud. I think they're more frightened about that possibility. Like his son, Al-Saud isn't known for his compassion."

"Even though he's decided to keep us alive, he could just snap and kill us?" Valerie said.

"I won't lie to you. It's possible." Ace shook his head. "Look, this operation is important, but like I said, I won't let you die. I won't go back on my promise."

"Thank you, Ace," E.J. said. "I'm assuming your name isn't really Ace?"

Ace grinned. "You'd be right. Detective Sam West."

"Then thanks, Sam."

Before he had a chance to say anything else, the door to the office opened and Mattan came rushing toward them, screaming curses at Sam. He was waving a gun, and his eyes were wild. Before anyone could move, he ran up and stuck his gun against Sam's temple.

CHAPTER
THIRTY-SEVEN

On instinct, E.J. started to stand up, but Sam looked at him and frowned. Although E.J. wasn't sure he should stand down, he decided to wait.

"What's the matter, boss?" Sam asked calmly.

"Don't talk to them. What are you saying? Are you talking about me?"

"Of course not, boss. I told them to hurry up. I don't want to be out here any longer than I have to."

"I told you to keep them alive," Mattan yelled, his face pale and shiny with sweat. "Not sit out here and have a party."

Sam shrugged. "I was just keeping my eye on them. If you want me to take their food away, just say so. It's no skin off my nose. I was only doing what you told me to do, boss."

Mattan stared at him for a few seconds, then slowly lowered his gun. "Just make them hurry up. Five more minutes. That's it." He walked quickly back to the office.

"Wow, you're right," E.J. said under his breath. "He's really losing it."

Sam nodded. "I don't see it getting any better either."

"Is he still planning to take me to D.C.?" Valerie asked. "I mean, I assume the grand jury won't meet since Senator Warren is dead."

"I wasn't sure if you were aware of that," Sam said. "I honestly don't have any idea." He looked at E.J. "How close do you think your people are to finding you?"

"Trust me, they know we're in trouble, especially after our widely filmed escapade on the highway." E.J. took another bite of his sandwich, chewed, and swallowed. "Sam, if Mattan goes completely off his nut and decides to start killing everyone, will you be able to take him down?"

"I doubt it. You know that big burly guy? The one you met when you got here?"

"Yeah?"

"His name's Waseem Bati. He's served Al-Saud for years. The man is completely sold out to the Al-Saud family. There's no way to reason with him—no way to turn him. He doesn't trust anyone. Especially me."

"Did you do something to make him suspicious?"

"Sure, I'm American, and he's of the opinion we're all devils. He fought Mattan tooth and nail when he asked me to join his happy little band of terrorists, but Waseem backed off when Mattan put his foot down. He wanted the cash and weapons I used to buy my way in."

"What?"

Sam nodded. "Donated by the U.S. government for this operation." He glanced back toward the office. "There are two other longtime Al-Saud men here I don't trust. I don't know their real names. One of them, the guy who brought you in,

264

is nicknamed Butch. The other man's called Mouse. I have
no idea why. He's certainly not timid. There are three others
too who came on only recently, but I'm pretty sure they're
all going to bail. They've been talking among themselves. I
don't think they're willing to wait until Mattan finally melts
down. If they go, I might have a chance of shutting Mattan
down. Of course, with Waseem watching my every move,
it's almost impossible."

"So what should we do?" E.J. asked. "Just wait here like
sitting ducks?"

"No. If Mattan decides to get rid of you, I'll go after him,
but Waseem will shoot me without blinking an eye. If we get
into a struggle and you can do anything to neutralize Was
eem, go for it." He shook his head. "I know I'm not building
much confidence in you all, but I promise to do everything
I can to get you out of here in one piece."

"You keep saying that, but this sounds more like bravado
than reality," Casey said.

"Nah, that's just commitment," E.J. said, nodding at Sam.
"I understand, brother. But please be careful. We want you
to make it out of here too."

The door to the office flew open, and Mattan screamed
something at them. Sam waved his hand at him. "You got
it, boss," he called back. He looked at E.J. "Sorry. Gotta tie
you up again. I'll leave you as loose as I can. If someone else
checks on you, make it look legit."

Casey took another pill from her pocket and stuck it in
her mouth. "Okay," she said. "I'm ready."

"Hey, those things are strong," Sam said. "I know I said
they wouldn't hurt you, but don't overdo it."

"I won't. But I have to be able to function if we get the chance to escape."

"Please don't get yourself caught, Sam," E.J. warned again. "If you get killed, you'll be no help to us."

Sam winked. "Thanks. Glad to hear you've got my best interests at heart."

E.J. quickly wolfed down the rest of his sandwich while Sam tied up the women. Then he put his hands behind his chair as Sam loosely wrapped the plastic line around his wrists.

Sam collected the remnants of their meal, threw it all in the trash, pushed the table back to where he'd found it and walked away.

E.J., Casey, and Valerie were left alone with their thoughts again. Sam's words made it clear their lives were in real danger. The enemy they faced was a psychopath who was capable of just about anything. It was almost impossible to come up with a plan of escape when dealing with someone as unstable as Ben Mattan.

After another hour, E.J. began to worry. He couldn't see Sam with the other men in the office. E.J. prayed he was okay and that Mattan wouldn't hurt him. E.J. kept working on the ties around his wrists. Thanks to Sam, E. J. was certain he'd be able to free himself. He still had the scissors in his pocket. Given the chance, he could also free Valerie and Casey. At this point, it was the only thing he could think of that might get them out of the warehouse.

Another door in the back opened, and several men came

out. They were moving quickly, heading for the front door. They didn't even bother to look at Mattan's three hostages. Seconds later, E.J. heard a car start and then peel out of the alley. Then the door to the office opened, and the big man, Waseem Bati, came stomping out. He reminded E.J. of a huge bull. He always looked angry, and he seemed especially irritated now. Throwing open the door the other men had just gone through, he stepped out into the alley and stared toward the direction the car had gone.

Sam came running out of the back. As he approached Waseem, he asked, "Did they leave?"

Waseem stopped and glared at Sam, not bothering to respond to his question, before huffing and walking past him. Sam watched as Waseem stomped away. He rolled his eyes as he looked at E.J. He'd just begun to head back to the office when Mattan came out—charging straight at Sam.

E.J. fought hard against his bonds, trying to wiggle out of them so he could help Sam if he needed it. But there wasn't time. Mattan rushed up to Sam and got right in his face. "Where are you going? Are you leaving too?"

Sam shook his head. "Of course not, boss. I was trying to stop them. You should know me better than that by now."

"Waseem tells me you can't be trusted. Is he right?"

"No, boss. He's not right. You can trust me."

Mattan took his gun out of its holster and stuck it in Sam's face. E.J. was afraid he was going to pull the trigger, but he didn't. After a few seconds that felt like an eternity, he lowered the gun and walked over to where they all sat.

"Maybe I'll shoot one of you," he said, putting the gun next to Casey's head. "I don't really need you, you know. These two are supposed to go to D.C." He waved the gun at Valerie and E.J. "But you're nothing to me." He leaned down, his ugly face right next to Casey's. "Why should I let you live?"

As Mattan clicked off the safety, E.J. decided to jump up even though he was still tied to the chair. He couldn't sit here and watch Casey die. But before he could do anything, Sam whispered something in Mattan's ear. He hesitated a moment, and then a slow smile spread across his disfigured face.

"Good point, Ace," Mattan said. "Thanks. Maybe you're on my side after all." He slapped Sam on the back before sliding the gun back in its holster. He leaned in close to Sam. "I have an idea. You, me, and Waseem can carry it off. It'll take care of my father's problems for good. Wait until you hear it. You'll love it!"

"Sure, boss," he said. "Let me give these people some water and then I'll be right with you. If you have plans for them, we'd better keep them alive."

Mattan stepped back and gazed at Sam for a moment, as if studying him. "I . . . I guess that makes sense. But don't let me down, Ace. I mean it."

"You don't have to worry about me, boss. I'll never let you down." Sam smiled at Mattan, who finally seemed mollified.

As Mattan walked away, muttering to himself, Sam came up next to E.J. "See what I mean?" he said in a low voice. "Those other guys left because they knew things are going south."

"No chance Waseem will abandon ship too?" E.J. asked.

"Never. Like I said, he doesn't waver. He's a machine. I've never seen him express feelings or thoughts. He's committed to Al-Saud; he'd rather die than turn his back on him. I don't know if he's truly loyal to Ben or if his real job is to keep an eye on him. In a way, he's even more dangerous than Ben."

Sam went over to the pop machine, pulled out a bottle of water, and came back. He carried the bottle to each person, letting them take a drink. When he reached E.J., he refused the water.

"Sam, I need you to get the scissors out of my pocket. Cut this line. I'll keep my hands together, but I don't want to be useless if Mattan points a gun at us again. Please."

Sam hesitated. "If they come out here to check on you, it could get us all killed. I'm not sure it's a good idea."

"But like you said, he's losing it. We need a shot at survival if things go wrong."

"Here, take a drink. Let me think about it."

E.J. took several gulps of water and wished it could be more.

"Okay," Sam said finally. "You're right. If Mattan starts shooting, you need a way out." He slid his hand into E.J.'s pocket and took out the scissors. Then, making a show of checking that they were still securely tied up, he cut the line around E.J.'s wrists. "I can't do this for anyone else. It has to look like you got free by yourself, in case you get caught."

"I understand. Thanks."

Sam carefully put the scissors back in E.J.'s pocket before returning to the office.

"Well, at least now we have a chance," E.J. said to the women. "I'm not going to let that nut shoot you."

Casey grunted. "Maybe *I'm* not going to let that nut shoot *you*," she said. "Don't be sexist."

"I wasn't trying to be . . ." When E.J. saw Casey's face,

he realized she wasn't serious. "Not an appropriate time to crack jokes," he said.

"Sorry. But I'm not completely kidding. You're not in this alone, you know. I might not be at my best, but don't rule me out."

E.J. looked at her in confusion. "I wasn't—" He stopped and thought for a moment. "Okay, maybe I was, but it's because you've been shot. You're not at your best."

"It hurts, sure, but I'm not incapacitated."

E.J. nodded. "Fair enough."

Casey was getting ready to say something else when Mattan came storming out of his office again. Ace was close behind him, trying to keep up.

"You!" Mattan said to Valerie, pointing at her. "You will go to Washington tomorrow. Together we will give the FBI exactly what they deserve." He glared at E.J. "And *you* will call your bosses and tell them to meet you and Ms. Bennett outside FBI headquarters at ten in the morning. Do you understand?" Without waiting for a reply, Mattan said to Sam, "Bring him to the office. Now."

Sam stepped behind E.J. with a large knife and pretended to cut his bonds. He grabbed E.J. by the arm. "Come with me," he said gruffly.

E.J. noticed that Sam quickly slid the knife into the waistband of his pants, most likely thinking Mattan was too strung out to notice. E.J. shot a look Casey's way before Sam pushed him forward. He saw the fear in her eyes. She was probably wondering the same thing he was. Did Mattan really want E.J. to make a call, or was the man planning to kill him?

CHAPTER
THIRTY-EIGHT

E.J. was led into the sparse office and pushed down onto an old padded leather chair in front of a wooden desk peppered with cigarette burns. It was obvious cigarettes weren't the only thing being smoked. The air was thick with the smell of marijuana. Mattan seemed to be mixing his drugs in dangerous proportions.

Sam stood next to E.J. as Mattan plopped himself down behind the desk. E.J. was thinking about jumping over the desk and grabbing Mattan by the throat when he noticed Waseem Bati standing a few feet away, a gun trained on him. Sam's words about the man slipped into E.J.'s mind. Bati's face was like carved stone. No spark of humanity in his eyes. As Sam had said, the man was a machine.

"You're going to call your boss," Mattan said, "and we'll be listening. So no funny business. If you say or do anything we don't like, you'll die."

"What is it you want me to say?" E.J. asked.

"You and Ms. Bennett will meet the FBI in front of their headquarters at ten in the morning. By the main doors. That's when you will hand Ms. Bennett over to them. That's all that needs to be said. If you add anything else, I'll kill both you and Ms. Bennett. And your pretty girlfriend too. You'll be of no use to me anymore. Do you understand?"

E.J. nodded.

Mattan handed him a phone. "Put it on speakerphone."

"It's very late. My boss isn't at work."

Mattan got up from the desk and walked over to E.J.'s chair. He slapped him hard across the face. "This is what I'm talking about. No lying. No manipulation. I know you can reach your boss. Do it now."

E.J. dialed his boss's number. As Mattan had guessed, reaching him wasn't difficult.

"Claypool here," a deep voice said.

"Hey, Chief. It's Deputy Queen."

"Queen, where in the world are you?"

"Just been keeping my head down, Chief." There was a brief pause, and E.J. prayed that Claypool would understand. He had no idea if the new chief knew about the code he and Casey had come up with, but it was all he could think to do.

"Actually, I was informed by St. Louis that I might not hear from you right away. I take it everything's okay?"

E.J. almost felt faint with relief. "Yeah, we're good. I need to deliver Valerie Bennett to the Feds tomorrow in D.C. Can I meet you and the FBI in front of their headquarters at ten o'clock in the morning? I'll hand her over then."

E.J. knew what a ridiculous request this was. If he hadn't tipped Claypool off, he would have come unglued.

"Sounds good. Anyone else with you?"

"No. I'm sending the Marshals from St. Louis on home."

"All right. Anything else I need to know, Queen?"

"No. I believe I've given you all the pertinent information."

"We'll see you tomorrow, then."

"Right. Thanks, Chief."

E.J. hung up the phone and handed it to Mattan. He wished the call had happened during the day. If he'd phoned Claypool at work, they could have traced the call. But on the chief's personal cell at night, if Mattan's phone was protected, there wasn't time for Claypool to locate them before ten. At least Claypool had responded correctly. He had to know it was a trap. They would be ready tomorrow. Now it was all in God's hands. There wasn't much else E.J. could do.

"Good job, Deputy Queen. I guess I'll let you live." Mattan's pupils were huge, and a little drool ran down the side of his mouth.

"Take him back," Mattan ordered Sam. "Then bring Ms. Bennett. We must prepare." He nodded at Waseem. "Go with them. I don't want any of them out of your sight. Is that clear?" Waseem only nodded.

"Hey, boss," Sam said with a frown, "you can trust me—I don't need Goliath here following me everywhere I go."

Mattan stood, his eyes glazed and hard. "Waseem is the only person I trust with my life. He would never betray my father—or me. I don't know you that well, and you're always trying to help these people. Like you care about them or something."

"I was just trying to keep them alive for you. That was my only concern."

"Really?" Mattan reached over and took a gun out of his drawer, then walked around the desk. "Shoot him," he said, nodding toward E.J. "Shoot him in the head."

"Sure."

E.J. remained still while Sam put the gun to his head. Was he really going to fire? E.J. was horrified when he heard the trigger click. But nothing happened. Sam pulled the trigger again. Nothing.

Sam checked the gun. "Hey, there's no clip in this gun," he said. "Load it and give it back to me, and I'll kill him. Anything for you, boss."

Mattan's low laugh gave E.J. chills. "That's okay, Ace. We need him for tomorrow. You take him back out there and tie him up. Then bring that reporter to me."

Sam yanked E.J. to his feet. "Let's go," he said gruffly.

As he pushed E.J. out the door, Waseem followed them. Obviously, even though Sam had passed the test, Mattan was still paranoid. There was no way to get rid of Waseem. For now, all E.J. could do was go back to the chair where he'd already sat for hours. Sam had to tie him up again.

Waseem stood back several yards, watching. While Sam wrapped the fishing line around E.J.'s wrists, he whispered, "I knew the gun was empty. If I can take down King Kong back there, I'll come for you soon. If not, we might have to go to D.C."

E.J. shook his head slightly. "No, don't fight going to D.C.," he whispered back. "Trust me on that."

Although he couldn't risk trying to explain to Sam with Waseem standing guard, keeping that appointment tomorrow was their best chance at bringing all this to an end and getting out alive. That was worth any inconvenience they might have to endure at the moment.

After securing E.J., Sam went over to Valerie. He took out his knife and cut her bonds. "You have to come with me. The boss wants to see you."

Valerie appeared frightened as Sam led her away. Casey and E.J. stared at each other. What did Mattan have planned now?

CHAPTER
THIRTY-NINE

"Doesn't anything look familiar?" Tony asked. He was getting frustrated with Martin. They'd been over and over the same area many times. Martin couldn't recall the names of the streets around the warehouse where they'd kept him. And he couldn't remember the name of the bus he rode when he'd made his escape.

"I'm really sorry, Tony. I thought I could find it, but all these blocks look the same to me."

"Is there any particular business you can remember? A coffee shop maybe, or restaurant?"

Martin sighed and shook his head. "I was so drugged up, I barely remember anything."

They'd been driving for a couple of hours. Tony pulled the rental car over to the side of the street and parked. His cellphone had been going off for a while. He knew he was in trouble, but he thought they'd find the warehouse by now. He felt strongly that their people were in need of help. He'd texted Tom right after they left to let him know what they were doing, but he hadn't communicated with him since. He checked his watch. Almost five a.m. His phone rang again.

"Look," he said to Martin, "I may have already tossed my career away. One more time around the block and I'm done. We have to go back."

At that moment, a large truck pulled up in front of them and stopped. A man hopped out, went around to the back, opened the big doors, and started pulling out piles of newspapers.

"Newspapers . . ." Martin said softly. He turned to look at Tony. "Newspapers. I walked past a guy loading up one of those newspaper racks right before I got to the bus stop."

Tony got out of the car and asked the man with the newspapers where there was a rack next to a bus stop around here.

"Only one in this area," he answered. "Go up four blocks, turn right. Three blocks more and you'll find the stop for the MLK East Busway. P Line. P for purple."

"Thanks!" Tony said. "I really appreciate it." He ran back to the car. "We're close," he said, thumping Martin on the shoulder. He picked up his phone and called Tom. When Tom answered, Tony started to explain, but Tom shouted him down. He was so angry, at first Tony couldn't even understand what he was saying.

Tony listened for a moment as Tom repeated himself a little slower. Tony was shocked by what he heard. "Okay," he said. "But I think we found the warehouse. If we move fast enough, maybe we can catch them before they leave."

There was a long silence before Tom said, "You're still in big trouble, but give me the address."

"I don't have an address, but I have directions." Tony looked around them and then read the street signs back to Tom. "We're halfway up the block on the east side of the street. Why don't you meet us here and then you can follow us?"

"Okay. You stay right there—do you understand me?"

"Sure. No problem."

"Did you get fired?" Martin asked when Tony disconnected.

"I don't know," he said. "It seems they've heard from one of our deputies. He wants to meet the FBI in a few hours and turn Valerie over to them."

"Well, that's good news, isn't it?"

"Not really. First of all, it doesn't make sense. I mean, he shouldn't be telling the Feds where he plans to take their witness. Secondly, he used a coded phrase as a way to let his boss know something's wrong. Sounds like a trap."

Martin looked at Tony through narrowed eyes. "Are they still going to check out the warehouse?"

"Yeah, but they think our people are already gone. It's almost five hours from here to the FBI headquarters in D.C."

"We missed them?"

"Probably."

"It's my fault," Martin said. "I'm sorry."

"You're not to blame. You helped us find it. Don't beat yourself up. You've done more to help find Valerie and our people than anyone else."

"Thanks, but I feel like I've been a chump from the beginning. I started all this."

"That's not true. Just hang in there a bit longer, and we'll get this all under control. I know Valerie will be happy to see you."

"Or she'll want to kill me for getting her involved with Warren . . . and Al-Saud."

"We'll see," Tony said with a smile, "but I bet I'm right."

They sat there silently in the dark, waiting for their backup. Finally they could hear the whine of sirens. Soon a car pulled up next to them. Tony rolled down his window. Tom was looking at him, his window down as well.

"Where is it?" Tom asked.

Tony relayed the same information the newspaper carrier had given him.

"Okay, lead on," Tom said.

As soon as the police car and two black SUVs had lined up behind them, Tony pulled out into the street. They were on their way to the warehouse. Tony prayed their people were still there.

And alive.

It was almost four-thirty in the morning when Mattan marched out of his office, Valerie in front of him. Sam was next to Mattan, and the big guy trailed all of them, his gun drawn.

Casey had felt better after the last pill, though the pain was coming back in waves. She didn't want to keep taking pills, yet she was determined to protect their witness. She'd do whatever she had to.

"Here they come," E.J. said.

He'd told her about the call he'd been forced to make. At least they would finally get some help, but she really didn't want them to leave. She couldn't read Mattan, couldn't figure

out what he might do next. In her opinion, he was border-
ing on the edge of a complete breakdown. She was afraid he
might kill Valerie and E.J., and she certainly didn't want to
be left behind with the man they called Waseem. No matter how tough she was, she probably didn't stand a chance
against a coldhearted giant with a gun.

She realized then that Valerie was wearing a coat. Some
kind of thick winter jacket. It was way too big for her and
quite unnecessary in this kind of heat. Although Casey wasn't
feeling well, she knew immediately what was going on, and
even in the stifling warehouse, a chill ran through her.

"We're going to leave now," Mattan said to E.J. "You will
come with Ms. Bennett and me. And you will stay here." He
was looking at Casey.

"I should go with them," Casey said quickly. "It's my job to
deliver our witness. Please let me carry out my assignment."

Mattan bent down until he was nose to nose with her. "No,
I don't think so," he said. "Ace tells me our friend Deputy
Queen is sweet on you. So . . ." Mattan signaled to the huge
man with the frozen expression. He came over and put the
barrel of his gun right on Casey's temple. "If Deputy Queen
disobeys any of my commands, I will punch a code on my
phone." He took another cellphone out of his pocket and
set it on the floor in front of Casey. "It will alert Mr. Bati
to shoot you. No questions asked." He straightened and
smiled at E.J. "So, Deputy, if you really do care about this
woman, you will do exactly as I tell you. Do we understand
each other?"

Casey was horrified to see E.J. nod. She was certain Sam
had told Mattan that E.J. cared for her as a way to save her

life. She was grateful but angry to be sidelined. "You put our witness first," she told E.J. "Don't you dare let him get away with this just because he threatened me."

"It will be okay," E.J. said. "Just pray for us."

"Well, how sweet." Mattan laughed. "Those better be some powerful prayers." He pointed at Valerie. "Maybe you're wondering why the lovely Ms. Bennett is modeling my winter jacket. Please, Ace, show them."

Sam carefully pulled Valerie's coat open. Even though she was prepared for what she knew she'd see, Casey gasped at the reality. Valerie had been forced into a suicide vest. It was loaded with enough explosives to take out a city block.

CHAPTER
FORTY

Tony and Martin followed the other cars to the warehouse.

"Yeah, this looks familiar," Martin said when they pulled up.

Tony noticed the look on his face. "It must have been terrifying."

Martin nodded. "I really thought I was going to die. It makes you reevaluate your life." He pointed at the other vehicles. "What now?"

"First we'll try to see what's going on. You wait here. And stay down."

Martin swore under his breath and slumped down in his seat.

Tony pulled his gun and got out of the car. All the sirens had been turned off as they'd approached the building, but that didn't guarantee those inside didn't know they were here. The FBI was obviously taking over the operation. He was thankful they'd finally decided to storm the warehouse. They signaled everyone to stand down until they could ascertain the location of Mattan's men and the people they'd come to rescue. The windows at eye level had all been boarded up, so one of the agents jumped up on top of a large trash dumpster. Then he slowly stood until he could peer into one of the windows at the top of the wall. When he jumped down, they all gathered close to him.

"Three people," he whispered. "A woman tied up. Long blond hair. Small."

"That's our deputy," Tom said quietly. "Who else is there?"

"A black guy, tall, well-built, short cornrows."

"That's our undercover officer," one of the detectives from Pittsburgh PD said. "Sam West. Is he armed?"

The officer shook his head. "Only one man is armed. Middle Eastern. Large guy. And I mean huge. He seems to be keeping an eye on both of them."

"Did you see any other way in?"

The question came from Officer Holman, who had demanded that representatives of the Cranberry Township PD be on hand for this takedown. No one in law enforcement would deny that request. Their brother had been murdered, and they had the right to see this through.

"There are some rooms in the back. I have no idea if we can get in that way. We need to take a look."

Agent Taggart waved his hand toward the back of the building, and several LEOs followed him to check it out. Tony, Tom, and one of the FBI agents stayed at the front entrance in case someone made a run for it. A couple of minutes later, everyone who'd left came back.

"Everything's padlocked," Willis, the other detective, said. "This is our only way in."

"Okay," Tom said, "just don't get our deputy killed. Please."

"We'd like to have Sam make it out in one piece too, if you don't mind," Captain Ramos added. "And try not to kill the other guy. He might be an important witness."

"We'll do our best," Agent Taggart said. "But if he fires on us—"

"Take him out."

"What made you change your mind about going in?" Tony asked Agent Taggart.

"Everything's different. We have no idea what Mattan has planned in front of our building in the morning, and we can't have citizens getting caught in the crossfire. Mattan has changed the playing field—and the game. We're willing to take what we have so far and call it good."

Although Tony was grateful the FBI was with them now, Agent Taggart's concerns were chilling. Just what was Mattan up to?

The other guy from the FBI brought a battering ram from their SUV. Everyone got behind him, weapons drawn. Agent Willis held up his hand, counting to three. When three fingers went up, he yelled, "FBI!" and the other man struck the door. It splintered immediately. They all ran inside to find the large guy holding a gun to Casey's head.

"Put the gun down!" Agent Willis ordered. "Now!"

The warning did nothing. The man with the gun just stared at them as if he didn't understand. His face showed no expression whatsoever, and his dead eyes gave the impression that no one was home inside this behemoth.

"Put it down now!" Willis yelled again.

The man turned to look at Casey. It was obvious he was getting ready to shoot, but before anyone could respond,

Detective West jumped out of his chair, a knife in his hand, and slammed into the huge man, trying to throw him off his feet. It was like a butterfly attacking a brick wall. Though the move had no effect physically, it did confuse the man for just an instant, and he swung his gun toward the detective. It was the last thing he would ever do. A hail of bullets brought him down.

Tony and Tom ran to Casey, who seemed too calm for the situation. "You've got to stop them," she said. "Mattan. He's meeting with the FBI in D.C. He took E.J. with him, and Valerie's wired with a bomb!"

Everyone was silent as Casey's words soaked in. Tony took a small knife from his pocket and quickly cut the fishing line off her wrists. She was getting ready to explain when she caught sight of someone over Tony's shoulder.

"Doug!" she cried. "I thought . . ."

"You were supposed to," he said with a smile. "Tony wanted Mattan's men to think I was dead. When you all left, I called for help. Thank God they arrived before Mattan's cleanup crew." He nodded at the sling supporting his arm. "Some broken bones, but I'll be okay."

When her hands were free, she got up and wrapped her arms around him. "I'm so glad you're alive, Doug."

"Casey, we need to know more about this bomb," Tom said. "What's going on?"

"Mattan is acting alone," she said, stepping away from Doug. "Al-Saud has cut him off. You know that Al-Saud is Mattan's father, right?"

"Yeah, we know," Tom said.

"Well, Mattan is drugged up and insane. I think he believes

that if he blows up someone from the FBI, his father will forgive him. I know it doesn't make sense, but that's what he's doing. He might also be thinking that if Valerie dies, there's no one left to testify against his father."

"Does he plan to be near the bomb when it goes off?"

Casey didn't know the man who asked the question, but it was clear he was FBI. The real FBI. "I have no idea. I kind of doubt it. He's a coward. Used men like this one"—she pointed to the dead man on the floor—"to do his dirty work."

"Where in the world did Mattan get this bomb?" another man asked.

"He's got all kinds of drugs and weapons here," Sam said. "Putting together a suicide vest is easy with everything he's amassed. It's possible he's even got chemical weapons. Might be a good idea to get this stuff secured."

Agent Willis immediately pulled out his phone. "We need to get the bomb squad and hazmat team out here now. I'll let them know we may also be dealing with chemical weapons."

"He's supposed to meet them at ten in the morning, sir," Sam said to one of the men. Casey assumed this was his boss.

"We'll be ready for them," Agent Willis said.

Casey tried to stretch her sore muscles.

"How about some water?" Sam asked.

"You've done enough for me," she said, tears filling her eyes. "You saved my life. I'll owe you forever."

"You don't owe me anything," he said softly. "Just doing my job."

"I know this isn't professional," she said before leaning over and hugging him. "Thank you."

"You're welcome." He turned to Tom. "She's been shot, and there's infection in the wound. She should be taken to a hospital right away."

Casey shook her head. "No way. I'm going with you."

"No, you're not," Tom insisted. "You're going to the hospital."

"Please, Tom. I want to be there. I need to make sure E.J. and Valerie are okay."

"Sorry." He smiled at her. "I know you think I'm being unreasonable, but I'm not. With everything going on, I don't need to be worried about you too. If your gunshot is infected, it could be serious. Don't worry. I'll keep in touch with you."

"But—"

"Sorry, being acting chief means you gotta do what I say. Period."

Another man stuck out his hand, and Casey shook it. "I'm Arthur Claypool from D.C. I think you worked for our service before I came on."

She nodded, then frowned. "How did you know about our code for assistance?"

Claypool grinned. "Your chief, Terry Osborne, told me about it. Thank God he did or else I wouldn't have known you were in trouble."

Agent Willis walked over to them, sliding his phone into his pocket. "I've advised the D.C. office about Mattan."

"Can you just take him out?" one of the police officers asked.

"No. The problem is we have no idea how this bomb is set up. Mattan could have the trigger. If we shoot him—"

"He might set it off," Sam finished. "You know, if you can keep him alive, he might turn on Al-Saud. I realize it's a long shot, but he's the one person who could bring an end to Ali Al-Saud. Even with everything I've found out here, I still can't prove a direct link between Mattan's operations and Al-Saud. He's very clever when it comes to making himself look clean."

"We'll do what we can," Agent Willis said. "Right now, though, I'm more concerned with how we're going to keep these people alive and protect anyone else near that bomb."

CHAPTER
FORTY-ONE

A few minutes before ten a.m., Mattan ordered E.J. and Valerie out of the car. E.J. was certain Claypool had picked up on his warning, but what had he done? E.J. didn't dare try to overpower Mattan. He had a phone in his pocket that could be used to detonate the vest strapped to Valerie. It was way too risky.

Valerie was quiet. Too quiet. E.J. kept trying to reassure her that everything would be all right, but she didn't seem to be responding. She'd been through so much, he wasn't certain how she was still moving. He was determined to save her and hoping to save himself as well. E.J. was furious with Mattan. This stupid dopehead had hurt too many people and caused too much destruction. E.J. wanted him to face justice. He realized the FBI might want him alive, but E.J. was past caring about that. Next to seeing Casey again, he wanted to watch Mattan receive the justice he deserved.

As they walked up the street, E.J. could see the massive J. Edgar Hoover Building. Many considered it a monstrosity with its odd angles and sections that didn't seem to fit with the rest of the structure. As they neared the entrance, E.J. looked around, trying to see if there were sharpshooters on the roofs of nearby buildings. He couldn't be certain, but he thought he saw slight movement from a tall building across the street. Even if he couldn't see the snipers, he knew they were there. But this was still chancy. One touch on Mattan's phone could take out the whole block.

Mattan stopped and said, "I'm not going on with you." His smile looked more like a sneer. "You two walk up to the front and wait. And don't try anything. If you do something I don't like, I'll push the button." He checked his watch. "If I don't call Waseem by 10:15, he's been instructed to kill your friend. So you really have no choices here, do you?"

"Why do you think we're going to cave in to you?" E.J. asked through gritted teeth. "You plan to blow this vest anyway."

Mattan shrugged. "Maybe. But the longer I wait, the more of a chance you have to try to outsmart me. Not that you'll succeed." He laughed so hard he snorted.

Mattan was clearly out of his head. He was so far gone, he was capable of anything. But the one thing Mattan didn't know was that the FBI was ready for him. Right now, it was the only thing he and Valerie had going for them.

Mattan walked away, crossing the street and leaving them alone.

"What are we going to do?" Valerie whispered, her voice shaking.

E.J. was glad she was talking. It was a good sign. "Valerie, the FBI knows what's happening here. When I spoke to my boss, I let him know that this is a trap. Whatever they have planned will work. I'm sure of it. We just need to keep walking."

"Oh . . . okay." She took his arm. "I hope they don't shoot him. He might accidentally set off the bomb."

"I'm sure they know that."

She stopped and turned to him. "Listen, E.J., I want you to stay here. Don't come any farther with me . . . just in case. Then at least you'll be all right."

E.J. shook his head. "I'm not leaving you, Valerie. My job is to deliver you safely, and I intend to do just that. Besides, if that bomb goes off, standing a few feet away won't help."

"Then run away." She looked up at him, her pupils dilated with fear. "Casey needs you. Please don't throw your life away when you don't have to."

"I appreciate what you're saying, and I know your heart is in the right place, but the FBI has a plan, and it includes both of us walking up to that entrance. If we change things, their plan could fail and we could both die. I trust them. We have to keep to the original script, okay? Do you understand?"

"I . . . I guess so."

He was touched that she'd offered to go on alone. And she might be right. If he ran fast enough, he might survive. But he had no intention of letting her go through this by herself. Being in law enforcement meant being willing to lay down your life if the situation called for it. He was willing . . . but he really did have confidence that the FBI had worked out something. He just wished he knew what it was.

As they began the last leg of their walk up Pennsylvania Avenue, E.J. noticed the crowds on the sidewalk began to thin out. Some men at the corner seemed to be warning people away. Pretending to be handing out flyers, they talked with each person, who then turned and went another way. Some of them looked a little spooked. E.J. was certain the Feds were trying to keep people out of the blast area. Just in case.

As they approached the front of the building, a group of men came out to greet them. One of them stepped up to him and held out his hand.

"Deputy Queen? I'm Assistant FBI Director Gerald Patterson. I'm very glad to meet you." He nodded at a couple of men next to him. "Remove the vest, please."

"Stop!" E.J. said, pulling Valerie away from him. "You can't touch it. Ben Mattan is watching us. If you try to remove the vest, he'll blow us up."

Two men held him back. E.J. watched in horror as the men he'd spoken to ignored him completely and took off Valerie's coat.

"E.J.?" she said.

Then one of them unhooked the vest. From around the corner, a man came pushing a bomb disposal container, and the vest was carefully placed inside it. The man rolled the container away.

E.J. wrestled away from the men who held him. He barely caught Valerie, who started to collapse. She leaned up against him and cried softly.

"How did you know that vest wouldn't go off?" he asked.

"Our experts checked out the supplies he had in his warehouse. It was obvious he planned to use a cellphone to detonate the vest."

"So?"

The agent grinned. "So we cut his cellphone service. It really wasn't that complicated."

E.J. stared at the man for several seconds and then laughed out loud. It was there in front of him all the time, but he'd been too busy trying to figure out other ways to stop Mattan. The final solution was so simple it had eluded him.

Several men with FBI jackets approached. They had Mattan in handcuffs. He was ranting and raving. He was convinced the bomb had exploded.

"He's got so many drugs in him, he doesn't know what he's saying," E.J. told them.

"We're hoping we can clean him up and get him to testify against his father," the assistant director said. "If he agrees, we'll be contacting you."

"You said something about the warehouse," E.J. said. "Is . . . is everyone all right?"

Patterson shook his head. "No, one of them didn't make it."

E.J. felt his heart tighten in his chest. "Who . . . who?"

"Don't worry. It was one of Mattan's men. Deputy Sloane and Detective West are fine."

E.J. was so grateful for the news, he had to blink away the tears that suddenly filled his eyes. "Where is Deputy Sloane?"

"In the hospital. We felt it was best if she got checked out. She wanted to be here, of course."

E.J. chuckled. "Of course. And what about Deputy Howard?"

The assistant director nodded. "He's fine too. He's with her."

"Thank God. I prayed he'd make it."

E.J. looked down at Valerie, who still leaned against him. "We could use some food, something to drink. Maybe some medical attention for Ms. Bennett?"

"You bet. Come with us."

E.J. turned to watch as the agents led Mattan away. "Just a minute," he said to Valerie. "I'll be right back." He ran toward the agents. "Hey!" he called out. "Hold on."

They stopped and waited for him. One of them put his hand on his gun.

E.J. put his hands up. "I'm not going to shoot him. I just want to tell him something."

Mattan stared at E.J. as if he had no idea who he was.

"I just wanted to tell you that no one gets away with this kind of evil," E.J. said. "Somehow, someday, you'll pay for what you've done. And I hope I'm there to see it." He smiled at Mattan before the agents took him to their car and placed him inside.

E.J. hoped Al-Saud would be next. It was time to bring an end to this terrible dynasty.

CHAPTER
FORTY-TWO

Casey was drifting off to sleep when the door to her hospital room opened and E.J. walked in. Doug got up from the chair where he was sitting and grabbed E.J. with his good arm, giving him a hug.

"So happy to see you," he said. "Thanks for saving my life."

"Thank *you* for not dying," E.J. said with a grin. "You had me worried there."

"You should have told me he was alive when we left," Casey said. "How could you let me think he was dead?"

"I couldn't take the risk Mattan would find out," E.J. explained. "If he had, he would have sent someone back to finish the job. Besides, I didn't want to get your hopes up in case Doug didn't make it. I couldn't tell how badly hurt he really was."

"Sounds like you two got rid of a lot of Mattan's people," Doug said. "That shootout on the highway was pretty dramatic. You may get a request from Hollywood for a sequel."

"Well, let's just say we were narrowing the field so we'd have a better chance of making it through this thing."

"So did the 'cleanup crew' ever arrive?" E.J. asked.

"Oh, yeah. But our guys were already there. We made them call Mattan's contact and tell him everything was okay. Then we arrested them. They'll get reduced sentences because they cooperated."

"Any connection to Al-Saud?"

Doug shook his head. "Not directly. Just another outside group contracted by Mattan."

"I spoke with Tom on the phone," Casey said. "He said they're talking to Mattan, trying to get him to testify against his father."

"They'd have to really clean him up," E.J. said. "He wouldn't make a good witness right now."

"You're right," Casey said, "but I think he'll do it. I mean, what does he have left? I don't think Al-Saud will take him back now. He messed up too badly."

E.J. came over and pulled up a chair. He sat next to Casey and took her hand. "So how are you doing?"

"I'll recover. They're treating the infection. I'm still pretty tired, but at least they're feeding me." She nodded toward the IV pole next to the bed. "The bad thing is, they won't give me coffee. I think I'm going into withdrawal."

E.J. laughed. "Well, if you don't get your caffeine fix soon, maybe I can smuggle a cup of coffee in for you."

"You're a truly wonderful human being." Then she frowned and asked, "How's Sam? Is he doing all right?"

"He's fine. He's with his people, giving them all the information he can. Their operation is over. They have a lot of evidence against Mattan, but—"

"They didn't get anything to nail Al-Saud?"

"Nothing solid. I'm sorry."

"We can't go through all this and not find a way to bring Al-Saud down for good. We just can't."

"Then we pray that Mattan will testify. That's all we can do." He squeezed her hand. "But for now, let's just concentrate on getting you back to full strength."

"I agree." She took a deep breath, trying to relax, but it would take some time to put the last few days behind her. She and God had some work to do. Casey was determined to stop punishing herself for the past. She knew God wanted her to be free and she had every intention of making that happen. "Where's Valerie?" she asked.

"She's with the FBI," E.J. said. "I don't know any more than that."

"Well, I do."

Casey looked toward the doorway. Tony stood there with a big smile on his face.

"I heard you were here," she said.

"Tom's here too. He's talking with the Feds, trying to hammer out a deal for Mattan—if he decides he's interested. At the moment Mattan's in a rehab facility. Not anywhere near here, of course."

"Is he going to be okay?"

"Sure. Just trying to sober him up. Boy, if we didn't need his testimony . . ."

E.J. walked over to Tony. "I'm E.J. Queen," he said, putting out his hand.

Tony took it. "I know exactly who you are. We're grateful for everything you've done. These two are important to us. We recently lost several of our people. Couldn't stand to lose anyone else."

"Not sure either one of them really needed me. These are two fine deputies."

"So what about Valerie?" Casey asked.

"After she's finished talking to the FBI, we're going to fly her out to Missouri to see her sister, Susan."

Casey's mouth dropped open. "You found her? You found Susan?"

Tony chuckled. "Well, I didn't find her, but the Feds did. She was in pretty bad shape, but she's going to recover."

"That's great news!"

"There's more," Tony said. "Martin Avery is alive too. He's been in hiding. When he heard that Senator Warren was dead, he contacted the Feds and offered to help. He's the reason we found the warehouse."

"Wow," Casey said slowly. "So Mattan lied to his father. Told him Avery was dead. When Al-Saud finds out, he won't be happy."

"He certainly won't. Seems Sam is the one who made sure Avery got away. According to Sam, Mattan chased Avery, but a couple of our boys in blue were parked on the street. Mattan gave up and went back to the warehouse. He was afraid to tell his father what happened, so he made him think Avery was dead. Then when he disappeared, it seemed to match Mattan's story."

E.J. laughed. "Those cops will probably never know they saved Avery's life."

Casey was silent for a moment. Some of her colleagues were dead, yet some people she thought dead were alive. It was weird how things had turned out. She waved Tony over to her bed. "Tony, I still don't know who all we lost in the bombing."

"Altogether, seven people died. Three people outside the building were killed by flying debris," Tony said. "We lost three deputies—Morrison, Edwards, and Grafton."

"Oh no." Casey's eyes filled with tears. "Grafton's wife just had a baby."

"I know."

"That's six. Who's the seventh?"

"Shelly Chambers."

"Oh, Tony . . ." Casey turned away. She couldn't stop her tears.

"Batterson's administrative assistant?" E. J. asked.

Tony nodded. "Batterson told her to get out immediately when he first ordered the evacuation, but she went back to make certain he was safe. That's when the bomb went off."

"I'm sorry," E.J. said.

"We are too. Another reason we need to get Al-Saud."

Casey turned back around. "I hate that we're offering WITSEC to Mattan."

"I don't like it any more than you do," Tony said. "But we have intel that Al-Saud might be planning something with ISIS. Something big. That's why he's been shipping weapons to the U.S. Of course, it's all been done in someone else's name. I've never seen anyone who has managed to surround himself with so many layers of protection."

"So now what?" Doug asked. "What's the next step?"

"Well," Tony said, "first thing, we let Casey get stronger. Then you both need some time off."

"I don't need time off," Casey argued. "I'm already feeling better."

"Sorry. Tom says you're taking at least two weeks off." Tony nodded at Doug. "Same goes for you."

"When will our building be repaired?" Casey asked.

"About a month at least. We're using parts of it. Just need to get the chief's office back up and running—and several offices near him. Our lunchroom is in bad shape and will have to be completely rebuilt." He winked. "Time to get that espresso machine we've been asking for."

Casey nodded. "Sounds like a plan. How is the chief doing?"

"Well, he's driving the hospital staff crazy. They want him out as soon as possible."

"So he's back to his old self?"

Tony chuckled. "I would say so. He's not happy I didn't tell him about Doug, but until I was certain he was going to be okay, I didn't want Batterson to worry."

Doug cleared his throat. "I think it's time for us to go, Tony. These two need some time together."

Tony smiled. "I agree." He started toward the door, but then he stopped and turned back. "Hey, E.J., I have a question."

"What's that?"

"What does E.J. stand for?"

"I'd like to know that too," Casey said. "You never would tell me." She was surprised to see him blush.

"All right. After everything we've been through together, I'll tell you. My mother is a very classy English lady. But the English love their mysteries. The *E* is for . . ."

"Oh no," Casey groaned. "You're kidding. Your first name is . . . Ellery!"

"Ellery Jackson Queen," E.J. stated. "And that doesn't need to leave this room."

"Of course it won't," Tony said with a grin. "Doug and I would never betray a secret, would we, Doug?"

"Heavens no," Doug replied, a slow smile splitting his face. "Never."

Casey could hear their laughter as they walked down the hall. "You know they're going to tell everyone they know, right?"

"Yeah. I got that. I guess I'll just have to live with it." He leaned down and gazed into her eyes. Casey felt her heart race. "Do you remember when I told you that when you were feeling like yourself and we weren't being held by people who wanted to kill us, we could revisit that kiss you gave me?"

"Yes, I have a very vivid memory of that."

E.J. glanced around the room. "Well, we seem to be safe, and you appear to be feeling better. Do you think this is an appropriate time to —"

Casey reached up and pulled his face down to hers. "Do you ever shut up?"

"Sometimes," he said gently. "Like right now."

EPILOGUE

Ben Mattan opened the door of the restaurant. He felt nauseous, as if he might throw up at any moment. He pasted a smile on his face and walked up to the hostess, who asked if he was eating alone. He started to answer her, but then he saw the man he was meeting already seated at a booth near the bar.

"My party is already here," he said, brushing past her. He nodded at his luncheon companion and scooted into the other side of the booth.

Ali Al-Saud put his menu down. "The food here is quite good," he said, hardly any hint of an accent left. Anyone in the restaurant would think two American friends were having dinner. Nothing suspicious in that.

Ben was surprised to see how thin Ali was. He didn't look well. "I've never been here before. Heard of it. Most people in St. Louis know about it." He hoped he didn't sound nervous. He bit his lip to keep from blithering. He was shocked that his father had agreed to meet him after ignoring him for months.

"I recommend the rib eye. Carmine's has the best steaks in the city."

"Sounds good."

A waitress came up and took Ben's drink order. Needing something to help calm him down, he ordered a whiskey sour. He knew his father's aversion to alcohol, but Ben really needed a drink.

"So you have had a busy time lately, my son," Ali said with a smile.

Ben nervously cleared his throat. "Things started out fine, and then they just went . . . wrong. I tried to fix it, but I made a lot of stupid mistakes. I'm so sorry, Father. I let you down."

Ali waved his hand at him. "I am not upset with you. You got inside the U.S. Marshals Office, set the bomb. It wasn't your fault Richard Batterson saw your face. You did your best to take care of that. It was the right thing to do. Of course, that did not go well either, did it?"

Ben leaned in so he could speak softly. "I injected him with enough epinephrine to kill an elephant. I can't believe he lived through it. Really, Father, I did everything I thought you would want me to do. I tried to protect you." He sighed again. "Batterson just wouldn't die."

"And when you found that Batterson had not called the FBI, you decided to fix this too?"

Ben swallowed hard. He realized now that he'd made a huge mistake, although at the time he couldn't figure out any other way to handle things. He blamed it on the drugs. Under normal circumstances, he would have worked diligently to come up with another option. "Yes, I . . . I was afraid that if the reporter spent too much time with the Marshals, she would spill the beans. I was just trying to get her on the road. On her way to Washington. I realize now that I wasn't thinking clearly."

Al-Saud picked up his iced tea and swirled it around in the glass. He took a slow sip while Ben drew a deep breath. He knew beyond a shadow of a doubt that Al-Saud wanted him dead. He was actually thankful for the Marshals—for their offer of a new life. He still wasn't sure why his father had agreed to this meeting. Ben had prayed to Allah for another chance, and soon afterward Ali called him. After he got his father to say the things the Marshals wanted to hear, he would walk out of the restaurant, free from Ali forever.

"But the men you hired to pick up the reporter let her and the deputies get away, did they not?"

"Yes," Ben acknowledged. "But I called one of my operatives, and he picked them up and took them to the warehouse. Everything would have been okay if they hadn't found us." He reached for his whiskey sour. His nerves were on edge. He just wanted this meeting to be over.

"You were discovered because Martin Avery wasn't dead after all."

Al-Saud said this as a statement, not as a question. Ben began to get irritated. Why was his father rehashing all his mistakes? Ben needed Ali to admit to his part in what happened, to say something the FBI could use to lock Ali Al-Saud away forever. The truth was, Ben didn't need to put up with Ali's garbage anymore. That knowledge made him momentarily braver. "I'm sorry I told you he was dead. I didn't expect to hear from him ever again."

Clearing his throat, he pressed on. "Look, Father, I'm truly sorry for my mistakes, but I did the best I could. If you wanted it done better, maybe you should have done it yourself." As soon as the words escaped his lips, he was sorry. Even if Al-Saud was going down, Ben still had respect for the man. After all, he was his father. "I only wanted to serve you well. It seems I've failed you more than once."

Ali acted as if he hadn't heard him. "I am surprised you got away from the FBI. How did you escape?"

Ben frowned at him. "I've already explained that while they were busy with the reporter in front of the FBI building, I managed to run away. They have no idea where I am." He stopped talking when the waitress came by.

"Are you two gentlemen ready to order?" she asked.

"Give us a few more minutes, dear," Ali said, his smile disarming. The waitress blushed and walked away.

Ben picked up his drink and took a couple of gulps. The warm rush of alcohol gave him courage. He took another deep breath and let it out slowly. "I did everything I could to follow your instructions," he repeated quietly. "I've always tried to serve you with my best efforts. This time . . . well, I guess I didn't count on how tough those Marshals would be."

"You almost sound as if you admire them."

"You know what?" Ben shrugged. "I think I do. They were determined to get the reporter to safety. No matter what. Even the threat of death didn't discourage them."

"And that is what I wanted from you," Ali said. "But I do not think you gave me that kind of commitment, did you?"

Ben felt the tension from earlier return with a vengeance. He grabbed his glass and emptied it, then held up an index finger to get the waitress's attention. When she looked his way, he lifted his empty glass.

She nodded and spoke to the bartender.

"You seem very thirsty today," Ali said.

"This whole thing was . . . exhausting and discouraging. At least we got what we needed from Senator Warren." Ben reached inside his jacket and pulled out the letter he'd picked up from the senator. "He left this for the FBI. It details everything, Father. How we kidnapped Martin Avery and the reporter's sister. And how we threatened to kill Warren's wife if he didn't go along with your plans."

"Actually, my son, I didn't do any of that," Ali said. "You did."

"But everything I did was according to your instructions."

"That may be true, but no one will ever know it."

"I'll never talk, and with our operatives dead, there's no way to link you to anything. You're perfectly safe, Father."

The waitress approached their booth with Ben's drink. She scooped up the other glass. "Are you ready to order now?"

Ali nodded. "Rib eye. Add a baked potato. Sour cream and butter."

"Same for me," Ben said. "Thank you."

She left to put in their order. She was almost to the kitchen when Ali shook his head and swore under his breath.

"My son," he said, "would you go and tell the waitress I also want an order of their grilled mushrooms?" He smiled. "It is the best way to eat steak. And please, if you would like them too, ask for two orders."

"I'd be happy to." Ben got up and went over to where the waitress had stopped to check on another table of customers. He told her they would like to add two orders of grilled mushrooms with their steaks.

"Sure," she replied. "Not a problem."

Ben thanked her and went back to the table.

"Thank you," Ali said. "So you are certain no one suspects me of being involved in this kidnapping?"

"No. No one." Ben picked up his fresh drink and almost downed it. "I would never allow you to be dragged into something like that."

"Thank you, son," Ali said.

Ben relaxed a bit more. It seemed everything was going to work out just fine. Now he had only to make it through dinner. After that . . .

"Ali Al-Saud, you're under arrest. Put your hands where we can see them."

Ben jumped at the sound of a voice behind him. He twisted in his seat to see two agents standing there, their guns drawn and pointed at his father.

"What . . . what are you doing?" Ben choked out. "You were supposed to wait until I left. Now he'll know I talked to you."

One of the agents, a man Ben knew as Agent Curtis, circled behind Ali, who held his hands up in surrender. "Stand up," he ordered.

Ali, staring at Ben with a half smile, stood to his feet. Agent Curtis slapped handcuffs on him and nodded to three other agents, who rose from a table in the corner of the restaurant. Dressed in street clothes, they blended in with the other customers. Curtis handed Ali over to them.

Ali's gaze never left Ben's. "Perhaps you noticed that I do not look well," he said. "I've found out too late that handling certain chemicals can be quite dangerous." He laughed. "Who would believe that a weapon we intended to use against the devils in this country would end my life instead? I suppose the Americans would call it *karma*."

"I . . . I don't understand," Ben said.

"I am dying, my son. I am content to see my life end in prison. You see, I felt it was worth it to see justice done. And today I have accomplished that."

"That's enough, Al-Saud. Time to go," one of the agents said.

As they led Al-Saud from the restaurant, Ben turned to Agent Curtis. "Now he knows I betrayed him. You promised you'd wait until I left before arresting him. I don't care how sick he is—Ali Al-Saud can get to anyone he wants to. Anytime. Even in Witness Protection, I'm not safe."

Ben wanted nothing more than to get out of the restaurant and go someplace where he could relax and forget about his father. He put a hand to his forehead and realized it was damp. He was sweating. Nerves.

The second agent, Doris Alvarez, sat down next to Ben. "Ben, Al-Saud put something in your drink while you were talking to the waitress. We tried to move in, but you drank it down before we could stop you."

Ben's breath caught in his throat. "You need to get me to the hospital."

"Do you know what he might've used?" Doris asked.

"I . . . I'm not sure. It might be Polonium-210. He . . . he's used it before."

He saw Agent Alvarez look at her partner. "Come with us. We'll get you to the hospital right away."

Suddenly the deal he'd made with the FBI didn't seem important anymore. Betray Al-Saud. Testify and go into Witness Protection. . . .

As Ben walked out of the restaurant with the agents, he was pretty sure he'd never make it to court. Although he wouldn't feel the symptoms right away, when they came, they would be terrible. And he would die. The words of the Marshal from St. Louis whispered in his mind. *"Somehow, someday, you'll pay for what you've done."*

As Benyamin Mattan was rushed to the hospital, he cursed the Marshal and the god who had turned his back on him.

ACKNOWLEDGMENTS

Thank you to my Best Friend for the gift of writing. You've gotten me through every challenge, even when I couldn't see a way. You've listened to me complain, all the time knowing You already had the answer. As you lead me through this journey, I pray I will always magnify You with every word I write. Thank you, Father, for loving me and never giving up on a child who lets you down almost every day. I love You more than any words I could ever write would express.

My thanks to retired U.S. Deputy Marshal Paul Anderson. I couldn't have written these books without you. I'm so thankful to God for bringing you into my life. I hope we are friends forever.

To Officer Darin Hickey with the Training and Community Affairs Division in Cape Girardeau, Missouri: Thank you for always being happy to answer my questions. I appreciate you so much and am so thankful for your service to the people of Missouri.

The medical information in this book came from Dr. Leah

Silver in Festus, Missouri. Finding a great doctor after moving from Wichita is such a blessing, and I am so thankful for you. Sharing a love of reading only makes it better! Thanks for becoming a "character" in *Blind Betrayal*. I hope I represented you well. God bless you.

My thanks to Elisabeth Baker, who actually suggested the title of this book. Great job, Elisabeth!

Thanks so much to my Inner Circle: Zac, Mary, Cheryl, Liz, JoJo, Shirley, Tammy, Bonnie, Lynne, Deanna, Breeze, Mary, Karla, Michelle, and Rhonda for your support.

As always, thank you to Raela Schoenherr for her excellent advice and support.